The "I'll be Brief" Series Overview

"I'll Be Brief " Series offers a variety of book titles that is written by featured Author's across all genres including, Children's Books, Fiction, Non-fiction, Poetry, Mystery, Comedy, Business Guides, Self Help books, Documentaries and more. What makes an "I'll Be Brief "Series book special? All books are rated "A" for anyone and most can be read in only one day! Enjoy reading a book from the "I'll Be Brief series."

"Open Minds Can Read Between The Lines"

As promised, "I'll Be Brief."

I'll Be Brief © 2015

Book Excerpt

This realistic fiction Novel depicts the life of a beautiful young girl born into a tragic inter-racial struggle. After her mother is brutalized and killed, she is forced to live with people she calls family, yet she has no legal ties to them. Ultimately her quest is to find her own heritage as she enters a world of lies and deception. Living in the shadows of her great pain in search of her true identity, she walks alone.

Being denied information about her true heritage keeps her imprisoned as she fights for the courage to break the chain of silence, she exposes what lies beneath the Blanket of Southern Heat which shrouds the only life she knows. While trespassing on a dying man's estate, she examines documents in his personal affects, and stumbles across hidden manuscripts written by the daughter of a slave owner from the 17th century.

Through this discovery, she finds her own family history and the truth about her life. She also finds the man who becomes her true love.

Victoria E. Kain

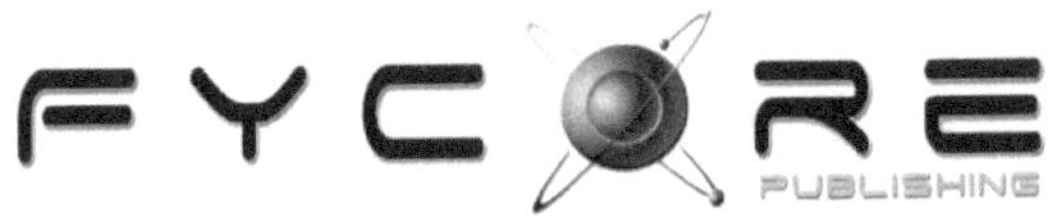

The Blanket Of Southern Heat

Author: Victoria E. Kain
Graphic Illustrations by: |www.gritography.com
Layout Design by: Fycore Publishing
Development Editor: Jane Adams
Publisher: Fycore Publishing
www.fycore.com

International Publisher Author Number: 15104855F2421
International Standard Book Number Hardback Cloth: 9781619100268
International Standard Book Number Softcover: 9781619100046
International Standard Book Number eBook: 9781619100251
Library of Congress Control Number: 2014931288

Additional Formats May be Available For Pre-Order:

PHYSICAL		DIGITAL	
Trade Cloth	$49.95	CD/MP3 (Audio Book)	$17.95
Hardback	$39.95	PDF Book	$15.95
Softcover	$18.95	eBook	$9.99

For Inquiries or Additional Orders:

131 Sunset Ave Ste E#353
Suisun City CA, 94585
Office | (800) 470-FYCORE
Facsimile: | (800) 531-0190
Email: | publisher@fycore.com

6th Book Edition from the "I'll be Brief" Series

6th Book Edition from the
"I'll be Brief" Series

Author: Victoria E. Kain

<u>Dedication</u>

I dedicate this book to my grandparents, Lee A. and Carrie B. Lane, who gave me my true start in life. With their humble beginnings and limited understanding of the world at large, they did not have all freedoms at their disposal during their life time. Despite that, they instilled in me principles and values on integrity, loyalty, honesty, and love. I have chosen to take these values and expound upon them by sharing with others that have been strategically placed in my life. I learned from them, the true meaning of love. "I loved them then and I love them now."

Victoria E. Kain

About The Author

Victoria found her calling while sitting on the old front porch swing at her grandparent's home during summer vacations. At the age of ten, she realized she would have a life time of amusing audiences for years to come. Victoria created exciting imaginary stories mesmerizing and amusing her siblings while her Grandmother prepared the family's dinner during those summer days. Her writings are simple truths and she believes that readers will choose to remember her stories.

Breaking all literary boundaries, Victoria brings readers to the main point swiftly with sincerity and truth. Humor will always grace her manuscripts keeping readers laughing, intrigued, enlightened and personally connected. She encourages parents to read to their children and adults to read more and "Become thirsty readers, who will always read between the lines."

Victoria E. Kain

TABLE OF CONTENTS

~ CHAPTER 1 ~

REWINDING THE SOUL

Rewinding The Soul

As I remember it, the South was always hot. It seemed that all the sun resided here in this beautiful God forsaken place where hatred and love was born and raised on each end of these old dirt roads. For decades, families struggled to live and make ends meet, that never did. All their dreams seemed to lead right back to nowhere for most of them.

There was simply no way of escaping the visible heat and the invisible oppression that was heaped upon the inhabitants of this lonely part of the earth. On many summer days, you could see weary travelers scurrying to their destinations on foot, wearing an old straw hat and shabby clothing.

The shabby designs were predicated by extreme wear and tear of not being able to afford new ones. They braved the heat waves that could be seen rising and falling in front of them on the highways like electrical currents. The soles of their feet were burning and their throats parched from the rays that grew hotter as they moved along to their perspective homes.

Old folk knew better than to test the suns treacherous scorching effects. It was common knowledge that during the hottest part of the day, it would be sudden death of a heat stroke if they exited the safe haven of the lean to porches and shade trees that surrounded the house. Water, in this instance, was considered a poor man's gold.

A precious commodity that most people had and understood the value of never wasting it under any circumstances. The dippers were always floating aimlessly in the buckets on top of cool spring water.

The Blanket of Southern Heat

Some folk submerged the dipper in the bucket to keep the aluminum cold so that when they drank, the water was even cooler. The bucket was always positioned at the end of the front porch near the family's well and only the grown folk could drink water from the dipper. It was an unspoken rite of passage to use this instrument for personal consumption.

There were also subtle reminders of the heat's destructive powers as observed by the thermometer that was strategically nailed to the side of the run down old shacks. It gave a grim glimpse of what the sun was capable of doing to the human body.

On occasions, when there was nothing else to do, you watched the oozing mercury drip down the side of the house from the instrument that once encapsulated it. Traditions were strange in the South. If you were not in the fields picking cotton, you were in them picking peas or greens for the day's supper.

You sat on the porch shelling those peas or cleaning the greens making sure you captured all the giant worms that might be hiding under the huge leaves that would later cook up nice and tender. To further pass the time away, you sat on the porch and watched everything that moved, creep by. This activity became a country boy's way of seeing the world.

He knew his chances of going anywhere was slim, so he watched everybody and everything that moved by him that was of interest. Examining it up and down allowing his brain to determine if the images he captured in his sight would be stored to his long or short term memory.

Author: Victoria E. Kain

Dipping snuff or chewing Prince Albert tobacco was comforting and relaxing for those old enough to partake of it or those too young but brazen enough to sneak a chew and think they were grown enough not to pay the horrible price for the after effects of it.

Besides yellowing teeth from a lack of oral hygiene, chewers received a heavy buzz from the processed tobacco. It was the only recreation most adult folk had during the light of day. Everything else happened under the blanket of darkness. It was the only time you were permitted to do the things you wanted to do but could not do during the light of day. Many lives were lost and found on these country dirt roads that were graced by many weary travelers.

Children that were too young to go to the fields, sat and watched the parched travelers slowly creep down the roadway. They wore open shirts with no buttons and were usually barefoot. If they had to walk in the sun, they grimaced, with one eye closed to shield the other, keeping the sun's rays from scorching their pupils. They would further place their forearms over the front of their heads shielding themselves from any part of the scorching rays that beamed down on them from every side like a solar blast from outer space.

Out of boredom they counted the travelers that passed by as they made their long strides hurrying to find cover from the treacherous heat. The strange thing was that it was only on a few occasions where you heard of anyone falling dead from the southern sun.

Most of the residents' bodies had acclimated to it over the many years of being conditioned by being in the fields picking cotton or plowing long fields for planting during the hottest part of the day for their masters. Either way, they respected the sun and its power.

When walking, people in the South only stopped out of necessity. They might politely request a glass full of water from a neighbors well to quench their parched palates. It was in the hopes that it would bring their internal temperatures down to a degree that would permit them to continue on their journey to the next shack down the road a piece.

Everyone knew the sun had a true presence in the South. This fiasco went on from sun up until sun down.

With all the variables of living in the South, it still was a wonderfully strange place to live and grow up, if you were not fortunate enough to be born anywhere else. You had many experiences that took you forward in life. If you were conceived after the civil rights movement era, there was much pain and extreme fear and suffering heaped upon you.

Fortunately, there were those of us who came along much later on the scene, but carried the same negative baggage and misery that most people encountered during the civil rights timeline. People longed to leave the South for a better life up north but most simply didn't make it out. For these, it was a life of being a hundred years behind the times until you accidentally caught yourself up by way of education, or someone up north sponsoring you by letting you live with them until you could make it on your own.

Any other way, you were in a pine box by special means. You understand. Either you survived, or you did not. But once you left, if you ever came back, you better have a good plan or you would fall right back into the dreaded rut of doom from the sun's heat rays drawing the life out of you until your dying day.

Looking back on my life has been as crazy and mixed up as those before me. I was one of the ones that got out, but I had a different dilemma. I was in the South but I was neither black nor white, but "other," as they called me.

Because of that label, I had no clue as to who I really was or where my real family might be that could shed some light on my true identity.

I was a misfit, trying to fit everyone's mold. Knowing how much I hated my life in the South, it seemed as if coming back here would be the last thing on my mind to do, but the truth is, I cried like a baby when I was forced to leave the only world I had known and later chose to make the South my permanent home again.

I learned quickly that the South either accepted or rejected you. You either fit the entire description of being black or white or you were an outcast on both sides of the fence. I like to use the term "tolerated." Being from a bi-racial descent was very challenging to say the least and tolerance is what you were always shown. The worst part was that no one would ever give you enough information for you to find out where you actually came from or belonged. They didn't want it said that they had mistreated one of Gods children. Even if you knew you didn't fit.

You were called everything, and a million assumptions were heaped upon you regardless of how you felt about it.

Resembling no one in your family but wanting to, caused you to conform to almost anyone's rules of what they thought you needed to be in order to fit into that group. At some point, it became a daunting task and you either gave up or conformed to the group you chose to associate with on a daily basis.

Telling my story of how I came into existence and survived as a human being from bi-racial descent is a difficult story to tell. The chain of silence had to be broken by someone in order to free me from all the lies I was told. Even though these lies were thought to be told as a way to protect me, it traumatized me for life.

I had to live though the multitudes of skeletons in my family's closet hoping to find my way home. I will tell my story first, as it was told to me. Then, I will tell it my way. We all have a beginning and mine was no different than most, but may be similar to some. It is clear to see the difference in how our lives are affected by the environments we grow up in, and how that experience shapes our future.

The one difference between me and others like me is that I have chosen to share my tragic beginning with the world. No shame or repulsion here. Only the sordid details of how I came full circle with who I was by way of a myriad of lies. Being conceived by way of my mother being raped by a man who was thought to be my father, was a very difficult thing to digest as a young child in the South, when people were still being lynched.

Later, I would be given more fragments of the tragic details of how my mother's attacker impregnated her. It was horrifying to have this data heaped upon my young brain. Not knowing what kind of person I would later become in life.

Author: Victoria E. Kain

It was said that the same man who violated my mother would have become her murderer as well, had it not been for another mysterious stranger walking into the same alleyway that dark night.

My mother had walked home alone that evening after working a late shift. She entered the alleyway which was a short cut to get home. Before she could get to the end of the alley which would put her on the street where she lived, she walked briskly through the musty dark place.

There were many uneven surfaces and potholes in the alley and one would have to walk carefully as it reeked of urine and feces from the many homeless people living there. They shielded themselves from the basic elements by making this their home. Sometimes, even prostitutes would bring their clients into this dreadful hole as a lonely place to do their business for the moments they would be there, ignoring the debauched conditions of their surroundings.

This night, my mother would not be the only one in this alleyway. Soon she would notice a very large man entering the same alley behind her. She quickly assessed that she was not alone. Picking up her pace to a brisk walk, she hurried to get to the other end of the alley to her street to be visible by others in the event something bad should happen to her. She had a horrible feeling that night.

As she walked briskly, so did the man behind her. Not wanting to break out in a stride for fear of embarrassment, if this man was only utilizing the alley for the same purpose she was, she simply kept her same pace. Sadly though, that was not the case.

The Blanket of Southern Heat

Before my mother could reach the end of the alleyway, the man broke into a fast sprint and grabbed her from behind clasping his large hands over her mouth. While striking her in the abdomen, rendering her helpless, he gained an advantage over her petite frame. He then brutally violated her.

The sadistic ordeal would end in him pulling a knife from his pocket to silence her forever in that filthy alley, ending her life and mine that night. As fate would have it, another man entered the alleyway and rushed the attacker and delivered a single blow to his temple and the man fell silent to the ground.

The man that saved my mother fled the alleyway that night realizing what he had done, assuming the attacker was dead. My mother was able to pull herself up on her feet and run screaming for help. She later was able to tell the police what the attacker had done and gave details about the man who had saved her.

The police found the attacker still in the alley laying on the ground unconscious. The description my mother gave helped them identify the assailant. She desperately wanted to know if they found out who had saved her life. No information was ever given about the man who saved her, but her assailant was taken to the hospital and survived the fracture to his skull.

My mother's attacker was found to be the son of one of the richest factory owners in the town. The man's son confessed to the brutal attack on my mother and went to prison for a short while. Being from a wealthy family, he did not serve a long sentence.

His father's business provided many of the people and their families in the town with jobs which made it difficult for any officials to hand down a harsh sentence for the rich mans' son.

Author: Victoria E. Kain

He only served one year in prison. Laws were different for different people in the South. The man who saved my mother was never located. A large reward was put out by the rich factory owner to find the man who had thwarted the attacker from getting away with murder. Weeks later, my mother found out she was pregnant with me and was devastated. She believed it was from the attack that night in the alleyway.

All she could think of was what she should do about the baby she was carrying. My fate was literally in my mother's hands and in her heart. After much deliberation and tears, she decided to keep me because she reasoned that I had nothing to do with how I came about and had a right to life the same as anyone else.

It was said that she prayed a lot before I was born and that she would rid her fears of the incident by getting to know me as her child. If there was anything good in that attacker, she also prayed it would be in me. This was her feeble way of trying to forgive what had been done to her. She would see how I would turn out as a child.

My Grandmother said that my delivery was difficult for my mother. That is why she named me China because I was fragile. Working on her feet ten to twelve hours a day in the same Mill for her attacker's rich father, did not help her. That may have been why I was born early. From that day on, my mother was very sickly. She was never the same after the attack on her life.

Our lives seemed good up until my second birthday. That is when I lost my mother and was still too young to clearly understand how I lost her. No one ever told me how my mother died but I felt the loss of knowing that I had no one in the world other than the woman I called Grandmother and my sisters.

It would be a long time before I understood the true relationship of the man that saved me and my mother that night in the alley. Either way, the woman I knew as Grandmother raised me and my sisters in a household of four children. There was me, the youngest, Pearl was the oldest and Gem was the middle girl and there was Franklin, Grandmother's brother, (Shane's) son.

Uncle Buddy was the youngest of Grandmother's family and was said to be a bit touched in the head. These were the only family members I knew of and grew to love for the years I lived in the South.

As I grew up, my mind always raced back to where I actually came from. It haunted me for many years about my father and I had nightmares about not knowing him.

Two years turned into four after we lost mother and Grandmother began taking me to a prison to see a man named Ed that I didn't know. Each time we took the trip, she dressed me up very pretty with matching shoes and bows for my long curly braids. When we arrived at the prison, the guards searched my hair and my coat when we went in. I wasn't sure why I had to go, but I went.

I was always given special gifts by this man she took me to see but didn't understand, or care for that matter, why I was receiving them, but enjoyed the benefits of taking the long trip on the hot bus each month. Finally Grandmother began receiving mail from the man in prison and bought me all sorts of pretty dresses and things I always wanted.

It was not normal for children of black families to be lavished the way I was and it created a bit of an issue for my sisters' Pearl and Gem. Pearl was the oldest and we looked nothing alike. She seemed to dislike me but Grandmother said it was because she missed our mother. I thought she was simply hateful.

None of the kids received what I did but I didn't care because I liked being able to get the nice things. Later, after many visits to the prison, my Grandmother thought it best that I share the toys I received with the other kids. I believe they would have stoned me to death in my sleep if she did not have me do that. I really didn't mind as long as the kids showed appreciation for me sharing and they were nice to me. It just made my life a little easier.

One day Pearl asked Grandmother, "Why does China get all the new stuff?" She was fidgeting with her skirt, and playing with her pigtail. Before Grandmother could answer, I chimed in, "Yes, Grandmother, why do I get these things?" I asked, thinking if I played with my hair like Pearl did, it would keep Grandmother from smacking us both for asking questions about gifts.

You were never were supposed to look a gift horse in the mouth. I guessed that Ed was the horse. Whatever that meant. She finally responded to me as if Pearl had not asked the question. "You get all these pretty things because someone loves you very much." Grandmother said smiling a toothless smile. Grandmother didn't like wearing her teeth at home if she didn't have company.

She called them "company teeth." When someone came to the door, she would tell us, "Go find my teeth, and hurry up."

Today she smiled a really greedy type smile as she sat in the old chair braiding Gem's hair. She always fussed when she did their hair, but never when she did mine. Pearl and I didn't ask any more questions and she kept telling me to be nice to the man when we went to see him again.   Naturally, I did as I was told and besides, it was only a visit, it wasn't like she left me there or anything.

The next few times we went to see him, the men in the cells would look at me with a strange look in their eyes. It frightened me so much that even my Grandmother held my hand a little tighter as a way to remind me to stay close to her as we walked down the long corridors with the rest of the people coming to visit prisoners.

By the time I was eight years old, I understood a little more about things, but still had questions. I didn't dare ask anything detailed about our visits to the prison for fear of being spanked for being womanish.

That was when you thought you were grown up and was considered being out of place as a child. The South was crazy for whipping children for stupid things like asking questions that really made sense to have answers to, but only the white children were permitted to ask questions in their households.

This time, when we went to visit Ed, the prison seemed to feel colder and dirtier. All the men wore the same uniforms and looked scruffy. I never knew how to address this man in prison and the only thing Grandmother told me was that his name was Edmondo. They called him "Ed" for short.

I was not allowed to call him Ed because of being a child and all, and I had to put mister in front of it but was able to give him a hug each time I went there. This time when he came out of the locked doors, he had the biggest smile on his face. He was always hesitant to hug me and looked at Grandmother first to get her permission before he touched me. Once she gave the approving nod, he picked me up and gave me a big hug.

The hug was strangely comforting. It felt like my mother's hug whenever she had hugged me when she was alive. The man looked at me intently and told me how beautiful I was. He commented on how much I had grown since the last time he saw me and then began talking to Grandmother. While they talked, I noticed the men behind the glass windows. Ed noticed me looking at them and looked back at them and pointed to me smiling, as if he was proud of something special.

He gave them a nod and they all began smiling adoringly as if they were happy for him for some reason. Grandmother had given me a Twinkie and I was more interested in breaking it open and getting all of the filling out without getting it all over my dress. I knew Grandmother would have had a fit if I did.

The two of them talked for a while and then Ed looked at me and smiled, "so, little one, what do you want Ed to buy for you this time?"

"Just tell me and I will get it for you," he said, with all thirty two teeth showing. He was excited about something Grandmother had said to him but I didn't hear what it was. I looked at Grandmother and she hurried and nudged me. "Go on girl and tell Ed what you want."

This was my cue from her to say what we had rehearsed. Grandmother wanted to have a room added onto the house and other repairs and didn't want to ask him to do it for her. She knew if I asked he would do anything for me.

"Well, I want my own bedroom with toys in it and a bicycle." I did want my own room because I hated sleeping in the bed with Pearl and Gem. Pearl hated me and pulled all the covers from me at night leaving me shivering in the dead of winter and Gem wet the bed. I actually wanted my own bed, but they could sleep in the same room with me. I just didn't want to sleep with them.

Ed's smile changed a bit, after I asked for the room, but you could still see some teeth. He looked at Grandmother and raised an eyebrow as if to let her know that he was aware that the request was not from an eight year old but more like a 50 something year old. He soon smiled again and lowered his brow as if to give in to the request.

"I will see what I can do about that bedroom and for sure that bicycle for you." Ed replied to me. He was searching my face for sincerity of the request. "You have to promise me you will write me okay?" He asked, smiling again in full force. I gave him an agreement to write and another big hug and this time before letting me go, he kissed me on the cheek and whispered that he loved me.

The statement startled me because he had never said that before. I didn't know what to say and said nothing at all, but I felt comforted that he was there for some strange reason.

The worst part of the trip was watching the guards usher him back behind the locked doors as we walked away. They seemed to treat him with respect, but I could see by his demeanor that it was hurting his pride. There was sadness in his eyes each time he had to leave. I soon began to feel something special for Ed but I didn't know why I should have.

He was becoming like part of the family and I looked forward to seeing him more and more the older I got. All I knew was that someone cared about me. I just didn't know why, but they were family and Grandmother was very gracious and kept her eyes on me at all times. She was very protective as we walked out of the prison.

The ride home was hot and muggy on the small and cramped bus. The roads were bumpy and many people were sweaty. All the people on it had been to the prison seeing loved ones. Mostly blacks and a handful of whites were there. There were other kids on the bus just like me. The little girl sitting next to me on the way home kept looking at the bracelet Ed had bought me from a previous visit.

She looked over inquisitively and asked in the most southern drawl I had ever heard in our household. "Where you get that from?" the girl asked, flicking her freshly pressed hair out of her face. You could tell she didn't get it pressed often because she paid so much attention to it. "Did your daddy give it to yah?" she asked.

While she was trying to touch my hair, Grandmother immodestly intercepted the motion and removed the little girl's hands from my head.

She didn't like anyone fussing with my hair but her. She had threatened anyone who even mentioned trying to cut or perm my hair which I didn't need at all.

I didn't know what to tell the little girl because all I knew was that the man that bought these things for me was named "Ed." Grandmother had heard the question and answered the little girl.

"Now, that's none of your business who gave her that bracelet, just tell her if you like it or not." she said, giving the girl a hard grown up look. I think she even rolled her eyes at the little girl.

The girl didn't ask any more questions but it made me wonder about Ed for the first time. Was this man Ed my daddy? I thought, looking up at the side of Grandmother's head as if the answer would pop out of it onto my lap. I didn't know anything about Ed and had never asked until now.

He seemed kind and I knew he sent Grandmother a lot of money for me. She was later able to add on two rooms to the house and get a new furnace. I did get the bicycle that Ed promised me and because Pearl already knew how to ride and I didn't, she had to teach me and got to ride more than I did.

I waited till I knew how to ride before I stopped her from hogging the bike. Ed always bought me the nicest clothes. I even got my own room when Grandmother had two rooms added onto the house. With all the things we were getting by way of Ed, the other children began to be vexed with me. Pearl and Gem began to scold me and pick fights with me behind Grandmother's back.

They talked about me and pulled my hair and called me Casper. One Sunday we were getting ready for Sunday school and had to sit on the porch until Grandmother was ready to go. Pearl went out and got mud from the flower bed in the front yard and smeared it all over my clean dress.

She then called out to Grandmother and told her I had gotten up off of the swing and gotten dirty. I couldn't do anything but cry. When Grandmother came out and saw my pretty dress all dirty, she immediately grabbed Pearl's hands knowing she was the culprit and saw the dirt under her finger nails. She snatched her up under her arm and threw her over her lap and whaled the dickens out of her.

Gem began to tattle on Pearl after seeing the spanking she got and told how Pearl got the dirt and wiped it on my dress. She wanted to make sure she was protected from getting what Pearl had gotten. It worked! From then on, she was the informant and Pearl would hide anything she was going to do to me from Gem because she would rat on her. I finally got smart and began to bribe Gem which protected me from many frightening things Pearl would try to do.

My dress was changed into another pretty dress and from that day forward Pearl hated me. Gem got along with me because she really didn't care and knew that Grandmother would spank her as well. Pearl, on the other hand, had an itch to beat my butt and I knew she would if Grandmother was not around.

Ed continued sending money and other things to us from prison. Pearl continued to be mean to me and coerce others to do the same. It was that same year that a terrible thing almost happened to me.

It would cause my Grandmother to have to send me away from the South for my own protection. I had turned nine that year and life seemed good to me. I couldn't have asked for anything better in my life. I had Grandmother and my sisters and Ed who was all that I knew as a male figure in my life.

Grandmother's brother Buddy was down the road but they always said he was a little touched in the head from birth. I never believed it though. His eyes always said he was as sane as the rest of us.

With Ed being the only father figure in my life, I had grown to love him for the kind things he did by providing for me and all. All the other kid's fathers in the neighborhood were doing nothing for them, but Ed always came through. I remember once when Pearl had an abscessed tooth and was in so much pain she couldn't sleep.

Her jaw had swollen to the size of a baseball. Ed sent the money to have it pulled. After Pearl was better, Grandmother took me and Pearl to see Ed. It was the only time she did that. I was jealous of the fact that Ed hugged Pearl. She seemed to love thinking she had somehow stolen my thunder and now was going to see Ed with me and Grandmother. She only went once and cried when she thought she was going every time, but she didn't.

I was glad she didn't go! My poor mother, rest her soul, had done the best she could with us girls, but we all had unique personalities and looked totally different. Maybe it had everything to do with our fathers but neither of us knew who they were. Mama was a beautiful woman from all the pictures we had of her.

Author: Victoria E. Kain

She looked like a White woman. Even the ones she took with me were very nice. Mama looked very sad on all her pictures though, but it would be all I would have as a memory of her as time went forward.

I looked like a white baby on the photos and Pearl hated for Grandmother to comment on how pretty I looked. One day the three of us girls were looking through the old box of pictures which we were not permitted to do without Grandmother, and Pearl got to one of the prettiest pictures of me and mama and tore them up.

I was upset that she tore up the one picture I loved of mama, but didn't dare say anything because we all would have been in hot water. We decided to let Grandmother find it on her own one day and hoped she never would, but she did. When Aunt Paoli, Grandmother's baby sister came from New York one year to visit and they all were sitting in the living room drinking and talking and looking at pictures, she realized that picture was not there.

She asked us where it was and I was so scared that I told that we were looking at the pictures one day and Gem, the informant, told that Pearl tore it up. Grandmother was so angry that she whipped Pearl right then and there. Pearl had large welts on her back. It was nothing to get welts on your back if she was really angry.

I hated for anyone to get a whipping because it reminded me of the stories Grandmother told us about slavery. The ones that I couldn't listen to because it hurt my heart. It hurt my heart when it happened to Pearl and I wanted to console her but she seemed to hate me more for trying to make her feel better, even though Gem was the one that told.

I was willing to take a beating with them that night as a team. I walked over to her to talk to her with kindness as she sat in the corner sulking. "What do you want Red!" She snapped at me. Grimacing through her teeth. I could still see the trace of tears that had washed down her face. Her eyes were crimson from the strain of crying as she made an ugly face at me when I stated as a way to console her, "Don't cry anymore Pearl."

"It was just an old picture." I said. Wanting her to see that it didn't mean anything to me that she tore it up.

"I always thought I looked like Casper the friendly ghost anyway," I said.

"Shoot, you did me a favor by destroying that thing." I just didn't have the guts to do it." Pearl almost laughed when I said that. It seemed to make her feel better, but she still looked at me with dismay. She looked up at my hair and then my eyes and my mouth, and when her eyes dropped again, a frown replaced the almost smile on her face...

"Get away from me!" She growled, as if I had done something wrong. It was as if her inspection of me brought distaste to her inner self.

"Get out of here!!! She screamed. Then added more insult to her statement.

"And take your Casper-looking self away from me...you *Red bone*." "You think you something," she said, jumping up from the seat and trying to adjust her slightly blood stained shirt, now strutting away as if nothing had happened. Pearl was used to hiding her pain but it always showed itself. We all could see it very clearly. Something was eating her at the core.

Her statement slammed like a brick in my heart. Thinking I had made a break through with Pearl was false hope. I thought we were back on the same sheet of music. Why did she hate me so? For the first time, I ran to the mirror and examined myself for a long time. I looked with intensity trying to see what she saw in me that she hated so much. It seemed that it wasn't enough that I was kind and caring to all of the family. After all, I did love them.

I looked at my hair and ran my fingers through it inspecting it as if it were an FBI exhibit A, trying to locate a clue to some hideous crime. It was long and wavy and I couldn't see anything wrong with it, so I let the curls fall perfectly around my face. Any frizz you saw only made it look windblown, but it was pretty to me, no big deal.

My natural brown highlights reflected the sun's rays that came through the window. It looked soft and smooth. Pearl's hair was very coarse and kinky, but I thought it fit her perfectly and it was pretty when Grandmother would fix it for her.

My eyes were hazel and almond shaped. My nose was narrow and not wide and my cheeks had a rosy tint with a slight dimple on the left side. I examined my lips and they had a fullness to them that I had never taken notice of. My lashes were long and my skin was olive tanned and flawless. This was the first time I had ever examined myself this way and it felt weird.

I was beginning to feel some kind of way about myself and started to understand some of the reasons Pearl may have felt the way she did because we were vastly different. But why would that make her angry enough to heap ill treatment on me since I was nice to her? I thought about this for the rest of the day.

After Pearl's whipping that day, I began to remember when Grandmother would talk to us kids about some of the things her Grandmother and grandfather had told her when she was a little girl.

These stories became fewer and further apart until she stopped telling them. It was as if it began to bring pain to my Grandmother's heart to talk about some of the things they endured. I often wondered why she chose to remember such dreadful things and rehash them over and over again.

I simply could not understand why someone would beat any human or animal for that matter until they would shed blood. The storytelling finally stopped and she no longer had to console me every time. I used to be the only one being sent to bed when these stories were told, but now, she would send the other kids to bed along with me.

I never liked hearing or seeing anyone get a whipping. I guess I was tender-hearted the way Grandmother used to say I was. That year I began to have a deep feeling of responsibility for the way I was treated at times. I felt that I must have deserved to be called "Casper, red, and high yellow, " and not just by the children, but some of the adults as well that lived on our road. There were many names they called me but I just tried to ignore it and fit in. It was difficult to do because in this household, if you didn't look like everyone else, you were picked on.

I was like an old pair of shoes that never wore quite right. At some point, you stopped trying to wear them anywhere special and wore them in the field to pick cotton or to walk on the back of the heels in the corn field or going to the outhouse at night.

They took the place of slippers which no one had in our household. So what would happen to me? I didn't know then, and I don't know now. I still never quite understood why I felt the need to feel this way, but accepted the only solution for me at that time which was to trust anything Grandmother said because she was wise and there was no higher authority than her in the household except God, and I didn't know him well at all.

I only heard his name when Grandmother or others cried, "Lord have mercy," when something went wrong, which was always. In fact, she was all that I had in the world that I knew, other than Ed, the man she took me to see every month in prison who sent me money. What a life that was.

After the examination of myself, Pearl decided not to call me just "Red, but started calling me red riding hood, like the fairy Tale. It was as if she needed to heap more insult to it. I learned to look at the imposed insults as compliments. I thought I was special because so many concessions were being made for me, but I was always apologizing for someone else feeling bad about something they did not have or could not do. Everyone seemed to envy each other for little things. If one person had more of something than another, the folks in the household would talk about them.

I got tired of it after a while and wanted to just live my life like everyone else did. My reasoning was that I didn't care if someone's skin color was different than mine, or if their hair was straight or curly or wavy. I simply didn't care about it. That's probably why I didn't get as many whippings as the other kids because of trying to stay out of everybody's way. It still hurt me though, to hear Pearl getting whippings with the switch.

It's not like Grandmother was killing her, but it bothered me. It seemed that in my mind, there was another way to get children to behave or do things you wanted them to do or not to do. After a while, Pearl seemed to deliberately get in trouble to vex Grandmother to whip her as if she wanted to feel sorry for herself. It was the craziest thing ever.

Saturday came around quickly in our household and I didn't want to be separated from the activities on the cold nights when everyone from down the road and in the household sat by the old fireplace and baked sweet potatoes in the fireplace ashes. "Go on to bed China, "Grandmother would say. "Your ears can't hear all this." I was older now and demanded to stay. "Grandmother, I am bigger now and my heart is tough!"

"I can take it," I said. Beating my chest, ever so gently so as not to cough from losing air. Even promising her I wouldn't cry when I heard the horrid stories. Why did they tell the children such stories to make them feel bad? I thought about this for years to come. Why not tell them the good things so they had something to hold on to?

With all that, she still wouldn't let me stay and listen. From that point forward, I stopped asking. I just went to bed. I rationalized that I didn't need to fill my head with beatings of people long ago and the unfair oppression that people endured. So I thought about positive things in bed.

I didn't go into the cotton fields or stay in the sun long and didn't get whippings like the other siblings did. If Grandmother did have to spank me, she always used her hand and would hit my butt and then rub it as if she was ensuring there were no red marks on my skin because I bruised easily.

Author: Victoria E. Kain

This became a way that all light skinned children were treated. It was as if the children's skin was taken into consideration because it would give a visual of what was done to them and no one wanted to be reminded of the fact that they were repeating the cruelty that was heaped upon other Blacks during the slavery days.

So, if you were darker, the welts didn't show as readily unless you really beat the person for a longer time. Either way, it was sad and wrong. I had to prepare myself for my future or there was no telling how the world was going to treat me. After that last winter when I turned nine years old, I didn't go to see Ed anymore. That year I felt I had lost someone special in my life. I had grown fond of him but Grandmother said they moved him to another prison farther away and we would have to take the train to see him because the bus would take too long.

It seemed that everything I loved or cared about left me for one reason or another. That year, I began to feel unloved. Even though I couldn't go and see Ed, I began writing him letters and would sometimes get two or three each week from him. He even sent money in them for me and that was fun. I would always give it to Grandmother. When Pearl found out there was money in my letters, that is when she began stealing the letters out of the mailbox and burning them. She would keep the money.

As she got older she continued to get meaner and meaner. When I watched her take the mail from Ed out of the mailbox, she threatened me and said if I told on her, she would kill me like Cain killed Abel in the bible. I never told on her, because I remembered the story that Grandmother had told us about Cain.

He was a bad man and God didn't like him much. Grandmother was also getting letters from Ed about the money he was sending me too and she was asking me where the money was and I had none to give her because Pearl was taking it. Ed had written a letter asking Grandmother if she had bought me a new coat with the money he sent. That's when she became suspicious.

She wrote him a long letter back asking, "What money you talking about?" He'd respond a bit abrupt, in another letter…

"Don't be losing your mind old woman!" He said. I knew this because I snuck in her room and read them off and on. I may have been timid, but I was smart enough to find out things I needed to know when it was clear that no one would tell me anything.

"You know I sent you money." he said, including a smiley face on his letter, so as not to make her mad at him. So, Grandmother didn't respond back, but began her spy work watching the mail box. One day she pretended to go to the store before Mr. Louie, the mailman, delivered our mail for the day. Mr. Louie, was always on time with the mail and knew Grandmother would be angry if she did not receive those letters. If she had boxes, he'd bring them to the door just for her.

She knew Ed would be sending me a letter today and he did, just like clockwork. Mr. Samson, Grandmother's neighbor from down the road always drove her to the store on Saturdays for groceries, but today she had him pretend to take her shopping and drive her to the back of the property.

Pearl was napping before she left but I was peeking out the window. Mr. Sampson couldn't figure out what Grandmother was doing, but dropped her at the back of the property anyway like she asked.

Once she got back there, she got out and crouched in the corn field and watched Mr. Louie put the mail in the box and drive off. She waited and watched. I know she had to be hot in that corn field because Gem and I were just watching her out the window. We knew not to say anything or we'd be in trouble too.

Finally, out came Pearl, waltzing to the mail box as if she was the lady of the house. She was swinging her hands and hips and her butt was rocking back and forth as she walked. She always had a big butt and thought it was fun to swing it like that, especially if boys were around. Grandmother didn't like the way she walked and called her womanish, because that's how grown women walked and swayed especially if men were about.

Today Pearl seemed to swing harder from side to side almost mocking Grandmother. She waited until Mr. Louie was way down the road to make the snatch. She took the letter out of the mailbox and opened it as if it had come for her and immediately grabbed the money out and kissed it, signifying she had struck gold!

She stuck it in her bra area like grown folk do and came towards the back of the house to destroy the evidence before Grandmother arrived. Pearl was pretty bold. She went and got a match out of Grandmother's kitchen cupboard where she kept her lighter for the stove and matches.

We were forbidden to go in that cupboard. But Pearl did everything she was told not to do. She went out the back door and took the letter where Grandmother burned old boxes and papers she didn't need and burned the letter in the old wood pile…standing watching it go up in a short flame and smoke like she was offering up a sacrifice.

As she came from the wood pile, Gem and I were spying out the kitchen window and saw Grandmother emerge from the corn field like a bullet, holding her purse as if she had been somewhere but was in a hurry to get to the back yard.

Pearl almost fainted when she caught sight of Grandmother coming out of that corn field. It was as if she had seen a ghost. She asked Pearl, in a winded voice, still breathing hard from the walking she had to do in the sun.

"Why are you in the wood pile Pearlie?" she called her name in a huff.

"Just burning some old paper I had from school Grandmother." Pearl said, nonchalantly. Grandmother asked her again and this time Pearl was nervous and repeated the lie she was telling her and Grandmother just reached in her bra where she had seen her put the loot and asked her,

"Where did you get this money from gal?" She asked her in a very loud and demanding voice now, having got her second wind. Knowing she was close to finding out the truth about the theft of this money from Ed. She seemed relieved that she was about to close the case.

She didn't want Ed thinking she was lying about the money he was sending for me. She was always careful to do exactly what he wanted her to do with some of the money and she could do what she wanted with the rest. She didn't want her name attached to anything negative where his generosity was concerned.

Now crying, Pearl yelled. "I found it on the ground outside, demanding that Grandmother believe her. But instead of believing her, Grandmother pulled a switch from the old peach tree and asked Pearl again where she got the money.

"If you don't tell me the truth, I am going to beat it out of you." She said. With one strike on Pearl's legs with the thin branch, Pearl began dancing around like an Indian chief about to go to war. She was crying, but still lying about the money.

Finally Grandmother dropped her purse to the ground. Gem and I looked at each from the kitchen window, "Oh, lord, please Pearl, just tell the truth." we said, under our breath.

"If you don't tell me the truth, I am going to braid this switch with two more and tear your butt apart!" Grandmother yelled.

Pearl began to scream and yell as Grandmother continued to swat her several times more. Finally she began to tell the truth…

"I took it, I took it!" Pearl screamed. "I took it all!!! I hate China and I hate you!" She said, looking at Grandmother as if she had shot her. Grandmother, stopped swatting her either due to exhaustion or just shocked that she had said that she hated the two of us. She asked Pearl, "where's the rest of the money?"

"Go get it!" Now!" She demanded. Wobbling over to the steps to sit down from the tiring ordeal.

Pearl ran in the house and me and Gem acted as if we didn't see a thing. She went in the room and got the money that was left and gave it to Grandmother. Pearl tried to pretend that nothing happened, but Gem asked her outright, "What happened Pearl?"

"Did you get a whipping?"

"Yeah, but it didn't hurt!" she said, acting as if nothing happened.

"I just had to pretend so Grandmother would cut it short."

"I know how to jump around and make the old woman tired and she has to stop so I get fewer licks with the switch." She said smirking.

She looked at me as I sat quiet, not wanting to let on that I saw anything. She pulled my hair and pushed my head on the wall as she walked back out the door. I said nothing. After that day, she never went to the mail box again. Grandmother was strange towards Pearl after that. She realized that Pearl had said she hated her and that didn't set well with Grandmother. She continued to tell the stories on Friday nights but not about slavery. Everyone listened to them but me. I simply took myself to bed from then on.

Time went forward very fast. It seemed that we all were growing up the same and school was becoming interesting to me. Grandmother didn't whip Pearl as much after the money theft ring was resolved. It was about September now and Grandmother always made hot soup on chilly nights. This night she had made a great dinner that night in September. It was not cold outside but at night it was cool and we all ate dinner and turned in early. I was a little sleepy anyway.

I felt very strange this night when I went to bed. It was nice having my own room that Ed had made possible and I did have my little animals in it to keep me company. Grandmother always left the window cracked so it wouldn't get musty in the room, she'd say. In the dark of this night, I laid very still in my bed. Sleep would be slow coming for me for some reason.

It was as if I had a strange feeling in my heart. I started thinking about when Ed might get out of prison and if I would ever get to see him again. I wanted someone for me in my life that seemed to care about me and not just about the money being sent.

Before falling asleep, I made sure that all of my stuffed animals surrounded me as if they were the protectors I felt I never really had.

Author: Victoria E. Kain

The stuffed animals would barricade me from anyone getting close enough to me to do any harm. I had always wanted my own bedroom, as every little girl does, filled with pretty dolls, tea sets, jacks and jump ropes.

White eyelet curtains were hung perfectly on my window and every morning the sun would shine brightly through that window. I would have my special friends over and would play with them for hours and they would be wowed by the pretty things that I had.

Well, I did have the room, but it was not very fancy or large, and I did have some of the animals that Ed had sent me, and I finally had my own bedroom, but this night, I would not share it alone.

As I slept like every other night, the dim light could be seen in the hallway coming from my Grandmother's kitchen. She always left one on in there. I could hear soft footsteps coming towards my bedroom door but thought nothing of it. I always closed my door at night when I went to bed, but tonight, it was slightly open.

Still groggy, from the light sleep, I peeked through my sleepy eyes, after hearing the footsteps in the wee hours of the morning. It was almost instinctive that I woke up just before the intruder entered my room. I sensed that something was about to happen, but fear froze me and I didn't move.

As I lay very still in my bed, watching the silhouette come closer to where I lay, I slowly turned on my side to face the door. Often Grandmother came in and covered me when I had kicked off the covers, but tonight I realized I was completely covered. My heart was now pounding so loud that I hoped someone would hear it beating and burst in the bedroom.

With every beat in my little chest, I wondered what would happen next, still afraid to move.

I didn't understand what was about to happen to me and could not see the face of the intruder, but could only hear them breathing as they came closer to me and then I could feel their warm breath on my skin. Their hands slowly groping at anything they can find under the covers.

I cringed as this ordeal intensified but it did not last long. There was an excruciating burst of pain as I tried to yell but a strong hand quickly covered my mouth so tightly that I could taste the salt from their skin. That is when I knew I was in trouble. I knew something bad was about to happen to me.

Even in the dark, my eyes moved mechanically back and forth. Searching for answers to what was happening. I could smell the fragrance of menthol on the intruder's hands as he placed them firmly over my mouth pressing my lips to my teeth.

It was as if he wanted to crush my face in if I said anything at all. From that moment forward, I would hate the smell of menthol along with the strange muffled sounds the intruder made.

I did not understand why he made such sounds, but when the intruder began the ordeal over again, I was certain he would kill me this time and drag my body out of the open window of my bedroom and no one would ever find my lifeless body ever again.

I thought about what Grandmother said had happened to my mother and prayed that someone would come and save me like they had saved her, but the only person that could, would have been Ed in my mind, and he was still in prison.

Author: Victoria E. Kain

I knew I had to get the courage from somewhere to take advantage of the seemingly weakened state the intruder appeared to be in. With his hand firmly over my mouth, the only thing I could do was breathe as hard as I could to get as much oxygen in my lungs through my nose.

Finally I felt cold steel on my leg from what felt like a belt buckle. I realized that the intruder was trying to disrobe and was about to strike, when I opened my eyes as wide as I could and opened my mouth as wide as I could and clamped my teeth down with all my might on the intruders hand.

It was so intense that my upper and lower teeth met, causing the intruder extreme pain and instinctively, he screamed and jumped up holding his pants. Still wrenching in pain, he stumbled as he got to the window, pulling down the eyelet curtains and fell to the ground outside, and began running. I screamed as loud as I could and woke up the entire household.

At that moment I knew I was free! I had halted the intruder's ultimate attack of completely violating my innocence. A few more minutes and he would have damaged me forever. But, he didn't get the chance. I heard a yell from the hallway in the room across from mine. Grandmother's voice was loud and strong as if she were not sleeping at all.

My Grandmother burst into the room with her pistol aimed in the air and turned on the light like an FBI agent. She ran to the window and fired a shot from her 45. She didn't know if she hit the intruder or not, but he would not want to come back if he knew what was good for him. She fired a second shot out the window as a reminder to whoever had come into the house, that if they ever came back, that one bullet would be especially for them.

It also put a secure feeling in my young heart that someone was there to protect me. I felt that, this night. Grandmother checked me out and saw that I was okay. I had blood on my lips which shocked her because she thought it was mine. Upon examination, she saw it was the intruder's. She looked at me deep in my eyes as if she wanted to cry. "You are strong, aren't you?" She said, as if she was surprised that I had the strength or the sense to fight back.

"I told you I was not scared Grandmother." China said. That night, she let me sleep with her the rest of the night. The next morning came too swiftly. Grandmother, Pearl and Gem and the neighbors all looked for the man the next day to see if they could find out who it was that had broken into the house. I told what I could remember about the person, but apparently it was not enough.

There was one thing I didn't tell. After the attack, Pearl laughed at me and made fun of me and told everyone I was raped. I wasn't, but I still felt dirty, thinking I had somehow brought the attack on. Pearl got in trouble for the lies she told and she couldn't go to the fair that week. Grandmother was very concerned for my safety and realized that someone wanted to harm me.

She had many hushed conversations with Ed over the phone and soon Grandmother told me that I would be going away to stay for a while with her sister, Aunt Paoli, in New York. Aunt Paoli had one daughter by a man who died in the war. He was said to have been a ruthless man but left her with a few nice things to include her daughter. Going there was like jumping out of the skillet into the fire. I didn't want to go at all.

Author: Victoria E. Kain

I cried and begged not to go. I tried to convince Grandmother that I wasn't scared and would always fight if someone tried to bother me. It was important that she trust me, but I didn't feel she really understood what I needed from her. Grandmother tried to console me but couldn't. Being desperate, thinking I would be sent away from my family, I mustered up the courage to ask her to talk to Ed first about this, as if she didn't know the right thing to do for me.

"Just go on now, gal!" she said. "I'll let you know when you leaving." You don't know what you are asking me to do, and stop thinking you are something!" she yelled at me. Something was strange about that statement to me and I continued to pester her to talk to Ed. After all, she had gone to him for everything else she needed, why not advice, so I asked her again.

That is when Grandmother turned around and slapped my face. She seemed unnerved that I even made the statement and for the first time she had struck me in the face as if I had done something wrong when I had only asked a question. My face turned beet red and her hand print was on my pale skin. "Lord have mercy child," Grandmother said, trying to rub off the hand print from my face.

"Just look at you now!" She was wearing the saddest look I had ever seen on her face. "Don't you go telling Ed or nobody you got slapped either." She commanded.

I didn't know anything about slavery and the stories she told the rest of the kids, but I eavesdropped enough to know that this is what slaves use to endure. Just asking simple questions got you slapped in the mouth. I cried very hard and then got quiet like an animal that had been beaten, although it was only a slap.

Grandmother soon realized she couldn't wipe the hand print off my beet red face. It was the thing she didn't want to see. "That's what I don't like bout you high yellow children."

"I can't whip you like the others!" She kept me in the room and made me lie down. It was as if she thought sleeping would make it go away. It actually did go down after I stopped crying. I took a nap and tried not to think about leaving for the rest of the day.

While I laid there in her bed, I heard the kids from down the road come and ask if I could come out to play. I heard her tell them a fib that I was not feeling well. For the first time I knew what Pearl and others felt like getting slapped. I could only imagine what a whipping felt like. I didn't like it and thought that maybe I would be better off not being here. I didn't feel as if they wanted me anyway.

That night, since I slept in the room with Grandmother again, I gave some thought to the day's events. I was very quiet, reasoning that Grandmother probably had already talked to Ed and he had advised her to move me and that may have upset her. That is why she slapped me…I was sure of it now. Having to sleep in the bed with her gave me access to the letters from Ed. I had read them before, but this time I didn't have to sneak to get in her room since I was already in there.

I felt it was time to take action and get answers to some of the madness I was experiencing. I knew where her box of mail was and got the letter out from Ed. I saw a recent letter on the side of the box that Ed had sent her and what I read sent chills up my spine.

Author: Victoria E. Kain

Dear Ms. Eloise,

I am very angry that this thing has happened to my China Doll. I told you to look after her for me until I get out and keep her safe since she lost her mother. I told you I would take care of you and her and have sent you money for her since she was a baby and am concerned that she may be in harm's way there. Please accept the money I have enclosed which is enough to move China with your sister in New York.

Since they moved me closer to New York I may be able to see China if she is there. There is over four thousand dollars to get her set up in a private school and I will send more. I will be setting up a trust fund for her as well when she is old enough, so she will be able to receive the funds herself if I am not out of prison by then. I do not want any daughter of mine in a public school.

I have other relatives that will be checking on her indirectly as well. I go before the parole board in three months. If all is well, I may be getting out soon. I appreciate all you have done for my daughter and hope you have kept me alive in her heart. I have much love and respect for you. Tell China that I love her very much and will ensure she never has to experience that again and will be writing her every week. Take care.

Edmondo

Dropping the letter quickly back in the box to ensure no one saw me, I jumped back in bed. I knew if Grandmother had any idea I had read the letter from Ed, she would surely beat me like she beats Pearl. I was nervous and said nothing while echoing the words "Daughter!"

"I am his daughter!"

"He called me his "China Doll?"

That was such an endearment to me. No one ever spoke of me in a positive manner that way. This was something special to know, yet I was never given these kind words from this man that I was just finding out was my father. Repeating the word "daughter" over and over again made me feel good inside. I couldn't believe that I had a father but was never told that he was that to me. What does it mean to keep these kinds of secrets from a child? Didn't I need to know that there was someone in this world that was related to me and loved me in this way?

I cried the whole night and was awake when Grandmother got in bed. I pretended to be asleep and wept silently as she farted all night and snored. Now I know that Edmondo is my father! I loved the thought of knowing I had a living parent. What would happen to me now? I knew I had to pretend not to know I had a father and the fact that "he" had made that decision and not Grandmother. Now I understood why Grandmother slapped me.

She didn't want me to go but she had to do as Ed asked since he was my parent. She didn't want me or the money to be taken away from her, but I still loved her, even though I never understood why they had never told me the truth. If Ed is my father, I must have other relatives just like me. I wanted to know everything…and I wanted to know it now, but would have to wait and see what other skeletons were in our families' closet.

Weeks went by and all arrangements had finally been made for me to leave. Pearl was already telling Grandmother she wanted to take my room. It was the first time I hated Pearl. She made me sick! I would find out later that Grandmother turned my room into a sewing room. She felt that Pearl would have been letting boys in her room through the window freely.

Knowing Ed was my father and that he wanted me gone from there for my safety gave me comfort. I accepted that he would know best for me. I also wondered if Ed may have known something about who tried to attack me that night and felt Grandmother was getting old and would not be able to protect me.

Maybe he thought the person might come back, the thought of which was beginning to frighten me. I was hoping the day would hurry and come for me to leave with that thought. Grandmother had told me not to tell anyone when I was leaving. She didn't even tell me. Days went by and then one night, she got me up early in the morning.

Our neighbor picked us up and already had my suitcase in their car. I was half asleep when we left that morning before day break. I didn't get to say my goodbye to Pearl or Gem or Franklin. Grandmother and I boarded the Amtrak train that morning and waved goodbye to the neighbor that drove us to the station.

I never knew why we had to leave secretly and Grandmother was very nervous. It was a long ride for us to New York. Grandmother looked out the window and I saw tears come up in her eyes for the first time. She pretended she was coming down with something. The White porter came over and looked at Grandmother and then at me. He didn't speak to her but asked me,

"So little lady, aren't we pretty today?"

"Thank you!" I said politely.

"Are you going home to your parents?" he asked, now very close to my face to the point that I could smell the tobacco on his breath.

I quickly responded, "Yes, I am!" I smiled as if it was the happiest day of my life.

Oddly enough, Grandmother didn't say a word or scold me, but smiled an approving smile as if she was glad I wasn't afraid to speak and had showed him what manners I had. Well, I was never afraid to speak…it was that no one had ever asked me anything.

The white people on the train smiled at me and were very generous. I didn't understand the difference in the treatment I received at the time or that of my Grandmother. They acted like she didn't exist but treated me very nicely, like I was one of them. During dinner time the Black people normally ate at their seats on the train. The Porter came and told Grandmother that she could bring me to the dining car if I would like.

"Would you like that, little lady?" the Porter asked me.

"Yes, please," I responded properly, again smiling nicely, to get the approval of Grandmother. Once I realized that I received extra desserts and juice on the train whenever I asked for them, I started getting things for Grandmother when she wanted something and they ignored her request.

We shared. When the power went out in the car where all the Black people were and we had no heat in our section, the porter came and took me and Grandmother to the car that had heat in it.

He looked at her and said that I didn't deserve to be cold. Grandmother had arthritis in her hands and knees and was so cold she couldn't get up to go to the bathroom. Why was I the only one deserving to be warm? I was cold too, but Grandmother was old. She had a horrible cold after that ride.

The porters all winked at me and told me to let them know if I needed anything. I was beginning to see what prejudice looked like. Grandmother used the money Ed had given her for us to travel but we got a lot of things free because I looked White.

Author: Victoria E. Kain

I got more hugs than I had ever gotten from Grandmother on the train. She knew that once we got to New York, she wouldn't see me anymore. Sadness kept coming over me throughout our trip. I didn't want to leave Grandmother and she felt the same.

I would miss Pearl, Gem, uncle Buddy as well as Mr. Louie the postman and even our old dog Tuff luck, who had followed us home one day from old Ms. Pembroke's house. Once we fed him, he stayed. My life would change in many ways once I was with Aunt Paoli in New York. Regardless of where I had been, I still wanted to know where I came from and where the rest of my family was.

I vowed to find this out once and for all. I wanted answers to questions I had for what seemed like forever… Forever would be a long time coming. It was a very long trip but enjoyable because I got to spend those few days with Grandmother. We bonded a lot on the train. She seemed very different. When we finally arrived in New York, Aunt Paoli's boyfriend Benny picked us up. Benny didn't say much in the way of greeting us.

"You all coming from down South huh?" he asked.

"That's right," Grandmother responded.

"South Carolina," she said proudly, trying not to have a southern accent.

After that, he said nothing else until we got to Aunt Paoli's. We got there and I was literally dropped off. Grandmother and Aunt Paoli sat and talked most of the night and I even heard them arguing a bit. I assumed it had to be over money and me being there. Aunt Paoli's daughter wasn't home when we arrived and my Aunt showed me where I could put my few things in a dark basement apartment she had in her run down Condo.

The Blanket of Southern Heat

As I looked around the room in dismay, Grandmother, snatched me and gave me this big hug. I really didn't want to let her go because I knew that I wouldn't see her any more after this day. The look in her eyes was a look of sadness for herself and for me. I know she wanted to cry but didn't so I wouldn't cry as well.

"You be a good girl to your Aunt Paoli, you hear?" she said.

"I will Grandmother," I said quietly. This was our moment and I wanted nothing to spoil it. I knew she didn't want to leave me and that she had no choice in the matter but I didn't know why. This was where I would sleep for the next few years and grow up to be a young woman. I only prayed I could come out unscathed as so many in the South didn't. The north was even worse with the thugs that ruled the streets.

Grandmother and Aunt Paoli left me to unpack my things and I put them in the cardboard chest that she had bought with some of the money Ed sent her. It looked as if it had already been used and I saw a roach come out of one of the corners and I crushed it on the floor.

Grandmother's house was not dirty like this one was so this would take some getting used to. I was so tired and got into the tiny bed which only had one blanket and a flat pillow. I noticed that the bed that was on the other side of the room that was supposed to be for Brendalyn was a new bed with clean sheets and two pillows.

It looked as if they had switched the beds so that she had the new one that was bought for me. I was furious just knowing this. I couldn't say anything to them about it, but I reasoned that this is why Brendalyn may not have wanted to be there to greet us, because they knew they had made the switch.

Author: Victoria E. Kain

Ed gave them a lot of money for me and he would not have agreed with me sleeping in a dirty bed like this.

The sheets on my bed didn't smell fresh so I took it upon myself to take the other bed instead. All the new stuff in the room was mine and I knew it so I figured if I didn't start now by letting them know that they could not take advantage of me, they would continue to get worse. I moved my clothes over to the new chest and packed them away neatly and got ready for bed.

I figured that if anyone was going to say anything about it actually being Brendalyn's, I would have Grandmother contact Ed and let him know and they would have to scramble because they wanted his money. The clean bed with the new sheets and mattresses felt wonderful. Besides, I was tired and mad that I had to be there in the first place.

But now that I was comfortable, I felt a little relief that I would stand up for myself and not let people take advantage of me. I didn't know what my living arrangements were coming to from this point forward, but I was prepared to fight if I had to. I knew Grandmother would be gone before I woke up which disturbed me but I accepted my lot in life.

It seemed that I would go to sleep as a little girl, but would wake up an adult, having to take care of all of my affairs myself from now on. Life felt like it was taking a turn for the worse for me. Only time would shed its ugly light on my part of the world. These next few years would tell the story about who I really was.

~ CHAPTER 2 ~

CHANGING GEARS

Changing Gears

Living with Aunt Paoli and her daughter Brendalyn was no picnic. It was like jumping out of the skillet into the fire with what I had to deal with concerning these two women. Naturally they would not like me either, for the same reasons Pearl didn't like me, but I was used to that.

Aunt Paoli and her daughter hated everything about me. They gloated at night in their rooms about the money they received from Ed and what they were going to do with it and cackled like old hens in a hen house. They really made me sick just watching them undulate through the house with the dirty robes on and curlers in their hair all day until the evening like Madams in a whore house.

My Aunt had no choice but to pretend to like me but I really didn't care. I felt that they owed me something for being the reason they received a free paycheck. When I felt the need to throw my weight around which was not often, I seemed to get results then and when I called Ed's name around them. They were afraid to make him angry. I knew that Ed wrote her often because I would see letters for her when he wrote to me.

I had to find the time when both of them were out of the house to sneak in my Aunt's room and read her letters. The one letter she received from Ed stated something that gave me a sense of complete confidence. I read the letter from him two months after I arrived and what he stated was interesting to say the least.

Ms. Paoli,

You are well aware that my daughter China who is living with you is very precious to me. I will stop at nothing to get there or send a suitable representative if "ANYTHING" should happen to her.

All of the money that I send to her, temporarily through you, "MUST" be used for her or I will send someone to visit your home unannounced, to express my disappointment in you.

I also give you the stipend of 1,500 per month as the caregiver for her and hope that she is well and happy.

If she does not receive my letters and respond to me, I will know that they are being kept from her and will do exactly as I have stated above. Please see enclosed the cashier's check for $3,000 for her specific needs. What she states that she wants, "get it for her!" If you do not have enough money for it, "Send me a message" and I will get it to you for her. Either way, she is to have whatever she asks for or this arrangement of money will stop immediately. Thank you for your assistance.

Edmondo.

Reading that letter gave me a sense of empowerment to know that someone loved me enough to stand up for me like that. It also made me feel good that someone was looking over me and I didn't know who this "representative" would be that was spoken of that he would send if I was harmed in any way. I felt good that Ed loved me like that. Even though he was not physically in my life, he had a powerful presence in the background. It gave me the much needed courage I would need in dealing with my current living situation.

I wanted to test Aunt Paoli and see if she would do what Ed said, so one night I went in her room and told her that it was really hot in the basement apartment. The air conditioning was not cooling the same down there as it did the rest of the house. I asked her if she could get a small window air conditioning for me. At first she came unglued.

"Why do you need an air-conditioner when Brendalyn has not said anything about it being too hot down there?"

"Well, Brendalyn is never here," I said.

"That's going to cost me too much money to do this for you. You are not even working anywhere either," she said.

I looked at her and held my head down as if I were sad and responded.

"Okay, I understand, I will send a message to Ed and see if he could send the money for it."

I busied myself with finding paper to send Ed a letter.

Aunt Paoli was very nervous. I saw her scratching her head and looking perplexed as if she didn't know how to say what she knew she had to say. Finally the words came out.

"Well, let me see what my budget looks like, I may be able to get one from one of those discount stores on 40th street on clearance."

"It sure is taking a lot of money to keep you," she said, scowling her face.

"I don't know why Ed is so concerned about you having everything you want," she mumbled, as she walked out the door fussing. All I knew was that it worked! She was going to do what Ed said regardless. Now I know. I really didn't ask for much else, but if I needed something, I went through the same routine.

The city was big and dirtier than any place I had ever seen. People were rude and we lived in a rough neighborhood. I was scared all the time and never went anywhere but to school and back home.

Aunt Paoli was extremely overweight and snored so loud at night that no one could get any sleep in the house, not even their dog Boots, who had fleas and ended up dying of Canine parvovirus, which is likened to Aids for humans.

Aunt Paoli was the wig queen and wore a million different ones. All colors and styles. She used to want to "do" my hair, but I didn't trust her with anything of mine and refused. Once again, she always said I thought I was something. The same statement I got slapped for at Grandmothers and I heard it from Pearl and other kids from around the road when I lived in the South. Now I just tell anyone who said that to me, exactly what I thought.

"Yes, that's right, I am something and don't forget it!" It always worked and that became my signature statement. I learned how to do my own hair so no one else would have to. Aunt Paoli did what Ed asked her to do for me out of fear and he provided well for me. We got new carpet in the basement and they remodeled the bathrooms so I didn't have to share with Brendalyn. Everyone that came to see her, used hers.

The room was divided so that we had more privacy because I told Ed about Brendalyn and her unhealthy habits. He must have said something to Aunt Paoli because she eventually put a divider in the room but I could still smell Brendalyn's side of the room because she kept it dirty. For some reason, Aunt Paoli seemed to obey Ed, but tried to be slick and buy me cheap things until I told him about the lack of quality in the items she bought me with the money he sent.

After that, Ed began sending me the money for my school clothes and such. Aunt Paoli spent the bulk of the money he gave her on her wigs, alcohol and cigarettes.

Author: Victoria E. Kain

She bought them by the case for her and Brendalyn. Brendalyn was quiet and didn't bother me, but she literally was a kept prostitute. The only thing she couldn't do was bring the men that came to see her through the front door. They came in every other way. She would have brought them down the chimney like they say Santa comes into a home, if they had one.

Brendalyn was very skinny, just the opposite of her mother. If I had to rate her beauty on a scale of 1-5, one being the highest, I would give her a 3, but she would knock that number down to a 5 because of her ugly conceited personality and horrid behavior. She thought she looked better than she did and had boys coming into the basement where we slept. I got so sick of the smell from the boys who were not clean coming in to be with her.

One night I realized she had changed from having boys to men coming in through the window. This one night an old man came in through the window and she almost had to call 911 because he thought he was having a heart attack trying to climb the fire escape. He stayed until almost day break.

She seemed to like this old geezer for some reason. I put ear plugs in my ears and an additional barrier up around my bed like Alcatraz and had to take it down each morning so Aunt Paoli didn't see it. I swore to her that I would kill anyone that came near me. She knew I wasn't lying.

My life was a living hell. The house smelled of smoke and old worn underwear. Aunt Paoli would take me to school in her raggedy car and kept her new one parked at the house for her dates. Her daughter continued to be promiscuous and finally ended up getting pregnant by the old man before she finished school.

Later, it was found out that the father was the old geezer who turned out to be Aunt Paoli's boyfriend who was sneaking in the basement. I never knew who the old geezer was and didn't really care, but knew it was something weird.

Once it was known that Brendalyn was pregnant, I sent a letter to Ed and he sent one to Aunt Paoli and Brendalyn was moved from the basement apartment. She took the room upstairs next to Aunt Paoli and they fought every night. I didn't care because the apartment was all mine and now I could keep it clean.

On another occasion, I read another letter where Ed had asked her to bring me to see him. She made an excuse about wanting to take me and as soon as I showed enthusiasm, she started a fake cough and said she was not feeling well.

She had been there to see him once and had said that the men in the prison sneered and booed her because she was so fat and unattractive. She didn't want to go there but she wanted the money and didn't want me telling him about the conditions I was living in. She knew that soon I would be old enough to take care of myself.

All she wanted was the money for her and her daughter, who was lazy and now pregnant. The saddest thing was that even though she was pregnant, she still had men coming to the house and they smoked weed all the time.

I didn't want a contact high, so I tried to stay in the library a lot to keep from getting one. I remember I was walking to the library after school this one day, when I noticed a man across from the library just standing looking at me. I kept walking, thinking it was my imagination that he was stalking me. When I got to the library door, I looked back and he was still there.

Author: Victoria E. Kain

I rushed in the door and looked out of the tinted glass window and he stared in the direction of the library and slowly walked away. That was spooky for me and I didn't come back to the library after school for a while believing he was watching me. I often wondered who this man was, but would not find out until years later.

Time was going by fast and the year was coming up soon for my graduation. I had worked hard and got excellent grades. I had even tried to help Brendalyn, even though she was home schooling, but she still failed and did not graduate. Finally graduation came. It was a wonderful time, but there was no one there from my family.

I would have thought that Grandmother would have but understood that her arthritis prevented her from sitting long periods of time and she refused to board a plane. Aunt Paoli lost her mind over the fact that her boyfriend was the father of her grandchild and the two of them fought like cats and dogs until her daughter had the baby.

Brendalyn ended up giving the baby up for adoption. Aunt Paoli hated me because I finished school with honors. During the graduation, all the classmates took pictures with me, but I had no one to take pictures with from my family. I still enjoyed myself, but a strange thing happened.

As the graduates walked out of the auditorium, I noticed the same man that I saw across from the library that one day. I did a double take as I saw him in the audience. He quickly turned his head and I had to keep up with the procession and could not stop. I reasoned that he must have had a child in the graduation or family member and let the thought go.

After graduation, I turned 18 that same year. I decided to move out of Aunt Paoli's. I contacted Grandmother and asked her to have Ed send me the money to get my own place. I had had enough when Brendalyn came back and forth in the house with different men.

Ed sent Grandmother five thousand dollars for me to move. It also would help with college books and tuition to get started in the fall. He knew that sending the money to someone else kept me safe from people targeting me for an attack in this big city.

He knew this city because he had grown up here. That was smart and considerate of him to do this for me as a father. I found a place for myself and started college the same year.

Each month I received money in an account and often wondered if Ed was wealthy because he sent so much money for me. One month he sent me 6,000, but I didn't get anything for another three months or so. I later heard that Aunt Paoli got very sick and was sad because the money stopped when I left.

My life was still very sad. I knew in my heart I could take care of myself better than she had done, but appreciated her opening her home to me. I felt sad for them as well.

After Brendalyn left, Aunt Paoli lost her new car and her house. Ed continued to give Grandmother money to help her but he sent nothing to Aunt Paoli. He appreciated what Grandmother had done for me and the fact that she never missed bringing me to see him. The first year after moving out went by fast in college.

It was frightening at first to be on my own, but I had learned how to maneuver around in the city and to stay out of harm's way.

Author: Victoria E. Kain

By the second year of college, I was really lonely. I guess my biological clock must have been ticking because I wanted companionship like all the other women I saw with their husbands or fiancés.

On those cold nights and warm summer days, I wanted someone to hold my hand and tell me they loved me too. Many men tried to talk to me but I was seriously confused about who I was and did not feel it was the right time to begin a relationship with a man… until I met Travis.

By the end of my second year of college, I met Travis. He also was a manager at a fine Italian restaurant I frequented. I seemed to gravitate to Italian foods for some reason and occasionally went for the Italian bread, but not often. Travis seemed nice and ran the local restaurant. He was very well known by the ladies in my classes and they mostly went there to flirt with him.

Some days I went to the restaurant by myself, and when he would see me, like all the other guys, he would stare for hours, neglecting his team and becoming visibly agitated when they broke his concentration from gazing at me sitting at the corner table, where I always sat.

He was a handsome man with smooth dark skin and a nice smile. Very muscular with a nice build and brown eyes. He wore his hair in a low cut and a trimmed beard. For weeks he watched me and sometimes sent extra things to my table, especially if other ladies were with me.

Once he sent extra items and I told the waiter it was not what I ordered and they pointed to Travis who was standing behind the counter, mouthing the words, "It's on me." Smiling an accepting smile.

I would accept it, but never ate all of whatever he sent because I didn't eat that much. If someone was with me, they gobbled it down. Finally, one evening I went in and he was sitting in the seat where I always sat. I found it odd, but immediately began looking for another seat to do my studying and just be out until I went home for the evening. It was my recreation time.

As I looked away, he beckoned for me to take the seat and he got up abruptly.

"I am sorry, I know you always sit here," he said,

"No, I can find another seat since you are working." China said.

"No." he said, "I insist."

"Well, if you insist," I stated, while moving my bag over to the opposite side of the table, but he did not get up from his side.

"What can we get you today Ms.?" He gleefully said, again hoping to prolong the conversation and get my last name.

"Well, a latte and spaghetti with meat sauce." She said.

"Will that be all, Ms.?" he said again, tapping his ticket with my order on it as if hoping for more time with me and to get a name to put with the Ms.

"That will be all." I said.

"And my name is China."

"Well, China, I will have this out to you, piping hot in 10 minutes if I may be permitted to sit and dine with you?" I was stunned by the request, but had seen him staring for weeks and welcomed the adult contact. I knew I had a strong attraction to him, but wanted to be careful.

I remembered what Ed had told me. I accepted the invitation and he had his employees take the order.

Author: Victoria E. Kain

We both had our dinner together that day and from that night forward, we got to know each other and he began to court me officially. I did what I thought was the right thing and wrote Ed about him, but he almost went ballistic in his letter back to me like a true parent, so I didn't say much about Travis anymore. I guess this is what dads do. I wasn't use to this type of response and didn't know how to take it.

I was really nervous and really wasn't sure about how fast we were moving. I spoke with a close classmate, Trisha, and some of the other girls at the college who thought he was all that and a bag of Doritos. Travis seemed to come from nowhere and said he was from the South originally which made us kindred spirits. It was nice to have someone in my life that seemed to understand some of my struggles having lived in the South.

We would meet after class before he went to work and had good simple fun. I didn't want to be intimate before marriage so I put him off a lot, but he seemed okay with the premise of chastity. It was difficult to hold him off because he was such an amorous man. He constantly referred to how beautiful I was and stated how much he wanted and needed me in his life.

While we talked about many things from his past and what we wanted to do in the future, there were still things I would find out much later that he did not divulge to me. Many nights I fought the urge to give in to his pleadings, but knew it was the right thing to do. I didn't want to disappoint Ed or Grandmother by conducting myself inappropriately even though I was a legal adult.

Many of my classmates in college were pregnant with several children and unmarried. It was difficult for all of them with no help from the fathers.

I didn't want to end up like that, so I chose to wait. It's not that I was a prude, but I would recommend chastity to any person who is unmarried.

I also remembered the cardinal rule Ed had given me as a father, about not letting a man into my apartment because once they were in, they would want to stay and take over and would never appreciate what you had done to secure your place. Let them work for what they will have and they will have more respect for it. For this reason, I wouldn't let Travis or any man come to my place.

Travis also didn't bring me to his place either. He said he respected me for my values and I appreciated him more and more. I received flowers and candy and phone calls all the time from him. It felt good to know that when I left school I had someone waiting to see me.

He would pick me up sometimes and take me wherever I needed or wanted to go. He was a comfort for me and I loved having him around. When he hugged me, I knew it was genuine because I could feel him trembling like he was afraid I would crumble from his strength. There was no man in my life before him other than Ed who technically was not in my life, and since he was still in prison, he couldn't protect me.

I never told Travis about Ed being in prison. I skirted around the subject all the time because I wanted to ensure that he was the one before I divulged that information. There were still questions I had about him, but I did tell him about Grandmother and my sisters, Pearl and Gem. I told him about losing mama when I was only two. Maybe that's why he didn't ask much about Ed. He probably felt he was like most dads and just disappeared.

Having no one to tell you to take things slow and not accept the first proposal you receive, our romance went from one thing that led to another and before I entered my third year of college, Travis asked me to marry him and I accepted his proposal. I did let Grandmother and the family there know about the marriage. I met his family and they seemed nice and accepted me into their family. His sister Janice was sweet and we became good friends. We were both in our early twenties.

Travis was ten years older than me and I didn't feel uncomfortable with this because I didn't want anyone too old or too young, but old enough to take care of me. That was a good age difference I thought. Since we were both in school, he said he didn't want to have a wedding but said we would go to the court house.

He promised me we would have a honeymoon later, but that would never happen. Either way, his family wanted to do something for us, so they had a small dinner to celebrate our marriage. Afterwards, we spent the night in my apartment together for the first time. Obviously the consummation of the marriage was new, exciting and challenging for me.

My husband seemed to know his way with a woman and made me feel very comfortable with our relationship and marriage. For the first time in my life, I felt as if I belonged somewhere. I no longer had to wonder what it was like to love someone and not know if they loved me back. Travis was very open about his love for me with everyone…especially me.

As time went on, Travis became more and more protective of me, but that only drew us closer together. His protectiveness was like a special extension of Ed's caring attitude for me.

The only difference with Travis was that we were closer because he was my husband now. I was Mrs. China Stone. Finally, I's was married! As the old country folk use to say. I was proud to change my name on all of my important documents. It made me feel special. It was as if I were starting a whole new identity. Like shedding an old skin and a new one was emerging all fresh and clean. I liked that feeling.

Each day we were together, it was like something out of a fairytale. I felt exceptionally special when he called me his "China doll." That was the thing that took my breath away when he endeared me with those words which took my feelings over the edge for him. Ed was the only person that had called me that when I found out he was my father. I thought this would last forever.

For months, we became inseparable. Travis took me everywhere with him and allowed no one to come near me. There were days when I went to the restaurant after class like I always did and the male employees would be cat calling and whistling at me when I walked in. Travis was so vexed about it that he threw the guys out of the restaurant, telling his boss they were harassing other customers, when they were only harassing me.

Upper Management began noticing that they were losing customers because Travis was throwing many of the male customers out because of the attention they were giving me. On one occasion, his boss walked into the restaurant, not knowing who I was and approached me and asked,

"Can I take your order Ms.?

"No thank you!" I said, looking at him with dismay… I saw the look he gave me and looked away, hoping he would just leave.

"Well, I am the owner, and if there is anything, I mean, anything you need, just let me know." He said.

"Here is my card and my personal number on the back." Now winking at me just as Travis came out of the back office and saw the whole thing.

Boldly walking up on his boss, he quickly made his move.

"I see you've met my wife," Travis said, proud and aggressive. Mr. Crenshaw had an embarrassing and sick look on his face! He just turned around and walked out as if someone had shot him for nothing. He never acknowledged Travis's statement.

That night when Travis got home, he asked me what his boss had said to me. I told him, but he didn't seem to believe me. It was the first time he acted as if I had done something wrong. I didn't like the feeling I got from his attitude about what he thought his boss said but there was a part of me that didn't want to tell him either.

This side of him was a bit frightening. He warned me not to come in the restaurant anymore, because it was causing too much commotion. When I asked why, he said, just because. Then he blurted out in an almost rage I'd never seen before.

"These men think because you look White that you are a White woman and when they see me, looking like Kunta Kinte, they become angry," I don't know if I will have a job long now because of you.

That statement hurt me very deeply and I began to cry. Travis was quick to console me and apologized and told me that he wanted me to be safe and that he was jealous of me. Why would Travis feel that my coming to the store meant he wouldn't have a job?

I agreed not to come to the store again and that seemed to make him happy. He always loved being with me and showed all of his love for me as my husband no matter who was around.

I felt very special and thought there was no one better than Travis. We got over the incident that evening and got through the night with flying colors. I knew Travis loved me and I loved him and knew that nothing could come between us. I thought I had finally found my true love and was understanding what it felt like to belong. I didn't want to jeopardize that and did as he asked.

As time went on, Travis was a loving husband but still became more possessive. He seemed agitated when any man looked at me or even paid me a simple greeting. I was not permitted to return a simple friendly acknowledgement. We occasionally argued about it and he began to stay later and later after work sometimes, but I never questioned him.

I was three years into college now and really didn't have any female friends. I missed Grandmother and longed for other female company. As the days went on, one day I was collecting the mail from the mailman and noticed a letter from South Carolina. I thought it was a letter from Grandmother and rushed to tear into it. It was actually from Pearl.

I was glad and shocked to receive it and opened it and read it fast, hoping it was something good because she always hated me. I had not heard from her since I left South Carolina.

In the letter, she was very positive and told me all about what had happened there since I left. She acted like the girlfriend I always wanted, but thought I would never find. It would be comforting for a moment because I had just wished for someone to talk to.

Author: Victoria E. Kain

She said the old tattling mailman had died and our dog Tuff Luck had run away because uncle buddy scalded him one day with hot water.

Gem was still Gem and doing well.

Then she said something I didn't expect. She apologized for the entire negative attitude she had towards me when we were kids and asked for my forgiveness. I was in tears and said I forgave her in my heart. She said she had missed me and wanted to know if she could come and stay with me for a few weeks. She wanted to move from the South and was tired of the hillbilly routine.

I laughed and agreed that it was rather country there. She said she was proud that she had a sister that was citified and as educated as I was and would love to come to New York and have me show her around. I was so excited that I jumped up and called Travis to see if he was okay with her staying with us for a few weeks. Since he didn't want me to have girl-friends from the college, he shouldn't have any problems with my sister, but I wanted to check. The apartment had two bedrooms and she said she would pay a little something to contribute towards the household.

We could use the extra money and Travis didn't have problems with women being around him at all. He was a good looking man and well-built and had a way with the ladies. It was known that he adored me so I didn't worry about other women. I made arrangements with Pearl to come up the next week and she arrived at the train station right on time.

When she stepped off the train, I almost didn't recognize her. She was very stately and beautiful. She had done something different with her hair and looked amazing. I gave her the biggest hug and Travis gave her an even bigger one.

That was odd for someone he didn't know, but there was no space between them in this hug and she didn't seem to pull back at all. Again, I didn't think much of the elongated hug, but thought since we were family it was legitimate.

We went to dinner that night at the restaurant and had a blast. She was so different, but I noticed the long stare she gave Travis and the unusual eye contact and sexual gestures. A couple of times, I caught her looking at me and Travis being playful. It was as if she was jealous and had that old mean look in her eye again, but quickly turned it around when she saw me looking at her.

"Okay, you two love birds, cut it out!" She said, putting her hand between us to separate us in a playful manner. We all laughed and ignored her as he planted a big kiss on my lips. Travis loved playing with me in front of women like that. He did it all the time and I watched him make women squirm knowing they wished they had a man to show them as much attention as I received. I believe that is why he didn't want men around me because so many were drawn to me. We all seemed to be getting along well. When we were at home and we played scrabble or other games with Pearl, it would be getting late and Travis would always say,

"Okay, it's time for me to take my China Doll to bed, and he would raise an eyebrow." "She needs her beauty rest." He'd say. Then he'd pick me up and put me over his shoulder. I would wave goodnight to Pearl as he carried me to our bedroom. Pearl always looked at me with a strange look as my hair fell across my shoulders and his and bounced back and forth. Travis always made me laugh as we closed our bedroom door. Several months went by and Pearl had not found work anywhere.

Finally I talked Travis into giving her a job in the restaurant. She was grateful to get the work and we needed the extra money. Some nights Travis and Pearl got in later and later. I didn't think much about it because there was nothing lacking in our relationship and working late was part of his job. He was always attentive to me and never wavered in his seeming devotion and always took care of what I needed materially and otherwise.

When women would come on to him in my presence, he would set them straight, "Aaaah, ma'am, as you can see, I am a married, rather, "happily, married man." "No crumbs here." He would say to them and embarrass the women for their cheap attempts. His loyalty was not in question.

Our lives seemed to be going really well and Travis had begun hounding me about having a baby. He had been promoted on his job but had told me he wanted to drop out of school to work more hours so he could buy the Condo we had talked about for years before we began having our babies. It was my last year of school finishing my bachelor's degree. Pearl and I were getting along very well and we all did a lot of things together. After weeks turned into months of Pearl being with us, we went on a picnic one Sunday and it was a very nice sunny day.

The drive to the park was a distance from us and the sun was beaming in the sky with the billowing cumulous clouds floating majestically across the sky. Pearl and I remembered seeing them when we were children and we tried to picture what the shapes were in the clouds. We did this that Sunday on the way to the park as adults trying to find a cloud that had the shape of something we could recognize and we laughed all the way to the park.

The Blanket of Southern Heat

We arrived and set up our picnic spot in a quiet place and other picnickers were about. After we ate a nice lunch, I had finals coming up and still needed to study and had taken books with me to get some studying in. I decided to read for a while and Travis and Pearl were running around acting crazy as usual, but this day Travis did something I found to be weird. He grabbed Pearl and picked her up and put her over his shoulder.

I stopped for a moment and looked up over the book I was reading and there it was…Pearl gave me the same look I gave her when Travis picked me up at night at home before he took me to bed. It wasn't just a look she gave, it was an "ah ha" look. I felt a surge of jealousy come over me with the quickness.

Travis reacted as if it were an after-thought and he quickly put her down like she was a hot coal and tried to laugh it off by making a joke about her being much heavier than me. He tried to pick me up from the blanket, but I pushed him away, pretending I was into my reading.

She didn't like the statement from him and playfully hit him and looked at me with that same look. I didn't like it and I could see his nervousness for some reason, as if the cat was out of the bag. After that Sunday, we never went on another picnic and they seemed strained not to touch each other in my presence.

I still didn't think much about it, but felt something strange was going on. Pearl seemed to be changing. Travis kept pressuring me to have a baby. He said it would complete our family and he wanted some little cute Chinas' running around the house. He insisted that our babies would be beautiful and seemed adamant that he wanted this baby and was even willing to trick me by not using any protection when we were together.

Author: Victoria E. Kain

I was not going along with it and ensured that I had another form of contraceptive in place. Too many women I had known said their husbands had tricked them that way and they seemed to end up pregnant and the husband would be having an affair. The pregnancy would keep them busy or tired and the husband was free to roam like AT&T. I didn't want that so I knew what to do. I wanted to wait until I finished school to have a baby so I could spend the time at home with it.

Pearl and I continued to do our girl talk from time to time and I had mentioned how Travis had been hounding me about a baby. Each time we'd talk about how he was, she would seem more and more agitated about the conversation. Finally eleven months had flown by and we had had a couple of conversations about her getting her own place.

She never wanted to talk about it and neither did Travis. One morning everything was at its usual pace. I noticed Pearl had been staying out of work a lot lately and Travis had already gone to work and the two of us were sitting at the breakfast table. Out of the blue, Pearl brought up an earlier conversation we had had a week earlier.

"China, why don't you go on and give that man a baby?" She asked, patting me on the behind as I went to the fridge for some orange juice.

"I really don't want to have a baby right now." Girl, you know I have one year left to finish this bachelor's degree and don't want morning sickness and huffing and puffing up flights of stairs at that University."

"Besides, he keeps me busy enough, if you know what I mean and I don't need two baby's to take care of at home right now." Chuckling, I pulled my hair up in a bun.

"He can wait until next year!" I said, smirking and sitting back down at the table.

"Then I will get pregnant and have his little China doll and he will be Mr. happy camper." Pearl was quiet and let me talk.

"After the baby is a year old, I will got into the Master's program for two years and finish that degree." I smiled and winked at Pearl, but the sentiments were not returned. It was like some sinister movie character that emerged from the deep when Pearl spoke.

"You think you got it all figured out, don't you, girlfriend?" Pearl said in a deep heavy voice. It was that same "You think you are something," tone she used when we were kids. I would always remember that tone. I was older now and knew how to answer her.

"No, I don't think I am something." "I now know that I am." I said. "And, yes, I do have it all figured out, I just know what I want to do with my body and how to make this man happy! Okay?"

"Listen, Pearl, I love Travis and want to give him babies, but now is not the time."

He wants to go back to school as well and I want that for him.

"I know that's right!" Pearl said sipping out of her juice glass and eating like a pig.

Thinking that the conversation was on even keel, I responded,

"Girl, you going to get fat eating like that if you don't stop."

Author: Victoria E. Kain

"I know, I better stop now before it's too late," Pearl said, sarcastically.

We talked for a few minutes more at the table and I began thinking about Pearls attitude and felt it was time to bring up the subject of her looking for a place. What I hadn't told Pearl was that we didn't want to start our family with her living there. Besides I still hadn't gotten over Travis putting her on his shoulders at our "literal" last picnic. It made me uncomfortable. Of all the women Travis was around, Pearl made me nervous around him.

I thought it was time for her to be moving, but Travis was just too okay with her being here now. I would break the ice this time. Besides, it was my house.

"So, have you looked for any places yet?" I asked Pearl, breaking the toast in half and dunking it in my coffee.

"Nope."

"Haven't looked for anything lately," she smugly stated. It was as if she were already in her own place and didn't have to go anywhere. It was something about the way she said it that made me listen more intently to her.

"Well, I know how you really want to get your own place and start dating and all." Still in the girl talk mode.

"I notice you don't seem to have any guy friends."

"Not that I think you are gay or anything, but you are a beautiful and smart woman." I said, trying to evoke some reaction from Pearl to satisfy where my thoughts were taking me.

"Naaah," Pearl said, "The guys try to talk to me, but I'm not listening." "I'm a happy woman right now!" She said, smiling as she turned the pages of the paper Travis had left on the table before leaving for work.

"You know, I can still smell Travis's cologne on this paper." She said, holding the paper up to her face and letting it linger there.

"Really!" I said. Now furious about her comment.

"So does that mean you will not be looking for a place?"

"Are you planning to go back South?" Now a bit more agitated about Pearls smugness sitting at the table eating our food.

"Well, I really don't have anything back in the South but I do have more here now, than I have ever had," she said.

"I like living here with Travis and you. She said, this time looking at me like I had two heads.

"Really, Why so?" I asked.

"What he charges you for rent you could get a whole place a lot cheaper elsewhere and have your privacy." Pearl became incensed, possibly due to her hidden condition. She must have felt it was time to let the cat out of the bag.

"I like it here with Travis." She said, bluntly, this time leaving my name out of the equation.

"Okay Pearl, what is your deal?"

"Let's be straight now with each other." You are sitting here getting fat and not really going to work."

"Your attitude is beginning to suck, and what's up with that!"

"You really do need to lose some weight girl, I said, trying to make light of the heavy conversation we were having.

What she stated next would almost stop me in my tracks.

"Well in a few months, I will lose some weight. Little sister!!!"

"Normally a baby is about eight or nine pounds, don't you think?" You are either going to be an Aunt or a step-mother by marriage.

"Oh, that's right, you wouldn't know about that!"

"You still trying to save your precious womb like the white women did during slavery, while the slave masters were in the other room having their way with all the young virgin slave girls they wanted."

I was furious trying to figure out what Pearl was saying to me.

"What in the heck is wrong with you and this white woman crap?" I yelled.

"Well, if you are too stupid to see it, I AM PREGNANT CHINA!!!" Pearl screamed at the top of her lungs.

I stopped in my tracks and just sat with my mouth open. "Pregnant????"

"Well, that explains the stinking attitude!"

"I thought you weren't having anything to do with anyone?" I asked.

"I wasn't, but someone just came along…" Pearl lamented.

"Obviously I don't tell you everything." Pearl said, smirking.

"Who is it?" I demanded, my heart now racing.

"You are still as stupid as you were when you were little…and naive." I am four months pregnant and you know who the father of my child is," Pearl said and we both were shaking now.

I couldn't speak for fear that my thoughts and emotions were taking over me.

"What are you saying?" China asked again.

"Better yet, why don't you call your baby's father and tell him you have to leave from here and he needs to get a place for you and his child to stay right now!!!"

"You are no longer welcome here!" I couldn't believe what I was hearing from this ungrateful heifer, but it would get worse as the conversation continued.

"You still don't understand, sister of mine!" Pearl said, with a facetious smile. Pearl repeated "STEP MOTHER!"

I began to scream, barreling towards Pearl with my fist in the air ready to strike a fatal blow. Upon arriving face to face with this monster I had brought into my home, I remembered that it was carrying a child. I stopped nose to nose with her like a 747 crash landing on a dirt runway and yelled a death growl. "TRAVIS?????"

"YOU ARE LYING!!! How could you do something like this as good as we have been to you?"

"Good to me???"

"What have you done for me?"

"It was Travis that was good to me! You only tolerated me."

"Travis picked me up from the Train station, Travis gave me a place to stay, Travis gave me the job, and Travis gave me this baby!"

China mumbled as she was tearing up, "you stupid fool, I was the one always speaking for you not to leave before now!"

"I should have let him kick your black butt out like he wanted to!" "You are so un-grateful!" I was in shock now, filled with tears and rage. For the first time, I hated my sister.

"Yes, this is Travis's baby!" Pearl said, with confidence. She would strike now while the iron was hot.

"Remember when we were kids and I got that whipping… "RED!!!" Pearl said that, reminding me of my insulting childhood nickname. She had not called me that since we were kids.

"Well, I vowed I would get you back and let you see what pain really felt like, since no one ever beat your butt!

"You never got whippings like you were some prize calf or something and I hated you for it."

I was crying now. The tears were creating a flood on my face. I sat with my face in my hands and just shook my head.

"What is this?" I asked, as if someone else was sitting in the room with us.

"I have never done anything to you," I screamed, slinging the dishcloth to the floor wringing my hands as if I wanted to hit Pearl but was trying to squelch the thought.

"You have always been ungrateful! When Ed would send me money, you stole from me!" I screamed!

"When he bought you and Gem clothes, you complained that they were not as pretty as mine."

"When he bought us all bunk beds, you carved pictures on the side just to mar it to show that you didn't care."

"What are you on the inside Pearl?" I asked, now staring Pearl straight in the eye as if all fear had left me.

Pearl stood back and rubbed her belly slowly to taunt me. It was clear that she relished in the fact that she was now carrying my beloved Travis's baby…the one I would not agree to have for him this year.

Pearl continued to jab at me with everything she had.

"Oh, about Ed, your supposed benefactor." Pearl walked closer to China and looked her in the face like a boxer to his opponent before he knocks him out.

"Did you know that Ed is actually your real daddy? "Humph, I read Grandmother's letter's and found out."

I didn't make any expression of shock which stunned Pearl who thought the low blow of information would shake me down. But in this round I actually won. I slowly turned to face Pearl again…

"Well, you fat hussy!" I already knew that Edmondo was my father!"

"Furthermore, I also know that your father was a drug addict!" "That's right, "the Jack Rabbit" they called him and I wonder why?"

"The one that stole from Grandmother's house and slept on the streets."

"What does that say about you?" I could see that Pearl was the one shaking at this time and I kept punching her. Pearl was agitated but tried to hold it together and could see that the old China was gone. I was no longer afraid to fight for myself.

In tears, I began expressing anger and frustration even further. I had nothing to lose now and let Pearl have it.

"So what is this baby going to be about?"

"Its' mother was nothing short of a prostitute when she was growing up."

"Well let's see, if it is a boy, he will probably be just like his grandfather." A simple thief, drug head and lier.

"Well wrong again, Ms. I'm so black and hip!!!" I said furious, and it manifested itself in every word that spewed from my lips going forward. I was on a roll and couldn't be stopped.

"Oh, and wait, if it's a girl, and I hope it is." I said, squinting my eyes almost to the point of them being completely closed.

"Your little girl with be as trifling as her mother!"

"She will follow closely in your footsteps and have all of the same crap on her feet in life as you did. She will be a stench, like you are to every one she comes in contact with in every phase of her existence. In the end, she will be as lonely as her mother is because everyone can smell crap a mile away and will do everything in their power to avoid it, China yelled."

"So, the bottom line is that your daughter will have nothing to look forward to from having you as a mother. You are just another cheap tramp of a woman who thought that by lying down with a married man was proving something. But, in the end, all tramps get is trampled on by men. The men get up, take themselves and their money and leave the tramp where she lay and possibly filled with another baby she can't feed. He simply tosses her away along with the instrument he used and never looks back."

Finally, after I gained my composure, I made one final statement. "I am sick of trampy women like you, thinking that you somehow have some invisible control over me."

"You can't hurt me any more Pearl! I am sick of you people trying to tolerate me because of your own prejudices. You have dogged me for getting something you couldn't get and because you benefitted from it, you still gave me no credit for making things a little easier for you by the sheer fact that I was there."

"You all were mad because what was given to you was not yours, but mine and you hated it, thinking I got what I did because of the color of my skin, so you wanted to dog me out for it!"

"You all capitalized off what was given to me and have mentally abused me long enough and I am sick it, and you!"

"So why don't you call your baby's daddy and get out of my house once and for all!" I turned my back on Pearl and started loading the dishwasher with the two plates we had eaten off of.

As an afterthought, I pulled the plate Pearl had eaten off of out of my dishwasher and broke it in half and put it in the garbage and spit on it. Pearl was fuming mad and wanted to have the last word, even though she was dumbfounded that I had told her to get out. She wanted to hurl one last mud sling at me. I didn't care and was ready for anything. I was mad as hell!!!

"Well, I don't have to get out unless Travis wants me and his baby out!" Pearl yelled.

"That's right, um having the baby that you thought you were too good to give him, I am going to give that to him!!!" Pearl said.

"You will now have to help pay for my baby's clothes even if you have one of your own little red bones, since he wanted you to have a baby so badly for him."

Pearl said, looking down at her belly, holding it like it was her ticket into the county fair or something. She continued to get things off her chest as well. This had been brewing since childhood.

"You wanted to make Travis beg for something he wanted so badly and you thought you were too good to get a little fat on your skinny behind," Pearl said as she was still ranting.

I still was silent because anger had taken over me. I did not even turn around to look at Pearl, which infuriated her.

Pearl went on to tell what happened. Most criminals want to tell someone about the crimes they committed and this was her opportunity to confess. She wanted to get another rise out of me and make me cry but I showed no signs of pain. She began to sling mud again this time closer to home.

"Well, let me tell you how it happened. I decided that night at the restaurant that I would give in to Travis and give him what he really wanted."

After making the comment, Pearl began to hyperventilate to the extent that she couldn't catch her breath at all. Initially, I ignored her thinking I would let her fall out, then I heard Pearl trying to breathe, begging for help. I turned around and got to Pearl before she fell to the floor.

I quickly called 911 and the medics came and picked her up at the apartment. The two men that put Pearl on the stretcher asked me if I wanted to come with her and I responded,

"No, I will call her baby's daddy and have him bring his trifling self to see about his mistress and his baby.

"You see, the baby belongs to my Ex-husband! The one I am going to divorce." Pearl had a defeated look on her face because she never thought I would leave Travis. The two medics looked at me and consoled me and not Pearl.

"Ma'am, I am sorry this has happened to you."

"Are you okay to call the father or would you like to give us the number and we can do it for you?"

Pearl lay on the stretcher as if she didn't exist. The Medics strapped her in and looked at her with disgust but did their job to ensure she was secured on the stretcher.

I gave them the number to call Travis and they took Pearl to the hospital.

I called Travis any way and told him what happened. I wanted to hear his voice and be the one to tell him. The conversation was short because he was in their breakfast rush. Instead of Travis going to the hospital first, he came home to me.

I was still in conflict with my thoughts and emotions when he arrived home. He tried to hold me, but for the first time, I wouldn't let him. I was in a fighting mode. In the past, I always welcomed his affections, but today, it felt like it did when I was a little girl with the intruder trying to violate me. My life had changed me.

I pulled away from Travis.

"How could you do this to someone you say you love, Travis?" I was so stunned that he had betrayed me right under my nose. He tried to explain what had happened with him and Pearl and stated that the incident meant nothing.

He told me that he did not love Pearl but still loved me. He disclosed that Pearl had not told him she was pregnant but that one of the other employees had told him and that was why she was sick a lot.

Travis had thought the father was Jake, a guy on the pasta station at his restaurant. He had always told everyone he really liked Pearl and wanted to marry her someday, but Pearl didn't like him because he had no money and was not attractive to her.

Travis knew he had only had the one time affair with Pearl and deeply regretted it. He knew he was wrong for what he had done and now this incident would cost him everything. He stood before me and was deeply shaken. Travis truly loved me, but his old habits had caught up with him. He broke down sobbing and I asked him to leave. He begged for a second chance, but I was not able to grant the request.

"What about the down payment I put on the condo for us on 15th avenue?"

"Well, I guess that is where I will live, since you, Pearl and your baby will need this apartment since she liked it so much."

"I don't want Pearl, I want you! Travis yelled, visibly broken."

"I think you have made your choice Travis. How can I even think about having babies with you now and you have done this terrible thing to me."

"I saved myself for this!!!" I began to cry.

I asked Travis to leave and he handed me a key with an address on it. He had just closed on the condo that morning and was going to give it to me as a gift for our upcoming anniversary. He now knew that Pearl did what she did on purpose. She was aware of the surprise he had for me.

The new condo was close to my school and would have been easy for me to get to after having the baby we were planning to have in one year. Now he would have to let it all go. He looked at the key one last time.

"I want you to have this!"

"You were a good wife and didn't deserve this, China. I have made the biggest mistake of my life, but know that I truly loved you, I really did."

I was very hurt, but still loved him and wanted to tell him that I would take him back, but I remembered what Pearl said about me paying for her child's life and hating me enough to do something as evil as this…I couldn't say the words. I didn't want to get in this triangle because I had no way of knowing whether it would happen again. I knew that after Pearl had the baby she would always hold it over our heads like the baby on Roots, dangling him in midair like a sacrifice.

Travis packed some things and left the apartment. I cried the entire night and couldn't sleep. Travis had mistakenly left his cell phone at the apartment and it continued to ring. I had never paid attention to it ringing before now because it was always people from the restaurant calling him or so I thought. This night, I looked at the caller ID for the very first time and it was a strange name.

Lowanda #2 came up on Travis's ID. I decided to answer his phone.

"Hello," I said in an inquisitive voice. My eyes searching back and forth in the room, hoping it was a work employee.

"Who is this?" the caller asked rudely.

"Who do you want Ma'am, you have called my husband's number." I boldly stated. Not admitting that I had just kicked him out.

"Well, all I need is this month's child support money!"

"His daughter needs pampers and milk and need medicine because she is teething," the woman said.

"Can you tell him to call me?" She asked. Now speaking in a more acceptable tone than when she first spoke. She seemed to realize that I could have refused to give him the message and it sounded like she really needed these items.

My mouth was open and getting dry again.

"What do you mean his daughter?"

The woman responded as if I didn't hear her.

"My baby is seven months old Ma'am, and he promised to make sure I had my money on time because I'm not working anywhere." She said.

"I don't know if this is a trick or what, but my husband does not have any children," I hesitated and added, "Yet!"

"Well, I don't know what he told you," the woman said "but Travis Stone has my daughter, and other children as well. My cousin has a little boy by him. You could say, he liked my family a lot," the woman chuckled nervously.

I was mentally wrecked at this point. I hung up the phone and called the restaurant to let Travis know he had left his cell phone, but before I could call, the doorbell rang. It was Travis.

"Aaah, I left my cell phone China. I just want to get it."

"Yeah, your baby mama #2 just called for pampers, medicine and child support for your daughter."

Travis almost fainted. I could see he was visibly weak in the knees. His secrets were out. The skeletons in his closet were dangling aimlessly and there was nothing he could do but watch them.

"That woman is lying!" he said. Trying to recoil."

It was an amazing lesson I learned at such an early age. While I understood that every man was not a liar, when people are caught in lies, they tend to keep lying. I remember watching Pearl when she was stealing the money Ed was sending me in the mail, it reminded me of what Travis was doing now. He was lying to save face. He just continued to lie.

"China, I was just helping her with her kid! That's all!"

"I really don't care Travis." You seemed to have had plenty of secrets. Take your phone and go. I will call you when the divorce papers are ready." I gave him the phone and closed and chained the door. I didn't want him breaking in and over powering me.

I didn't want him thinking he had any rights to any part of me or anything that belonged to me at this time. This night, I was devastated. I cried and wondered about my life and asked God why this had happened to me. Still feeling love for Travis, I wanted to call him but my heart wouldn't let me. I finally overruled the thought and picked up the phone.

When the phone rang three times I was about to hang up when a woman answered. It was the same woman that had called about the baby earlier and I could hear Travis in the back ground trying to console his teething child.

I hung up the phone and cried all night.

The things I wanted to say to him I wrote in a poem. These words reflected what I felt about his perceived love for me and I would bury the skeletons where I found them.

If You Loved Me

If you loved me, why couldn't you
Help me out, and see
That everything I did for you, I did the same for me.

If you loved me, restraint was the word
Which so many fail to use
They act first and reason last
And the wrong decision they choose

If you loved me, why couldn't you
trust yourself and me together
For in our lives we'd worked so hard and
withstood all kinds of weather.

A day or two longer, a night for sure
And we would have had it all
But fate swiftly came in the dark of night
and caused us both to fall

Fate left a rubble of our lives as a ghostly thing to see
For if you had love me it could not have touched
the love you had for me

The Blanket of Southern Heat

The words that were in my heart that night I carried with me for the rest of my life. They reflected how I felt about the man I loved and his inability to use constraint in an unnatural situation. People don't seem to understand the effects of infidelity. So many are hurt very deeply and the pain never seems to go away. Life had once again, thrown me down and steam rolled over me.

It wasn't enough that my mother had suffered a violent attack as a young woman and gave birth to me under those conditions, but she still was cut short in her young life and is gone forever, never being able to live and know true love or to love me.

I couldn't fathom why my life had to be so difficult when I had only wanted to love and be loved by the people that were in it. It would be a long while before I could give my heart completely to someone else as I had done with Travis.

I was determined not to take anyone else for face value or trust completely until they showed who they were. Even though my past was as dark as a stormy night in winter, this poem was like a bright light that I could reflect on for strength. I put it in a box and neatly packed it away like everything else that caused me pain.

After my failed marriage, time moved swiftly on. Winter was beginning to approach the city and the days and evenings became cooler as the night approached. The year had already gone by, and graduate school was just getting started. If for nothing else, I could say that Travis had great taste in the selection of the condo he had picked out for us. It was breathtakingly beautiful.

With each day that passed, I thought back to better days when we laughed and he would carry me off to bed at night. Those were the times I missed the most. He was a generous man and didn't mind giving me anything he could afford.

Author: Victoria E. Kain

I wondered if I would ever find another man as generous as Travis was. Sometimes I found myself wishing it could have worked. Thinking that if the baby had not existed, I might have been able to salvage our relationship.

It is a shame that many seemingly decent men sometimes are deceptive and fall prey to desperate women who will stop at nothing to give in to a man's fleeting desires only to destroy them and be destroyed in the process.

These same men give up the real life for the placebo, allowing the thought that a woman will allow them any pleasure without consequences. They trade their lives of sunshine for a life of darkness. The superficial closeness of the one night stands and feelings of imagined love, shows itself to be the perfect recipe for disaster.

In the end, people are left naked and stripped of their pride and all self-worth, wondering where they went wrong or where they will end up. Now it was time to put the past behind me in order to take my next plunge into deeper things in my future.

~ **CHAPTER 3** ~

LIVING ON MY TERMS

Living On My Terms

Adjusting to single life once again these next years would prove to be very difficult for me. Realizing what it felt like to have family and then to have none again, would prove to be harder than I imagined. It seemed that school was all I had now to drown my sorrows in. The University was literally a stone's throw away from my Condo.

On a good day, I could walk to class, if I felt particularly frisky, which lately was not often because of my school load and work. I wanted to get as many classes out of the way during the summer months so that the winter was a bit freer for me. Since childhood, I was plagued with sinus issues that kept me out of the winter weather.

When kids played in the snow, I had to watch from a foggy window in my bedroom, laughing when they laughed but not being able to feel the joy they felt. My life seemed to always be lived through the eyes of someone else.

Grandmother always said my sinus issues was because my nose was pointy. She'd laugh a sweet old lady type laugh about it and then would kiss my nose to make me feel better. She didn't know it, but the kiss never helped. I always felt like something was wrong with my nose since it was not like everyone else's. Still, the Condo was my first real home and it felt good.

I glanced at my surroundings and saw tree lined streets and coffee shops along the way to school. Outdoor cafés were abuzz during the day which gave the feeling of being in a ritzy neighborhood crawling with the rich and struggling students attending the magnificent universities.

From my window, I could see people on Segway's, bicycles, skates and skateboards and anything else that posed as transportation for them. The big city was a strange place to be but very interesting.

I also was in walking distance to the train station as well. I received the deed for the Condo that year as well with a final plea for a second chance from Travis. I still filed for the divorce. I finally accepted that he had too much baggage in his life that would rob us of any peace we could have had. The deed to the Condo secured it for me so that his children's mothers could not get any part of it for support.

It was nice to know that he wanted me to have a place of my own. His note to me stated that I deserved more than he gave me, and that he wanted me to have the Condo because I gave him something he had never had before. I was his first love.

It was as if he knew I would keep the Condo safe for myself. I found out much later that the woman that had called my house the night I put Travis out, I believed this was the same one that he was supposed to have married after we divorced. I had heard many things about Travis that people wanted to throw up in my face and I finally wouldn't listen to anything else people said.

I couldn't understand why these women were so free to drop all these babies on a man who had other women already. "I guess that's why I don't have a man." I thought, quickly shrugging my shoulders and rolling my eyes up to the ceiling, running my fingers through my massive curls.

It always seemed to relax me when I had to make decisions or was stressed.

I loved the new Condo and thanked Travis and his new bride in silence. I sat in the oversized chair gazing out of the large bay window watching people scurry to their destinations on foot. The living room was spacious and I had made a fire in the fireplace. It was the coziest I had ever been, being alone. It wasn't often I had a day off from class, so I took advantage of it to pamper myself with a little R&R.

Scanning my living quarters, the view was clear into my spacious kitchen. It was to be a great place for entertaining for me and my Ex-husband, but since I now had no friends, it was just a matter of enjoying the scenery myself. The kitchen had a very functional island and all the latest stainless steel gadgets along with beautiful hardwood floors.

The bedrooms were large and spacious, but lonely at night. I was always reminded that the extra room was to be for the baby I never had for Travis. I made this into my guest bedroom, thinking that one day I might have a child or two with someone special.

I was still able to enjoy the condo along with knowing I had the deed for it. A sour note was that I also received my final alimony payment from Travis as well. Now I would have to ensure that I found a job very soon. Work was hard to come by in the city because everyone was looking for the same jobs. I knew I needed to find work quickly but nothing was coming up and the options were slim to none.

That same afternoon, I was looking in the newspaper for any openings for work and had exhausted all resources and stumbled across the card from Travis's boss at the restaurant where he used to work. I felt elated and remembered what the man had said to me.

With a sly grin he told me if I ever needed anything I was not to hesitate contacting him. I didn't waste any time picking up the phone to call him and felt that it was time to let these men start putting their money where their mouth was or to keep it closed.

I didn't want to work in a restaurant and had decided that if he suggested it, I would never call him again. The call was picked up fairly quick. Only two rings and I had him.

"This is Newman Crenshaw, how may I help you?" He said.

I introduced myself again and Mr. Crenshaw began to stammer remembering that Travis worked in one of his stores. I quickly recanted.

"Mr. Crenshaw, Travis and I are divorced. I am looking for a job and ran across your card."

Mr. Crenshaw quickly changed his tune. He was more open to talk after the divorce word came across.

"Oh, Ms. Stone, is it?"

"How are you? It's good to hear from you."

"Same here. I am fine, thank you." I said calmly. I told Mr. Crenshaw that I was looking for work and he jumped at the chance to help me. He appeared elated but tried not to let on. He made some calls and got me in to see a close family friend of his right away. This person was a high level Executive in a prestigious downtown firm. I had an appointment set for me and the location was not far from my home.

It is great knowing someone. After interviewing, everything went well. There were 18 people in there for that same job. I was nervous at first but soon realized that Mr. Crenshaw was behind the scenes pulling strings for me. I didn't care, I just wanted a job.

They just happened to have a position become available in their corporate office and did a second interview with me the following week. I passed the interviews with flying colors and was given the basic tour two weeks later. I was finally going to be able to take care of myself. Ed was not sending as much money these days, but he sent some ever so often. As I met with the staff at the new job, I noted that there was a lot of tension in the office with the other females as I walked through.

I was accustomed to this type of treatment from women and men for that matter so I was right at home. I deduced that the men all seemed pleased to meet me and gave the cup over hand shake. That's where they take one hand to shake it and cup the other hand over the hand being shook. I called it the "slick" down payment move, but didn't care as long as I got the job.

Ms. Diggs, the V.P. of the department was old as dirt. Very prominent and sophisticated. I even noted that she wore Prada items and was very frail but seemed to take no mess from any of the male executives. I knew this by the way she spoke to the men as she introduced me.

Jim was the first executive she introduced me to. She took me right up to his door and put her hand out in front of me to prevent me from entering. "Jim, this is the new cutie, Ms. China Stone." Before he could respond, Ms. Diggs continued;

"She is pretty and single, but I want you to remember that she is here to work, and work is what she will have to do to stay here."

Jim looked embarrassed, but wanted to flex his muscles and show me that he was not afraid of the old coot.

He was gracious and got up from his desk and approached me and did what Ms. Diggs didn't want him to do, which was, "touch" me.

"Hello Ms. Stone."

"Welcome aboard," he said, as he continued speaking…

"And regardless of what Sara Dianne Diggs says, please let me know if there is anything I can do to assist you."

He had called Ms. Diggs by her full name denoting that he knew her well enough that she couldn't get him fired. He then winked at her which seemed to make her feel better that he had given her some attention. She blushed and we walked to the next door.

"Cameron, this is Ms. Stone, our new Administrator for the firm."

"Hello Ms. Stone, welcome aboard," he said, not really making much eye contact but adjusting his pants for some reason.

I found out later that he had some identity issues. Ms. Diggs didn't say much about him though. There were no warnings for him.

Ms. Diggs seemed elated to introduce me to all the men and told one of the ladies that worked in the file room that if she had a daughter, she would look like me.

I took that as a great compliment from her since she had showed no other outward emotion towards me as we walked down the long hallways. The firm was huge and very elite.

We got through all of the introductions and finally came to the office of one of the Managers of the intake department. Brigitte was introduced to me and gave one of the limpest handshakes ever received in the world. Ms. Diggs introduced us.

"Brigitte, this is China Stone," Ms. Diggs stated. I noticed she gave her my first and last name and to all the men she gave a more formal introduction. Brigitte looked me up and down and spoke in her best office voice.

"Hello, Ms. Stone, is it?" she asked.

Before I could answer, Ms. Diggs received a phone call and asked Brigitte if she would take me around to meet the other ladies in that department.

"Sure." Brigitte politely responded giving me the evil eyes.

No sooner than Ms. Diggs was out of ear shot, her claws came out to claim her rights to her territory. Apparently Brigitte thought she was all that. She continued staring me down.

"So, do you have any kids?" she asked, in a snide voice sizing me up.

"We require our team members to be on time every day."

"Also, are you married?" if you aren't, we don't tolerate dating team members in the company, it affects productivity." She tried to get all of her questions in but the next ones stopped me cold.

"Is all that your real hair?" she asked.

"A lot of women here wear weave or wigs, but as you can see, mine is real." She takes her hand and rakes it all the way down to the scalp and pull the hair out to the side to show that there were no tracks in it.

At this point I was disgusted and needed to put this chick in her place. The old China had gone and the new China lived here now. Brigitte's attitude reminded me of Pearl and I lit into the woman.

I needed to respond and shut the situation down immediately and leave no traces.

I was sick of people thinking that because of the color of my skin, eyes and hair, I was somehow deemed as soft and easy. Not anymore. I was tired of people referring to me as if I were some Martian or something. I made sure Ms. Diggs or no one else could hear me and waited until we got into the break room and there were no others within ear shot and I was going to blow Brigitte out of the water.

"Brigitte, why don't I answer all of your questions and put you out of your misery completely." Brigitte was shocked and looked around to see if someone else had entered the break room. She had not expected the response she was receiving.

"No, I am not married and I don't have any children. As you can see, my hair is down to my butt and it is real and so is my butt." I took my head and flipped all of my hair forward bringing all of my curly locks up in a ponytail and let it all fall back down to my backside again.

"Bet you can't do that with your "Hair." I continued…

"My eyes are hazel, and these are NOT contacts, I was born with them."

"My lashes are real, not fake and these are my real teeth. No veneers, caps, implants or partials."

"By the way, the metal is showing on yours. I'll give you the name of my dentist to fix that for you."

"I am a perfect size…7 on a good day. So, I guess you could say, I am "all" woman and can fit into clothes you only dream of fitting into!"

Brigitte was standing in shock and looking at me go through my antics. She never expected me to respond that way and realized she had bitten off more than she could chew or swallow.

Author: Victoria E. Kain

She tried to regroup and began firing back.

She peeked out of the break room door to see if the coast was clear and began her next attack

"The man on the second floor, belongs to me," she said pouting and licking her lips and batting her fake lashes.

"I won't tell you his name, because you will know him when you see him."

"He is the finest one in the building! Hands off, or you will be getting a personal beat down at your home address," she said with a scowl on her face that was supposed to scare me. What she didn't realize was that I was reared by a black woman and knew all the antics and the antidotes for any poison she thought she wanted to serve me.

I was furious at this point. Again, I remembered how Pearl, my supposed sister, had literally destroyed my marriage by being low down and trifling. She had taken my kindness for weakness all because I wanted to believe she was sincere about being mature and had gotten over her childhood hatred of me. I learned my lesson and was not going to let this go so easily.

I told Brigitte my final statement on the matter.

"If you have any more questions, you need to swear me in, before I can answer."

"As far as your "Fine man" is concern, you may want to talk to him about "HIS" hands being off limits where I am concerned."

Just when Brigitte was about to step forward towards me, Mr. Pemberton, the President of the company walked into the break room.

Observing both of us talking, he approached me and completely ignored Brigitte. Even with all the bull this woman had just spoken to me, stupid me felt sorry for the way the President had just dissed her.

Part of me wanted to balance it out for her because I knew I had his complete attention, but the other part of me had learned a valuable lesson in heifer attacks and let her take the hit. I was through trying to bind the wounds of those who made it their life's goal to wound me in the process of showing them generosity. I let his jab stand.

"Ms. Stone is it?" the Vice President asked.

"I am Mr. Pemberton, Vice President of The Brief Publishing Co. Welcome aboard!"

Brigitte, stood very still and I shook Mr. Pemberton's hand. He too did the cup over on the handshake and Brigitte was furious. She knew what that meant coming from a man and knew that I was in complete control. I wanted to show her that I knew very well what to do with the power I had just been given by this man. I responded professionally.

"Thank you Mr. Pemberton, I am very excited to meet you and grateful for this opportunity." All the while, looking at Brigitte, who was now mortified since Mr. Pemberton did not acknowledge her existence in the room at all. He could not help staring at me, the one who captivated all of his attention. Brigitte was clear that I had won that battle.

"Well, China, as a matter of fact, I am on my way to the second floor and would like you to meet Philip, who is one of our brightest leading Editors here at the Brief." Brigitte almost fainted when Mr. Pemberton called Philip's name.

This was the person she considered to belong only to her, and now Mr. Pemberton was taking me directly to him.

"I would like for you to work on his team with a special project we have coming up shortly." Mr. Pemberton said.

"I would love that." I responded with an effective smile. All of the dental work Ed had paid for over the years was paying off today in a big way.

I saw the dejected look on Brigitte's face when Mr. Pemberton mentioned Philip Masterson. Mr. Pemberton excused the two of us, as we left Brigitte standing in the break room holding the fake cup of coffee. As a way to nail the coffin, I turned and whispered to Brigitte, "Be nice, or you won't have a man or a job!" I turned and outwardly thanked her for the introductions. She watched Mr. Pemberton open the door for me and reminded me not to get my beautiful hair caught in the door.

Brigitte looked as if she had been left in a burning building. I did one last thing, "Thank you for the tour Brigitte!" I look forward to working with you." I said, smiling as Mr. Pemberton escorted me out, still not acknowledging Brigitte's existence on the earth.

I felt revived. I felt as if I had fought a battle and won like I did the night the man attacked me when I was a little girl. I was tired of hiding my feelings and allowing people to walk all over me. Even though I knew I didn't have a man in my life, I knew I could have any man I wanted and was never going to allow women to trample over me again. Or men for that matter.

I met the man Philip that Brigitte was raving about and Cameron met me coming out of his office. I knew where that may have been going and wished Brigitte well. I certainly was not interested in him and he wasn't all that.

They showed me to my small office which was only large enough for a desk and a chair. Since I had my bachelor's degree, it put me ahead of the others in the department even though they had been there longer. I was also in my first year of graduate school. With education, I was overqualified for the job and it only paid 60k, but there was room for advancement.

My goal was to get as far up the ladder as quickly as I could using everything I had. Except that. I later thanked Mr. Crenshaw for the referral and assured him I would do a good job. I worked hard from that day forward. Brigitte became my quasi office friend after the break room cat fight in our first meeting.

She rationalized that I was liked by all of the top men in the firm and she wanted an edge. I considered her as just another person like all the rest in my life that wanted to ride on part of my coat tail. I let her ride though. I too realized I needed an ally at work and she would be it. Being the new girl, I needed to know who all the saboteurs were and what the temperature was in the company culture. Brigitte became my eyes and ears.

Things were going well and I was acclimating to working and going to school at the same time like the rest of the world. The first weeks went by fast and now feeling the effects of working and going to school was catching up with me. One Saturday afternoon, I ran into poor old Aunt Paoli in the mall. She looked haggard and run down. Her wig was matted and she smelled of cigarette smoke. She actually seemed glad to see me and immediately asked me for money. She felt the need to tell me all the gossip about Pearl saying that Pearl tried calling Ed, to get money for her rent.   She was put out of me and Travis's old apartment when Travis moved out and left her there.

Author: Victoria E. Kain

Ed knew what she and Travis had done to my marriage and he gave Grandmother some money and told Pearl to ask her for what she needed. Needless to say, Grandmother did not give her any money at all but she did give her the number to Child Services. Aunt Paoli said that Travis did not help Pearl with the baby at all. I was surprised about that, but they said he was never the same after I left him. Paoli went on to give her opinion that she didn't think Pearl deserved any help because her situation had been brought on by herself and trying to be spiteful.

Aunt Paoli was giving all the information for the money she wanted. I guess she felt that she had to do something to earn it. I really didn't know how much of this was truth or lies. I learned to take it with a grain of salt as they use to say in the South. She went on to say how Travis refused to see the child Pearl bore him. He left his new family and moved out of town. As she stated, he left all his baby mama's. She laughed the hearty laugh and stated,

"God don't like ugly now!" she said with emphasis. I gave her some money and she scurried along like a woman on crack. I later found that the marriage mentioned to me at the Mall about Travis, was just a rumor. The fact that he had another baby by the same woman he was with when we were married was true.

It was also found out that Travis had six other children, all by different women. He began drinking and never went back to school. I began to feel sorry for him. I was again stunned when my attorney finally divulged that Travis owed over 60,000 in back child support. I was very glad I was not with him and having to help pay for his indiscretions.

One thing about Travis was that he kept his word to me and sent the deed to the Condo to my attorney. It was finally mine.

I accepted that he had made many mistakes in his life and it was unfortunate that he had found the right woman, but didn't treasure me enough to say no to temptation.

All the lies were surfacing and now I know why he dropped out of college. His Federal grants were frozen because of back child support. He had told me he stopped school because of working to buy the Condo to start our family.

Those days he worked over, he did put money aside for the Condo, but the late nights supposedly working was spent with different baby mamas.

I do know that he loved me. That was a bit of comfort, but there were so many lies told in the relationship that I feel like I was a prisoner being promised a parole that never came. This was not the life I wanted to live.

I missed him a lot but believed that someone higher was looking out for me. Maybe I was beginning to know who God was at this time of my life. This could have been a disaster if it had continued. My life was like a patchwork quilt. So many places in it that needed mending, but also many pieces were missing as well.

As time continued to move forward and the winter and summer came and went, the one thing I learned was that marriage out of a need to have someone to take care of you, never works. My ugly past would soon be unraveled by yet another man who would wander into my young life and openly expose more secrets from the skeletons dangling in my family's closet and their own.

I had grown up watching those same skeletons mature day by day living as shadows in my head and there was nothing to be done about them except be shocked over and over again as they manifested themselves at inopportune times in my life.

I would soon have new acquaintances coming into my life that would expose my past, but also expose their own involvement in my family's history which shockingly unveiled who they really were to me, over time. My untimely involvement with someone else would reveal my true feelings and intentions that were not clear at first, about the effects of love.

The fire would be set ablaze in the depths of my soul once again. This would create an insatiable blanket of heat that would envelope my entire body at various times and would comfort my soul in my hour of need.

Often in my life I fought to protect myself from my enemies. I was now ready to do it again. The only nemesis to this life's saga was that there were many that haunted me for no apparent reason. Who are these people that come into our lives at birth and create the only existence we know and then toss us aside like old shoes?

I felt that way when I was sent away as a child. Like the scarlet letter was placed around my neck. Why had the first man in my life come in unannounced bearing all the right gifts along with his own sinister reasons for drawing me into himself? I fell prey to a man once, but would not let it happen again. The skeletons must be destroyed but they were large and long overdue for exposure. They awaited their redemption from the shackles they had worn for so many centuries and so did I.

The pain of living these kinds of secrets in relationships, uncaps issues that plague many of us throughout our lives. It is the reason why so many people in past generations did not reveal their secrets and chose to bury them in their graves where they would lay silent forever.

As I continued to rationalize my thoughts, feeling that people "learned" responses from the slave masters of old became prevalent in my mind. I didn't know a lot about slavery except what I had heard growing up, but the bits and pieces I gleaned from eavesdropping from my bed, taught me how people learned behaviors and handed them down through the generations whether they believed in what they had learned or not.

The masters knew the behavior they required would leave many lesions on the souls of generations coming into this oppressed race of people and they would have no choice except to repeat the same mistakes over and over again creating a vicious cycle, crippling each generation as it went forward carrying the negative banner to be worn by all in its path.

I continued to think about how I wanted to change my life and understood how to wipe the slate clean and start anew. We know that our lives mimic many of our ancestors and we still wear the shroud of pain and suffering the same as they did. The difference is that in our society today, that shroud contours to immolate the century in which it is being worn.

These thoughts left me thinking, feeling and wondering about my own heritage and legacy. I understood that, when we unearth and unleash the truths never told before to us, no one will ever be able to tell the same lie again. They will simply cease along with the secrets that were kept, only benefiting those that keep them!

"Tell us the truth for once in our retched lives!" I thought! Today, the shackles have moved from our feet to our minds. What will happen to my children someday if I take these same lies I have been told and give it to them and expect them to carry them forward?

My grandchildren and generations coming from them will perpetuate only lies. I want to tell the truth about how I see things and understand them. How I am affected by something has a bearing on how I react to it and how I live my life. We are still trying to be forced into a mold that no longer fits us.

I don't want to be called mulatto, mixed, bi-racial, black or whatever. I chose not to be labelled just because I don't look the same as someone else. Or because I have one part of a culture and a hundred parts of another, but the one part constitutes who I am.

What about the fact that in the black cultures, they don't believe each other, "first." They have been taught to despise, suspect and distrust their own and believe others first. It's not really the way they want to be but it is what they've learned.

Many do not show the support for one another and put each other down, taking advantage of those in their own culture who do lend them their hand for support.

Thinking that the only way to get revenge on the system that may have failed them is to take advantage of their own people, in order to feel the strength to step up from the crater they have been forced into.

We should support one another and break the chains within our cultures, regardless of how we may long for success, or to be as smart as, or as talented as the next person. We should stop putting others down as a way to ensure that they go no further than we ourselves may have gone. This is not how we survive and grow our community.

I realized that I was different than anyone in my family. I could see that my thoughts were deepening as I matured and moved forward in life. It went further than simply not looking the same as someone else, but, it was thought that courage sometimes skipped a generation. That may be true, but there were many before us all that were braver than we ever could be and they still died taking secrets to their graves that could have spared so many the unnecessary anguish and trauma we still see today.

Even though I don't rightly know who my ancestors are, I believe that our forefathers taught their offspring all the things they were permitted to teach them. It is up to us to decide what information to keep or discard that we receive. We are the ones responsible now for what happens.

Not the cadavers of long ago. Depending on what we teach now, the generations after us would produce an even stronger people within our society in the future. When someone else tells "your" life story the way they want others to see it, the entire story belongs to and only benefits them. It also changes who you become in the eyes of others.

Author: Victoria E. Kain

Only when you can stop the telling of the story and change its direction of how it really is supposed to go is when the story comes alive and reflects who you really are. No one can tell someone "how" to tell their own story because the teller of the story must own it, embrace it and must have lived it.

Many could have been saved if only they had the strength to stop the cycle of madness. Sometimes my soul cries out for revenge, yet there is a calming spirit within me that wants to bind the wounds of those who wail in the night for freedom.

It was my goal to make it my personal quest to do something about the untruths or lying that was done in my lifetime for the sake of saving face and family reputations which were already tarnished. Most of us believe in calling a spade a spade, so I say, "if the shoe fits," walk a mile in it before you criticize its wearer for not dancing to the same tune that you dance to.

We now show our courage with the goal of coming out the victor by telling the secrets from deep within. We should not allow another generation to come forth cutting their teeth on the same lies we were told from centuries ago. For each truth that is told, it is like a suture to an open wound. Each stitch will cause a "healing" of our children's souls for generations to come. All of this misery ended one full phase of my life.

I realized that my study of human history had unlocked a desire to know more about the plight of the people in my life. I was sick of it all. I couldn't figure anything out and didn't know who to trust or to ask questions. When no one would openly share information, who will I trust tomorrow?

What face is like mine? Who am I and where do I belong? I began a new phase of my sad life.

Alone again in the world and trying to make it. This time it was on me to make the right decisions. I prayed that I would. The doors to my freedom were being unlocked, yet it was evident that someone else still held the key.

Another year passed like lightening and I was still reflecting on my lost heritage. It was early in the morning, before the sun rose. A time in my life when I realized I had literally come full circle with myself. My sordid past was now heaped with a mountain of lies and deception from childhood to a failed marriage. All this in my early twenties. Never being permitted to bond with the only relatives I was told I had and was left grappling for companionship almost wherever I could experience it. All because I needed to know the true feeling of being wanted, needed and loved.

How is it that you can go through your entire life wanting to be normal, knowing it may never happen? Feelings of shame came over me when I stood amongst my own peers and family members and looked around for some remote commonality and found nothing. It was like looking in a mirror and someone else's face appears. You begin to doubt yourself and wonder if you belong on this earth at all.

To not know enough of a mother's love to be able to weather the storms of life can take a toll on you. You look for any reassurance to get you to the next point in your existence. I wondered why I was not permitted to bond with the only father I thought I had. Even though he was locked away as a criminal by the world, to me he would have been a saint and loved dearly.

However, I was never permitted to be held or consoled by him on my worst days of depression and loneliness.

Children only know that they want to be loved and cherished by their parents, or at least one of them. Instead of receiving the nurturing I needed, I received bits and pieces of love in the form of money and gifts. Always fed and clothed but never truly loved. Then I was sent away from the only place of solace I had known and left to grow up on my own.

Who would love me now and tell me it would be okay when I cried in the middle of the night for my lost childhood? Who will hold me and share my pain? Must I die never knowing what true love feels like? Or simply live in misery all the days of my life. At that very moment, I woke up in a cold sweat and sat straight up in bed in my Manhattan Condo.

I realized I had been dreaming about my life which was not uncommon. The betrayal of my husband Travis would never seem to leave my heart, but I hoped to be able to move forward and have a real life with someone someday. Being harassed by scores of male college students looking for that "right" someone in their lives was becoming cumbersome to digest.

In order to deal with the myriads of proposals, free lunches and dinner dates from freshmen to Deans and professors tossing out hints on my exam papers, I had to devise a scheme. They were tripping over themselves trying to find the opportune time to make their move on me only to no avail.

Now I knew what I wanted in my life and it was to mean something to someone. I no longer wanted to be a "trophy" for someone to possess and not know or care how I feel about anything. Going into the last year of graduate school I had come to understand some of what people felt when they looked at me.

I saw the outward beauty that women envied and men adored. The nervous looks on their faces when they stood before me, having a difficult time looking me in the eye without shying away and pulling back in order to regroup. Afraid to ask for a date for fear of rejection, and some tried to boldly command unwanted attention from me by insults. Many could not even keep their eyes on my face. Checking me out completely and giving me a clean 100% all woman, no flaws rating.

I knew I wanted someone special in my life that would love me and wanted to live their life with me faithfully. I vowed not to go into a serious relationship until I found the man that truly turned my head since I knew I would turn his. Having had many classes in psychology, philosophy and humanities, I decided to create a pseudo engagement with a nerdy classmate named Jared, who was third year medical student.

He was brilliant in the books but very simple and plain in his personal appearance. He had a good heart and actually came from a well to do family which drew a hoard of fire ant like women who would kill to snatch this young doctor in training. They would devour him and rip him off in every way possible leaving a shell of a man or whatever was left of him.

We both agreed to the terms of this pseudo engagement and pretended to be an item on campus. This would ward off evil relationship seekers. Jared became my quasi Fiancé. To date, the plan has worked like a charm.

Jared receives no benefits whatsoever for being in this relationship other than to get out of school unscathed by the plethora of bats that would swarm him and pick him apart before he could receive his medical degree.

Someone would pump out a baby and present it to him whether it was his or not and by the time they finished taking him through the ringer and he realized the kid was not his, his money, reputation and virginity would be down the toilet leaving only a shell of what he was in a heap on the floor for some other poor soul to pick the rest of his skeletal bones.

This was the best idea yet for the both of us. People knew it wasn't real but they dared not challenge it. For now, we were a couple. Tonight, Jared was sound asleep on the loveseat in the living room. He lay there, lifeless with one sock on the floor beside the seat like a 15 year old and the other on his boney foot that hung out from under the cover aimlessly.

Even though we knew nothing was going on, I felt comfortable with Jared being here. I knew he would protect me and wouldn't want anything in return. We had study hall today and time took a toll on both of us. We both had been studying for finals all night and fell asleep in separate rooms.

It didn't happen often, but I trusted him. Much of my life was still in shadows from the ordeal of the attack I endured by an intruder that came into my room as a child and tried to take my life. I still have these nightmares about that night and want answers as to why this man wanted to harm me and I had to be sent away.

Having these traumatic dreams caused me to be very guarded. Even in my marriage to Travis, he had to help me get use to revealing myself to him. I was never comfortable with that, although he was very happy with my anatomy. Even though Jared is asleep, I know he hears me moving about in the condo.

I tried not to disturb him with the hopes that he would stay asleep so I wouldn't have to answer any questions as to why I was up so early. I didn't like explaining things to him about my personal life and he wouldn't pry.

Jared rolled over on the sofa and kept snoring. I didn't want to have to explain why I was having nightmares again and didn't want him to try to console me either. I knew in my heart that Jared was not the right one for me and was okay with this charade. For now, he was the safest one I could find to keep the wolves from pressuring me.

Being single, living in Manhattan in graduate school, attractive and no kids, was big trouble. Jared was my friend and although some thought I was using him, I knew I was not and so did he. Jared would do anything for me to be permanently part of his life and I could clearly see that he was falling for me, but it was all in vain.

I was not interested and was waiting for that special someone. I thought many times to break off the fake engagement so Jared could find someone that really would be into him as he was to me. My decision was to wait until we finished this last year of college before I broke off the fake engagement and we set each other free.

I was not sure of how I would do it but there are many females at the University that would love to have a man who is about to be a Doctor. I only hoped he met someone that really loved him because he was a sweet and generous man. If he doesn't find the right woman, he will be miserable forever. We both reasoned that the fake relationship was actually a protection for us.

Even though we were close, I could never tell Jared about how I had the dreams about being attacked by the stranger who was trying to kill me.

I remembered that the intruder had whispered in my ear something strange, the night of the attack. "You are a white man's baby." He said, with a low death growl of vengeance in his voice. "You don't belong here with us."

I never told my Grandmother this or they would have certainly known who this intruder was. This was the beginning of the secrets and lies. All for the sake of protecting the reputation of the family. They had enough issues with an almost White child in their midst.

This night, I decided to get out of bed even though I had to go to work in a few hours. I walked down to the kitchen and got myself some hot chocolate to soothe my nerves, sitting quietly at the counter thinking about why the ugly ordeal had to happen to me during my childhood. What was more distressing was that I never saw the perpetrators face. This left me with the haunting thoughts of what he looked like, or who he could have been. He had to know which room I slept in.

I even wondered if he would have had a kind face that no one would suspect or if he was grotesque and just had lost his mind in some way. Many thoughts plagued my mind at times but it was not enough to keep me from functioning normally. After the ordeal as a child, I remember Grandmother whispering about me going to live with someone else up north because it wouldn't be safe for me in the South anymore. Apparently the person she spoke with didn't want me there either and I ended up with Aunt Paoli.

I remember eavesdropping as all kids did back then. I heard Grandmother say she thought the intruder was a relative of the White man that raped my mother. If that were true, that may have been why the man wanted to kill me because I was the only reminder of the attack on my mother that night.

Ed was in jail and my mother was already laid to rest and then there was me. I fit all the description of a White man's baby but was never sure because no one told me the truth about anything. I had to guess and piece information together as I grew up. I really was sick of it and felt that everything I thought was wrong.

With one hand, I ran my fingers through my soft hair as the other hand filled the kettle with milk for the hot chocolate. I placed the kettle on the stove and turned the fire up high to hurry and raise the temperature quickly. I didn't want the chocolate too hot so I watched it closely.

I sat on the tall bar stool with my head in my hands leaning over the massive granite counter top in the oversized kitchen. The Condo would always be remembered as my divorce settlement hush money. I felt I didn't do too badly.

Many times I thought about the marriage and if it could have worked. "Could I have weathered the storm and take Travis back?" I asked myself that with bitter sweet feelings. Having to leave your husband after only a few short years of marriage was difficult. I thought I had been in love with him and wanted to spend the rest of my life with him, but realized that his obsession of women in general was always going to present a problem.

I was glad I did not have a child in that union. It was time to move on. Even with the fake situation with Jared.

As I waited for the milk to heat up for my cocoa, I still tried to figure out why I chose to keep Jared around. The simple answer was that Jared was only for safety to keep suitors away.

Finally the tea kettle whistled and I snatched it off the eye of the stove to keep it from getting louder and waking Jared. I mumbled to myself as I pulled the hand mitten out of the drawer that was long overdue for cleaning out. It was stuffed with everything from grill forks to measuring spoons and pizza coupons that I never used.

I poured the milk in the huge coffee cup and dropped in a handful of marshmallows and watched them float aimlessly in the cup. Stirring it gently, I glanced over at the old clock Grandmother had given me, and realized that I only had three hours before I had to get ready for work. I quickly drank the chocolate and tiptoed back into the bedroom to try to get a few hours of sleep.

I was exhausted but managed to settle in and nestle deep under the cover. The chocolate had somehow made me feel warm and cozy. I made sure that I closed the door before I got into bed… and locked it... sleep finally took over.

The next morning, I awakened from a sound but short sleep. Jared had already left for class and that made me happy because I didn't want him questioning me about possibly hearing me get up in the middle of the night. Jared was good for pretending to be asleep, especially if he wanted to eavesdrop.

He was from a wealthy family and always found it to be an interesting conversation when I vaguely talked about my family. He wanted to dig for more details, but I never would give him any more than the basics.

I really didn't think he needed more than that. Besides, I was reared that way and I couldn't understand why everything was so secretive in my family. No one wanted to talk about anything they did, were doing or were going to do. It was as if we were from royalty or something and we were just the opposite. Dirt poor!

Jared was one of the privileged ones who had parents that paid for his College. They paid in advance and all of his dorm tuition fees, bought him a car, paid for books and everything was paid up front. I on the other hand wasn't that fortunate. People used to think I was rich though. They always said that I looked like I came from money.

Who knew what that even meant? Here it was that I was going into my last year of graduate school and up to my neck in debt. Getting to work, though exhausted from the late night studying and the nightmare, was enough to call out sick. But I didn't.

The good news was that I didn't have class today and only had to work for a few hours. Having had very little sleep the night before, I simply dragged myself through the day which turned out to be a literal nightmare.

I knew my sleeplessness would slow me down and cause me to miss lunch and other important deadlines that the Director for the department had announced would begin at 3pm. I had only been reminded three times of this meeting and would be in hot water with the boss later if I was not there. I could not get over the dream I had again and realized they were becoming more frequent than they ever had been before.

I couldn't get the thought out of my head as to why I never told Grandmother about what the intruder had whispered in my ear that night when I was a little girl. I hated lying.

Even though I understood that in the attack he didn't completely violate me, but there were still mental scars that haunted me. As I sat at my desk at work realizing that I was still thinking about what had happened to me as a child. I reasoned that I was fortunate that it was only that one time, and that it did not go as far as it could have if I had not fought back. Even knowing that, the dreams still made my life miserable because I could not identify my childhood perpetrator and still felt a sense of violation and fear from what took place.

For this reason, I protected myself from everyone. I was tired of hiding to get dressed or not wanting to be touched by anyone. Even though I had been married, it was very difficult to be an adult and have these types of issues. It was especially true of a man like my Ex, who could not keep his hands off me.

Even friendly hugs from close friends caused me to involuntarily pull away. Not meaning any harm, but it simply made me uncomfortable. It still would cause me to cringe, or a simple holding of someone's hand made me feel strange. I would find myself sweating in my palms and just letting their hand go limp and could see their reaction from this.

"When would these thoughts end?" I thought quietly. People started asking me if they had body odor or something, when they would hug me and I'd pull away. I made a joke and kept going. Over time, I got good at skating around the issue.

I was glad that Jared never asked for a hug but would welcome one if I volunteered. Which I never did. I realized that some of my shyness about affection was that I didn't receive much in Grandmother's house.

I knew I was loved because they fed and clothed me, but they would always put us girls down by telling us we were fat, or say things like,

"Sit your ugly self-down somewhere!" Later, I found that it was a way many African American families kept the girls from thinking too much of themselves when someone else saw their beauty.

Lord forbid if you were complimented as a young girl! That was such a punishment for black children. But for those who were lighter in complexion, it was even worse because everyone already "thought" that you felt you were all that, when you just felt like your normal self. Whatever that was. With all the negativity thrown at you, it is no wonder most Black children had such low self-esteem.

Many were not permitted to feel good about themselves for any reason. They seemed to want to keep the children thinking like "children" as long as they could. That innocent state was very important and for many young girls, very short lived. I began to think about that and the reason why I felt so negative about myself and my own body. Not that there was anything wrong with it.

I was tired of living this type of life and wanted to get to the bottom of it. I sat at my desk at work trying to look busy but continued writing notes to myself for when I got home. I jotted down things that I wanted to know about myself and my family and their lives because I was confused and always had been about why I looked so different than the other siblings in the family.

I wanted to know why my hair and skin color was so different than everyone else's. I had a million questions.

No one would ever tell me anything, but they would always tell me to "hush up" child, there is nothing wrong with you, or, you just got red bones like your kin folk from way back. Then the older folk would go into a story of sorts about somebody that was high yellow. Even then, I felt normal, but was treated different.

I understood the term high yellow, but knew that many people wanted to be the complexion I was. Everybody always commented on how fair skinned I was to the other kids. But after their comments you could see eyes meeting and heads nodding like they knew a secret.

Even the kids treated me special and would let me play the games first as if I were superior to them, especially if they were brown skinned or darker. I grew up beginning to like some of the positive attention I received, but not the negative kind.

I thought about all these things and really wanted to know the truth about my family. I remembered Buddy, "Grandmother's brother" who always used to come by the house to see her. Buddy was two years younger than Grandmother and was handicapped. As a boy, his hand was accidentally cut off in a sugar mill.

My Grandmother had him live near her in an old shack down the road from where she lived. We had to take food to Uncle Buddy in a syrup can. We were always afraid of him because he looked so scary to us.

Grandmother always told us that buddy wouldn't hurt us but we never went inside his house. We'd just knock and leave the can at the door. When he'd open the door, he would look at us long and hard. There was something about his eyes as if he were locked away from the world. We just ran back to the house.

Buddy would always try to come to the house when he knew Grandmother was gone to the grocery store. I wondered about that as well. Was Buddy the intruder? I would think to myself. Not really knowing or believing that he was, but I was still suspicious of everyone. Sometimes he would come right after Grandmother had left to go to the store.

One day, Buddy came to the house just as Mr. Freddy had picked up Grandmother and pulled onto the main Highway. Buddy came up on the porch and I remember that he slowly crept towards me asking, "is sis home?" He called Grandmother that because she was the only girl.

I looked puzzled, since they had just left and you could still see the car on the highway across the lake. I know Buddy had to see it, but I was polite and answered him…"no sir, Grandmother's not here, she went to the store." As I began to think about Buddy again, I remembered how he would systematically come by when Grandmother would leave home.

That one Saturday when Grandmother had just left, Buddy came to the house and as soon as he started talking to me on the porch and grinning and poking fun at me, he made a noise like the noise the intruder made when I was attacked as a child in my room. Buddy asked me to go inside and get him a glass of water.

We were to always obey adults in the family, so I got up to go inside and get his water. Just when I was going into the house, Buddy followed me. I became scared because I thought I was going to bring the water back to him…As soon as the front screen door closed I was getting more nervous when he said to me, "your hair sho' is pretty, China."

Author: Victoria E. Kain

He mumbled in an infantile type guttural voice. I was shaking and nervous now. I knew Grandmother was not there and I was not to let anyone in the house…as a matter of fact, I was supposed to sit on that porch until Grandmother came back and Buddy knew Grandmother's rule for us kids. Just when Buddy reached out to stroke one of my long braids, the front screen door slammed like a sonic boom.

The sound of the heels on Grandmother's shoes echoed on the wood floor. They could be heard like thunder coming across the living room and then into the kitchen. Grandmother came through the kitchen door with the force of a runaway locomotive. With one hand, she snatched the old kitchen broom handle and began to beat Buddy out of the house. Buddy was hollering and ducking and running all at the same time.

He was much larger than Grandmother, but Buddy never tried to resist the beating. She told him that if he ever came near the house again while she was not there she would "kill" him. She loved her brother and knew that he had mental problems, but she also knew he wasn't completely crazy and he knew that she knew this about him as well. Buddy ran from the house crying, screaming and ducking. He looked back at me with a pitiful look in his eye as if he wanted to say, "All I wanted to do was touch your pretty hair."

It was as if he was "sick" or something, he had that far away, glazed over look in his eyes. I actually felt sorry for him now that I didn't have to be afraid anymore. What was wrong with some of these men in the South had a lot to do with their upbringing and some of it was simply mental illness.

Sex seemed to be the only thing some of them knew even if they had mental problems. The females always had to be protected or they would never make it through puberty without becoming pregnant by someone that didn't even want to take them as a wife.

I stopped thinking about my life for a moment and realized that I was still at work and had completely stopped writing on the report I was to finish before I left. I thought back for a moment and just dropped the pen on my desk.

"Good grief," I said.

"I am so messed up in the head!" On one hand I knew I loved my family but on the other hand I didn't really feel as if I knew who I was or who my family members were either.

"I must find answers to these questions I have or it will drive me plum crazy!" I said.

I put the pen and pencil away and got back to work. My boss Ms. Diggs was a gruesome old woman who tip toed about down the hallways to each of her direct reports offices. Since she was the contact that (Travis's old boss) had sent me to for this job, I respected her greatly to show my appreciation for him helping me get the job.

Diggs son was some political figure and she used every bit of his power to control everyone she could. The other women that worked there snickered at me because I did not dress the same as they did, because I was more thrifty and because I did not have the same position as they did. I was still working my way up and was finishing up my degree and they were not aware of that which would later put me in a better position for a promotion.

I was excited to have gotten the job and planned to finish college and move into management soon. I didn't care that I didn't have much rank in this new office but I would soon out rank them all. I considered myself very fortunate and knew it would not be a long time before I climbed the corporate ladder.

I closed the door to my office and determined that I would sort out my life starting from the beginning. I was determined to do what most people didn't have the courage to do and search their family tree. In my family as I knew them, no one seemed to know anything about anyone in the family. It was the weirdest thing you ever wanted to experience.

I was determined to find out about my heritage. I didn't care where it led me. I would start by asking questions of all the old folk in the family I could find that were still alive. I did not know if anyone would give me any information but I would begin the quest. I finally felt good about something I wanted to do.

It was time to do something to make myself feel better about the person I was. Finally I looked at the clock on the wall in my office. It was almost time for me to go home for the day and I hadn't accomplished anything, but really didn't care today. I was tired and wanted to go home and get the much needed sleep I had missed the night before.

I began to quickly close my computer down and clean off my desk. It was cold outside already but I looked forward to the long train ride home which would give me time to write down the things I wanted to do about finding my ancestral roots.

I left the building and said good night to all the ladies in the office even though I didn't like them. It was courteous to do so.

I finally got to the elevator and hoped no one was getting on with me so I wouldn't have to talk to them but that wasn't the case. I got on the elevator and everyone in there were Vice Presidents or high officials. I squeezed to the back of the elevator like an amoeba and they all talked over my head as if I were not even there. I couldn't wait to get to the ground floor to the garage.

Everyone on the elevator said goodbye to each other like real human beings and walked towards their BMW's, Mercedes and Audi's. Beepers were going off like an FBI festival as they automatically opened their doors to enter their already warm vehicles. Well, I was the only one that walked slowly to the exit of the garage to enter the snow filled streets and began making my way towards the train station.

The elevator trains were mostly above ground unless you were going in a specific direction. There was a tunnel that you might go under, but for the most part it was above ground. I walked as fast as I could without falling on the slippery ice. At least I had bought a good coat for the winter.

I was nice and cozy in the down filled full length coat. I searched for my train card and approached the booth to pay my fair. Once I passed the turn styles, I moved toward the freezing platform to wait for the train to arrive.

Scores of people are standing in front of the elevator train track but I dare not stand in front in case some fool decided to push someone on the tracks as the trains came by that day. People did some crazy things in New York. I always thought about the "what if's" in life and I had done that ever since I was a kid.

On this cold evening, the snow finally began to fall. I bundled my scarf over my mouth and only my eyes were seen by others, but what a pretty pair they were. People still stared at me like they could see my whole face, assuming it was as beautiful as the part they were privileged to see. I prepared myself for what I always encounter at the train platform. I knew that there would be the long staring looks from the men on the platform which always made me nervous.

I could see the twinkle in their eyes as they nodded their heads and mouthed the words, "hello" as if waiting for me to return the courtesy. I gave a fake side grin that said, "Hello, but no thank you." I can't count the times men have tried to pick me up on this platform. I was so sick of it, but I realized that that is just the way it was in the big city.

As I glanced over the crowded way, I realized that the man who had smiled at me as I approached the platform had gotten a little closer. He was a tall handsome gentleman. He was well dressed with a briefcase (leather) to be exact. I could overhear his conversation with another older man and I heard him say that he was an "Attorney."

"Hmmm, I thought, if I am to get information about my heritage, I will need someone to help me legally. The wheels in my head began to spin out of control. I was not afraid to take advantage of a situation in my life and so as the train was approaching our station, I glanced over at the man again on the platform and this time I smiled, with teeth showing.

I stood in line with everyone else and then the doors opened slowly. Everyone raced in for a seat otherwise you'd have a long ride standing until someone next to you got off the train.

Once again I did not get a seat, but the "man" from the platform beaconed for me to take his seat. I initially was going to say no but decided to accept his offer. My feet were tired anyway from all the walking I did at work.

I said thank you and sat down. He stood in front of me like a sentry protecting his queen. Besides, it was the only place he could stand. He was tall enough to hold on to the strap that hung high above his head. He began to strike up a conversation with me and I felt obligated to at least talk to him.

"This weather is really getting messy out there, don't you think?" he said, smiling. Lo and behold, a dimple formed on his left cheek as if the smile wasn't enough distraction.

Eager to speak now since I realized how handsome the man was, I felt a bit more comfortable talking to him.

"Yes it is getting rather bad out."

"I hear it's supposed to be in the teens tonight!" he said.

"Yes, I heard the same thing before I left my office." I responded.

"By the way, my name is Bradley." What is yours? He asked, now looking at me with that "look" in his eye.

You know the look that a man gives you before he wants to kiss you or something worse. I knew that look all too well and had turned them all down many times. Well, I had no choice but to be nice to this man and responded.

"I'm Ms. Stone," not wanting to give him my first name because it would be too easy to find me if I did. Then something came over me about keeping unnecessary secrets and I decided to go ahead and tell him my full name.

I realized that he might come in handy for some legal advice in the future. It's always good to have connections. Besides, what would it hurt? "China Stone," I continued. He didn't make a cheap remark about my name and seemed very appreciative of that piece of information.

"Well, since we are giving full names, I am Bradley Steinberg." The fact that he gave me his full name spoke volumes about his professional demeanor. I perked up because I remembered that I had overheard that he was an attorney and now remembered a commercial for the law offices of Steinberg, Madison and Lowe, criminal attorneys. Before he could say anything else I quickly asked,

"Are you by chance the same person in the Legal commercial on television?

Bradley, smiled with an accepting smile, and said very eloquently,

"Yes, but the picture does not do me justice, I think I look much better in person, don't you?" I laughed and nodded, in agreement making a lasting eye contact with the stranger. Maybe this ride won't be as boring after all I thought, anticipating the rest of it.

He had at least twenty minutes or so and Bradley seemed to keep talking. He asked me where I worked and I hesitated telling him because I did not want him to know all this. One part of me wanted to tell him, and another wanted to keep a secret. I lamented in my head, "no more secrets!" Remember what you want to do in your life living on your terms." I had to think fast and responded…

"No, you go first, where's your law office?" Bradley hurt himself telling me not only the location of the building, which was one street over from where I worked, but it was right next to my favorite restaurant, that I could not afford to frequent very often.

He then reached in his pocket and eagerly hands me a business card. I was impressed and at that point didn't care about the fact that I had no rank on my job. I told him what I did proudly and then told him that he was one block over from my building. Bradley seemed elated.

He didn't seem to care that I was so far below him on the career ladder, he seemed happy that he was just talking to me. We talked and laughed and I began to forget about how tired and hungry I was. It was even warmer on the train tonight than it ever had been.

By now, some of the people were staring at the two of us because we were the only ones talking and seemingly enjoying the ride. The fact that I looked mixed and my long wavy hair fell past my shoulders, my hazel eyes and beautiful lashes mesmerized anyone looking at me. I had finally begun to accept that I didn't have to be ashamed of how I looked regardless of what others thought. Bradley couldn't help being attracted to me. He was certainly from Italian decent. His tall frame looked strong and muscular.

Not an ounce of fat in sight on his body was seen, not even through his overcoat. It was clear that he worked out often. He appeared to be protective of me even when people stared too long. He would give a long fixed glance over towards them as if to say to them,

"You've listened enough, now butt out of this conversation."

Strangely enough, the people would look away as if he had given them a legal subliminal message. I liked the feeling that he commanded that kind of respect. But even I knew that they still eavesdropped hard.

The next stop came up and an old man got off the train that was sitting in front of Bradley so he rushed to sit down beside me. He had a great smile and sense of humor. I wondered what he would be like in court handling a murder trial which is what he did.

I knew there had to be another side to this man, there always is. Finally as the next few stops went by, Bradley asked me, very anxiously, "so, do you always travel this route each day?" I hesitated because I realized that I didn't really know this man, but I really felt that I was attracted to him. Not once did I think about Jared, my so called fiancé. Can I trust this man or should I be skeptical and give him this kind of information? I was so guarded remembering my life with my ex-husband and how I was brought up. Well, if the man is on T.V., if he did anything crazy they would surely find him anyway.

I nodded yes, and recanted, "I am working on getting me a car soon."

"That's good." Bradley said.

"But the traffic is horrible coming from downtown, that's why I take the train." He stated.

"I park my car at the station and then drive home blocks away."

"Well, that is what I will do as well," I lamented with a smile. The next stop was Bradley's and he seemed nervous. It was as if he didn't want it to be his stop.

Maybe he wanted more time to say something but was afraid to. I had already told him what stop I was waiting for which was the one after his…Finally, he got the courage to ask.

"Do you want me to drop you off at home?" That way you don't have to get off the train alone?"

"Whew, I said it!" He looked nervous, hoping not to be rejected by a beautiful woman in front of all the people eavesdropping. I graciously stated, "thank you, but my family is meeting me at the station!" Although I was lying through my teeth.

He apologized for being so forward and excused himself to get up for the next stop. I decided to get up as well since my stop was next and people sometimes can clog the doorway and you can be stuck on the train if you are not at the door already before they reach your stop. As I stood facing Bradley, he reached out to shake my hand as if he just wanted to "touch" any part of my beautiful frame. His hands were shaking as if he were a young school boy standing in front of the girl he wanted to go steady with.

His warm palm engulfed my dainty hand… then, in an almost mechanical love struck tone, Bradley muttered in almost a whisper, "your hands are very soft," as if he had forgotten where he was and what he was doing…he continued his sentence as he adjusted his voice and stated,

"That's nice to have soft skin," he said, as if he had been awakened from a deep sleep. He then quickly let my hand go as if it had leprosy and walked to the door. Naturally, I was thoroughly confused by the contradicting actions that I had just witnessed…regardless of how I felt now, it was still nice to have someone hold my hand as if it were worth a million dollars.

Author: Victoria E. Kain

Bradley said his goodbyes and stepped off the train and onto the platform. He didn't begin walking fast like all the other passengers did as they got off the train. He walked slowly and looked back at me in a strange way.

I watched Bradley continue looking back towards the window where I stood. He walked very slowly as if he wanted to stop the train from taking off.

I made sure I was not the first to be noticeably looking his way…besides, it wouldn't be lady like, or what the old folk used to call being "proper." Whatever that means in this day and age with women showing every part of their anatomy from the bottom to the top. I guess it was these old ways of doing things that were handed down for generations. You just did them. It wasn't like you agreed or anything. You just followed suit.

As the train slowly began moving down the tracks, I felt safe enough to slowly glance out of the window so that it didn't appear that I was desperate. My eyes met his once again and this time, I smiled and waved at Bradley who eagerly waved back.

At this point, it was evident we had made a connection because neither of us took our eyes off one another until the train had taken us out of each other's view. We gazed until we naturally could no longer see each other anymore. I realized that I had waved until Bradley was out of sight.

I was even more perplexed as I stood leaning on the rail and this grungy man sat down next to me as if he couldn't wait for the seat to be empty. I was just glad that I was getting off at the next stop and was determined that I would just deal with his funky body odor…he smelled of week old arm pit and whiskey… "why" I thought.

I let my mind divert back to Bradley. I realized that it was the only thing that made this trip enjoyable. It was becoming more common for Caucasian men to show public interest in women of a biracial culture and just start a conversation the way Bradley had done, especially since he was an Attorney.

Had I given off some silent signal? Or, what was that about, "I thought." "Good grief," why couldn't it have been that he was attracted to me, I thought, and why do I always think the worst about every situation in my life?

I waited for my stop to come up next, and gazed out of the window looking at my reflection against the black night. For the first time I realized that I really didn't look black at all.

I was wondering if I would ever see Bradley again and wished I could. The conductor was calling the next stop too soon for me to finish daydreaming about someone that had just walked into my life and I knew we had made a connection. It wasn't like when I met my ex-husband. This was different. I had just met someone that I would have liked to know better…oh well, it's time to go back out in the cold. "My stop is next." I said.

Just as the train pulled into the platform at the station, I looked out of the glass doors of the train before it came to a complete stop… scores of people were standing on the platform waiting to get on. It was cold outside and people were rushing to get out of the snow that was beginning to fall.

I looked through the crowd and saw Jared, as goofy as ever, waving frantically as the doors open as if he is seeing me for the first time. It had only been last night since we saw each other. Jared was like a little puppy that just wanted to go home with you whether you fed him or not.

He just wanted to be there. You just can't hurt people like that because it would crush them to death, so you pretend to feel the way they do even knowing that you are void of those same feelings. I make my way through the crowd and Jared grabs my hand and gives me a big smile.

Still holding my hand, I couldn't help thinking about Bradley's warm strong hands. I quickly compared the difference in what it felt like to hold Jared's hand. It felt like an ice berg. His hands seemed petite and skinny. His fingers were long and clammy on such a cold evening. "Ugh!"

Oh, well, I thought, at least someone is here to meet me at the station, which is truly a plus. I also knew that Jared was in puppy love with me and that was okay with him. But I knew in my heart that we would never get together permanently, I just didn't know how to let him down easy and besides, I really wanted him there for me until I finished school at the end of the year.

Having anyone to meet you at that dreary station was better than having no one at all… I thought about Bradley and how nice it would be if he were there to meet me every day. He appeared strong, confident and even a bit aggressive which didn't frighten me at all. I stopped thinking about Bradley for a moment and focused on listening to Jared go on about his boring day at the University.

I still felt that I would love to have someone to cuddle up with in front of the unused fireplace in my condo on this cold day like today, but settled for what I had with hopes of having it all someday. "Maybe later in my life,

"Maybe later."

~ CHAPTER 4 ~

GOING BACK HOME

Going Back Home

The next week went by fast. I looked for Bradley but did not see him. I finally stopped looking. I felt that today would be a different day to take in life and its unexpected events. The new acquaintance with Bradley had sparked new feelings in me and I looked forward to the weekend. I still had homework though, so I was not completely free. Being more rested I could try to set a good schedule and get some things done. That kitchen drawer was still in need of attention with all of its eclectic items within it that didn't belong.

I thought about Bradley being an attorney and had dreamed we had become close but the likelihood of this happening was slim to none in my mind now. Since I didn't see him at all this past week, I figured he had deliberately driven to work to keep from running into me since I refused his offer for the ride home. It was a beautiful dream either way, but I soon realized that this was just another phase in my life. I couldn't wait for the day to be over and my weekend to begin. I had a late schedule for work today and had some chores to do around the house before I went in to work.

Breakfast consisted of a cup of hot chocolate and a bagel. I collected my dirty laundry and loaded the washer. I opened the pantry to clear out the things that were not being used that caused disarray. The drawers were also difficult to close. I took canned goods to the rescue home down the street. They liked receiving donations for helping the homeless. I sat down for a minute after I returned and the phone rang.

Normally it does not ring in the middle of the day like that unless Jared calls from school telling me about some dumb professor's attitude in his biology class or something. Or it could be pesky telemarketers! I was irritated that I had to stop what I was doing to answer the stupid phone!

I leaned over and looked at the caller ID and looked at the area code and it was a South Carolina area code which was where Grandmother lived. I had not seen Grandmother in years but I never thought the call was about her. Finally answering the phone on the last ring.

"Hello?"

"Is this China Culpepper?" the voice stated. I hesitated because the man had not identified himself nor pronounced my maiden name correctly thinking he might have the wrong person. Instinct moved me to answer affirmatively. Just in case it was serious.

"Yes, this is she." I responded.

The voice then identified himself as my Grandmother's brother, Jimmy and he continued to speak in a solemn tone.

"I know you don't remember me child."

With a fond smile, I assured him that I did remember him, and then he said, well....there was a long pause, "Your Grandmother passed away."

My smile turned solemn and I sat down slowly on the leather sofa in my living room. The handle of the vacuum cleaner hit the floor. That dreaded call had finally come. I realized that I now had no one in this life but Ed and my uncles.

It was odd that there were no tears but I felt a heaviness in my chest.

Author: Victoria E. Kain

As far as Ed was concerned, I rationalized that obviously I didn't need a father if he was not going to be in my life, and that apparently all I needed was the sperm and egg that it took to get me here. And here I am, I would take it from this point apparently. All those years hurled by me and now that day was upon me.

The woman who had raised me was gone. I thanked Uncle Jimmy and got all the information for the services and the call ended. I knew this trip would be a long one for me and I wasn't sure how I would feel coming back to what was home for me as a child. But what I did not know was that this trip would change my life forever.

I sat down leaning back on the soft leather couch. I closed my eyes gently so as not to dredge up any tears. This concerned me that I couldn't really cry because I loved my Grandmother so much. She had protected me and took care of me when mama died and my dad was never really there physically but was in prison but still played a big part in my life. They kept him alive in my head by speaking about him to me as if he were in the next room. I often wondered why that was so important to do that.

I continued to sit in a quasi-shocked state, finally getting the courage to call Jared at school, the only friend I had, and tell him the bad news. Jared was always busy in the library or tutoring other students on campus. He couldn't come to the phone as usual because they were working on a team project for a student's class.

I left a message for him and he quickly called back as if he was there all along and just wanted to feel as he had made me wait a moment or two for him.

"China, I am so sorry I didn't get your call but I did listen to your message and I am sad to hear about your Grandmother," Jared said. "I know how special she was to you."

"Yes, she was special to me. I'm really in shock Jared! Not because she is gone, but because I knew she was getting old and I did not take the time to go and see her when she was still young and remembered me as a child. I never got to say goodbye to her after I was sent away. I don't know if I was angry that I was sent away and the other kids got to finish growing up with her."

"It was hard for me as a child to be torn away from everything that I knew. I was ripped away from my loved ones for reasons I never understood. I was always told after I left that Grandmother had changed and didn't want me there."

"I never believed it but had no other choice but to accept what I was told. I kept purging my soul to Jared, my only close friend and family member now." He was glad to be there for me in that way. He quietly listened as I went on and on trying to let go of my sad past and the thoughts of Grandmother.

I realized she never got to see me again after I left. I was only nine or so and had promised Grandmother I would write and I did for a while, but then time and life took over and the rest is history. I kept babbling and I did not even hear the rest of what Jared was saying. I just sat on the couch, now leaning on one arm until it had gone numb lying on my side.

I told Jared I would see him when he got home and I just hung up and lay there staring up at the ceiling fan.

Author: Victoria E. Kain

The day seemed to slip away after the phone call, almost as quietly as my Grandmother had slipped away from me. I really didn't want any company, but would allow Jared to come by. Time slipped by and the doorbell rang. Jared came in and grabbed me and gave me a man size hug. It was the first time that I even remotely felt something for him. I needed the companionship at that moment, but I hoped he didn't think he was getting anything else in my moment of weakness.

He was a gentleman and I knew he wouldn't try anything. I thought he was a virgin myself. He gently kissed me on the cheek and went to the kitchen to find something to eat. He was always hungry.

Jared finally came back into the living room where I was still slumped over on the sofa and sat next to me eating a huge sandwich loaded with everything from the fridge. He offered me some of the other spoils he had confiscated from the kitchen and I refused and just lay on his shoulder. I listened to him crunch on the chips and then just thought about what I had to do next…this was a hard day for me. I wondered about Bradley from the train and wished I had his shoulder to lean on.

Hours had gone by after Jared finished snacking and I had fallen asleep in his arms. Finally I was roused by him trying to get me up to go to the bedroom to stretch out on the bed. He lightly rubbed my shoulder as if he was afraid to startle me from my sleep not realizing that I was already awake. I sat up and just looked at him and he hugged me again, this time with a bigger hug which made me feel better. All of a sudden, out of nowhere, the tears came crashing down. I burst into a very hard sobbing.

I sobbed so hard I almost could not catch my breath. It was as if I was crying for everyone that I had lost in my life. My mother, my Grandmother, my dog fluffy and even for the father I never really got to know. Jared seemed to know exactly what to say at that moment but I couldn't understand why the tears had not come when I first heard the news but were coming now. It didn't matter as long as I had somebody here for me right now.

I decided to ask Jared if he would spend the night, sleeping on the couch of course, and he agreed. I did not want to be alone right now and did not want to be desperate and call Bradley, a total stranger even though I was gravely attracted to him and felt assured that he would come, but I didn't know enough about this man to trust him alone in my house in my weakened state and remembered what Ed had said about men in my home. Jared was an exception that Ed might approve of.

Jared was geared up about staying over because he never had been asked before but had only spent the one night studying here with me. He may have thought it meant something, but it meant nothing to me because he was truly just a friend to me. Jared ran to his dorm to get a tooth brush and a change of clothes and got back with the quickness. He set up the sofa sleeper like he was truly at home.

Against all odds, I wondered if I should give Bradley a call and strike up a conversation, but again was confused about what I would do if he asked to come over and I would have to kick Jared out which would kill him. Jared looked down at me as if he read my mind. "I love you China Doll. You are my best friend and I am always here for you." he said, only Ed and Travis had called me that name and it calmed me completely that evening.

It was just what I needed. I reached for his hand and held it tight anyway. This time I didn't pull back. It was the first time it had not happened. I knew all I needed right now was someone to console me.

The next morning, I got up and noticed Jared still asleep on the couch. He had taken it upon himself to take off from class and had not told me he was doing so. Jared, rolled over in the oversized sleeper and scrunched up a pillow in his long arms and greeted me as if they were in the same bed. "Good morning, honey."

"How are you feeling this morning?" I looked at Jared as if he had looked at my under garments and replied, "I am ok, and what's with the "honey" bit like we are married," I said, almost sarcastic. Jared reached for his glasses because he couldn't see anything without them. I knew I could have been naked and he never would have known it without his glasses, but of course I was fully clothed.

Jared then rolled over to the side of the sofa sleeper and sat up and put on his slippers. I wondered, but didn't ask, how he managed to have a pair with him, but knew that he kept clothes in his car because he crashed at anyone's house when he was studying for finals. Finally he blurted out, "I am going with you to the funeral China." I was really in shock now. I never expected him to say that and I didn't k now what to say to him.

Did I really need him to go with me? Was he just being inquisitive, trying to see who my family was? I had not talked much about them to Jared. Jared never really paid attention to much, but if he wanted to do this…so be it. After all, I knew I would never marry Jared. That was the stark truth.

The anticipation of making the trip was becoming overwhelming. My initial thoughts were to take a leave of absence from my job for one reason and later face the dilemma about the rest of my life and just leave the company. Besides, it didn't seem that any promotions were coming anytime soon. The one position I had applied for months ago hadn't been filled yet and they probably would give it to one of the little twits in the office, so maybe I could make a job change and use the death of my Grandmother as the excuse to leave.

I wasn't sure about how I would feel about seeing Ed after all these years. Uncle Jimmy told me in another call that Ed had been paroled two years earlier and was living down South. My emotions were all over the place and there was nothing I could do about it. I was tired of wondering who really loved me and the thought of not really knowing was getting the best of me. Often I wondered if other people felt like I did. People often say they love you, but what did that really mean?

The funeral was the next Saturday coming up and it was coming up on the weekend. Already, I would need to make the reservations for the trip soon. I really did not have the extra money for the fare but never let on that my budget was that tight since Jared wanted to go there with me.

I wondered for a moment why he really wanted to go and thought about the fact that many of my old childhood friends still lived down South and might want to take me around. Yeah, that's probably why he wants to go…but who cares. I just don't feel like taking the trip alone. Jared would be the only one to go with me, but would he mind taking the trip?

Author: Victoria E. Kain

Jared had taken it upon himself to take the days off from school and had decided to take the trip with me like a true friend. I decided to go into work later, to let my boss know in person that I had lost my Grandmother and would be off for at least the following week.

I made our flight reservations and told Jared to give me his credit card to put his fare on it so that we would travel together. He gave me the card and shocked me. "I'll pay for both our fares China." He stated. It's the least I can do for you protecting me from the she wolves that I know would be after me and my tender loins." he smiled.

I was dumbfounded by the offer made and graciously accepted. It was the first time he had offered to do something like this for me and I was very impressed. He had really been a standup guy during this time and I soon saw a different side of him. I realized that he was more of a man than I had given him credit for being.

It helped me to see the other side of him and I no longer felt guilty thinking he was being used because he clearly stated he really appreciated me protecting him the way I did. Even when he woke up this morning before putting on his glasses, there was something different about him that made him look more attractive and manly.

With all the positive thoughts about him, I still made sure Jared was out of the condo before I left. I was very private and didn't want him snooping around in my things. Just in case that was another part of his personality. I was not willing to find out about that part of him right now.

The Blanket of Southern Heat

As I went into my den where the other computer was to finish making the reservations, I decided to start considering what I would pack for the trip. I was nervous thinking about all the memories as a child. Wow! Grandmother was actually gone! I did not get to hug her or say good bye. I loved her so much...she was everything to us.

I began taking items of clothing out of my closet that I would pack for the trip. Still holding a summer dress clutched in my hands, I let it lay across my chest. Looking up at the ceiling, I began to remember being a kid, sitting in front of the fireplace waiting for Grandmother to come and sit down by the fire and slice the delicious apples up for us.

She would get the oranges out and cut them up perfectly and give each one of us a slice until we wanted no more. The smell of the apples from the tiny closet that appeared to be huge to us as children was a sacred place. We never took anything from that closet as most kids would be inclined to do when they had not had enough of something. We always had more than enough at Grandmother's house.

It was the only place where we all felt completely loved and cared for. I quickly reminded myself that my mother had cared for me before she passed. It was as if someone was listening to my thoughts and could hear what I had just said about being loved by Grandmother so much that I didn't want to leave my mother out.

I realized that my mother was not much older than I was right now, when we lost her. She did not have enough time to give me all the love I needed, but my Grandmother's place was the place where my siblings and I became who we really were as people.

Author: Victoria E. Kain

I continued to pack for my untimely trip to say my farewell to my Grandmother. I knew she had loved me dearly. I carefully made sure my dresses were not too short because I knew that Ed probably wouldn't like to see me in short dresses, even though they weren't that short.

Jared had the nerve to voice an opinion about his preferences in my dress. I packed one short dress for myself, almost as a way to defy what I knew Ed and others wouldn't like. I reminded myself that it was a new day and what I did going forward was for "China!"

I frowned and then put another provocative dress in the suitcase. "Now, I feel like I have made the decisions I wanted!" Smiling a big smile, I walked out of the massive walk-in closet. The day seemed to go by very fast and Jared had gone to the dorm to pack his suit and other necessities for the trip.

Men never had much to pack when travelling. He told me that he packed one casual outfit in and could interchange his clothing. I shrugged my shoulders as if to say, "Why is it so easy for men to decide what they want to wear?"

"I guess as long as it has zippers and buttons, it really doesn't matter to men." Finally we were packed in our separate locations and ready for the next phase of making the trip.

Even though I had said I was going into the office at work to let them know about my loss personally, I went ahead and called first and they had put me on bereavement leave for the week. During that call, there was a message from the Vice President to call him before I left for my trip.

I wasn't sure why he wanted to speak to me, but I called him back. I figured it might have something to do about the downsizing that was going on and I certainly figured I might be the one to be let go because everyone else was in the click.

I called Mr. Pemberton and got his Administrative Assistant, Leigh Ann. I cringed as Leigh Ann meowed, in her munchkin like voice "Mr. Pemberton's office, how may I help you?" It wasn't a real voice but Mr. Pemberton didn't care as long as she brought her size 40 DD's in each morning for him to stare at all day. He wouldn't have minded if she were blind.

"This is Ms. Stone, returning Mr. Pemberton's call." I stated.

"Hold please!" Leah Ann said. As I waited for Mr. Pemberton to come to the phone, I wondered if they had revoked my request for leave or were they going to ask me to come back on Monday. I was prepared to fight for the extra days if they did that. I had never been out of work before now. Just when I had hyped myself up to fight for what I felt was mine, the voice came over the phone, "Ms. Stone,"

"Yes, Mr. Pemberton. I received a message that you called." I said, getting very nervous.

"I am sorry to hear about your Grandmother and let us know if you need more time."

"You are a valued employee to this company." My heart was racing a little less, but I was still nervous, wondering why he wanted me to call him.

"Thank you Mr. Pemberton." I enjoy working for the company. "Well, that is one of the reasons I wanted to call you myself."

"I wanted to let you know that we have made a decision about the new Director position in the Marketing department. We unanimously decided that you would be the best candidate for Director for this new division and your Degree fits the requirement perfectly."

"You've done exceptional with the projects and accounts you have managed over the time you have worked here." I almost dropped the phone. I was actually speechless.

"Well, thank you very much Mr. Pemberton."

"I must either pinch myself or ask, are you serious about this?

"Of course I am, Ms. Stone."

"We are offering you the opportunity and would like to discuss the salary and other benefits today or when you return."

"This is a great opportunity and we look forward to you working with the new division. Are you interested in taking the job?" he added.

"Well, yes of course!" I almost shouted.

"Thank you for this great opportunity."

"Well, it's a lot of work Ms. Stone, but you have shown you are not afraid of work and the publishing company was impressed with the last article you wrote. We are still getting compliments on that piece you did on African American History.

"Will you be able to come in and speak to HR Generalist before you take your trip so we can get moving on the training you will need when you return?"

I was elated and confirmed I would come in. I had not wanted to go in but would do so under these circumstances. I welcomed nothing more than to look in the witches faces in the office who thought I was going nowhere and they all had applied for the same job, but didn't know that I had secretly applied as well. This was the worst and the best week of my life. I quickly hung up the phone and did the victory dance. I decided that I would change clothes before I went to my new office.

"I can't wait to see their greedy little faces."

I snatched up one of the fancy suits I had packed and decided to wear it to the office. Today I would wear my matching pumps that I never wore to work but felt that this was the time to show those witches what I was made of… all woman!

I decided that I would call Jared when I came back from the office. I didn't want to do anything different than I had been doing. "Isn't this something?" I thought. This must be something special for me. I changed my outfit and gave one last look at myself before I went to the train station. The company had been very generous and I was feeling great for a few minutes until I thought about my Grandmother. I quickly walked out of the door and took a deep breath.

I arrived at work and walked into my small office. I sat at my desk and twirled around in my tiny chair for the last time. Before I could get my things to go to the HR office, Martha the office snitch came to my office…

"What are you doing here?" I thought you were on leave today?

"Well, I am," I stated.

"Don't worry, we will take care of all of your work while you are gone," Martha said with a smirk, looking at the other ladies in the cubicles. "It will be a mess without you here to do this, but we will manage." "Maybe we will get a temp or something. Oh, well, hurry back."

Martha didn't know why I was taking a leave of absence so I didn't tell her. I just smiled and thought about how they all will start their cycles simultaneously when they find out that Mr. Pemberton picked me to head up the new department and my new office will be four floors above theirs. I couldn't wait until I returned.

I wanted to run through the building screaming!!! I did it! "I did it!" I got promoted! But I quietly waved at everyone as I walked to the elevator to go to the fifth floor to Human Resources. Once I got in the elevator, before the door could close, the witch on the second floor they called "Maisie" stopped the door from closing.

She had with her the other witches. She was the witch with an itch. They called her that because she always had an itch for all the men in the building. It had been said that they all had gotten their small promotions to Leads because of their shenanigans in the office.

The elevator door closed and they both looked at me and sneered as if I wasn't there. Even though I was dressed like they were they acted as if it was nothing.

They got off the elevator on the same floor as I did. They stopped and looked at me for a moment wondering where I was going.

Maisie asked, "oh, didn't you get off on the wrong floor?" the administrative area is level 1?"

"No, I said, with a bit of a smug look. "I know exactly where I am." They both just looked at each other now, a bit puzzled but then snapped their fingers,

"Oh, that's right, you are requesting leave…

"That's right. On to HR."

"Sorry about your loss," they smugly whispered.

"Have a safe trip."

I felt strong! I felt as if I wanted to scream to the top of my lungs and tell them that I had the new position. As they walked down the hallway, the two of them passed by Mr. Pemberton, who nodded,

"Ladies…" and he winked at me!" I smiled a shy smile and walked into the Human resources office. Mr. McDaniel beaconed for me to come in. "Have a seat Ms. Stone."

"I am sorry to hear about your loss," Mr. McDaniel said.

"Thank you sir," I stated in a gracious tone as I sat very ladylike in the oversized leather chair. I couldn't help squeezing the arm of the chair just a little. I liked the feel of the expensive leather.

"Well, congratulations on your promotion. I think it's time and you are an excellent choice for this new role". Mr. McDaniel gave me the paperwork to sign. I was not aware that a contract would be needed, but when Mr. McDaniel told me what the salary was I understood.

I had no idea that the position paid quite as much as it did. "You will report to Mr. Pemberton and Mr. Walsh. The salary range is 102,500 with a quarterly bonus of 10,000 if all marketing sales numbers are met at the publishing company.

There are stock options and perks, special parking in the upper garage. You have 10 direct reports and will have some travel but that won't begin until next year when the new office is up and running in Japan.

I was in shock. It was a lot of responsibility but this was going to be worth it. Mr. McDaniel continued. "You may have the option of hiring another Assistant Manager for your group. This position is the Director for the division and is a three year contract. If all goes well, in the three years, you would be eligible for the Asst. Vice President to Mr. Pemberton.

"How does that sound?" he asked. I was almost speechless.

"Yes, this is an amazing opportunity." I said. Before I could say anything else, Mr. Pemberton walked into Mr. McDaniel office.

"Mr. McDaniel spoke personally to Mr. Pemberton.

"Bob, Ms. Stone has accepted the offer and we are closing the contract now."

"So, how does it feel Ms. Stone?" Mr. Pemberton asked.

"Well, I am speechless, but will say thank you for this great opportunity."

"I will do my best to make the company successful."

"Well, before you leave, let me take you to your new office which is right next to mine." Mr. Pemberton said. I was nervous getting up from my seat. Mr. McDaniel made one last statement. "Ms. Stone, we will make an official announcement shortly so that people will know before they leave today and the rumors can stop about who they think has received the position."

"Thank you Mr. McDaniel." I shook his hand and walked out with Mr. Pemberton.

As we walked out of the H.R. office down to Mr. Pemberton's office, he stopped at the desk of his admin and asked her to send the announcement out immediately about the selected candidate for the new position. She smirked a side grin, but sent the very short message out. Odd as it was, the two witches were standing in the hallway making small talk with another V.P. when Mr. Pemberton passed by again, this time with me. They looked very nervous.

"Mr. Pemberton?" Maisie said, trying to be coy and show that she was not afraid to talk to him in my presence.

"When will the decision be made on the new position?" She asked, smiling with her capped smile.

"Well, as a matter of fact, the decision has just been sent out, it should be in your inbox now." He smiled like they had gotten the job. They smiled a nervous smile, and walked briskly down the hall to the elevator. Once again, sneering at me. But for the last time.

Brigitte and the other women are going to burst when they see that I got the new department promotion. Mr. Pemberton opened the door to my new office for me. "Unbelievable!" I thought. I can't believe I am actually here.

And, next door to the president! That's a good and a bad thing.

"Well, what do you think?" Mr. Pemberton asked.

"This is wonderful!" I said. I had almost forgotten about my sadness.

"I can't wait to get started Mr. Pemberton!"

"Well, you take your time with your family and we look forward to seeing you return. It's a lot of work but I know you can do it."

"Thank you sir!"

"I will have my Admin send flowers for your family. "

"Thank you again." I said.

"Oh, and here is the key to your new office."

I almost tripped getting out of the door. I was so elated I didn't know what to think. When I walked back down to my old office, I saw the witches slumped over their crowded desks, filled with files and papers they had to finish processing. They looked at me for the last time in the tiny office corner space. Maisie and her hoard looked as if they had all been crying. They probably had read the announcement about the promotion.

Brigitte, my first nemesis, winked at me. She knew about the promotion, but also knew that I would need a new Manager and wanted to let me know she could keep her mouth shut. I waved goodbye and strutted out of the office. As I walked down to the train station, I realized that with the new job I would be able to buy a car and finally finish up my last year and some months of Graduate school.

Today, I walked a little bit taller and more confident, knowing that I had been promoted. All of my hard work was finally paying off for me.

Even though I had been sad earlier in the day about Grandmother and the thought of having to face that ordeal, I also had a sense of accomplishment in my life. I knew that finishing school was to be my first big accomplishment, but it looks like this was the trump card for me.

I never thought that this would happen so soon. I smiled more at the same people that I used to sneer at because of my exhausted mindset with what was not happening in my life.

This time when I got on the elevator with the V.P.'s and Directors, they all spoke to me. Imagine that. Was it that I was dressed differently or did they already know? It was probably the latter. They all called me by name. "Have a safe trip Ms. Stone." They were instantly treating me as if I were one of them.

As I walked out of the building onto the snow one last time, I got to the station and paid my fare for the train and walked slowly through the turnstile up to the platform and took my place like all the other people waiting for the elevator train. The platform was getting crowded with people getting off work as usual, but today was a little different for me. My viewpoint and mindset was changing and I knew it would affect everything about me.

It was still chilly this evening, but the snow had not stopped completely. I stood there for a moment thinking about what I was about to do. Going back South was a true trip because of having to face all the people I left behind as a child and seeing the man Ed, the only dad I knew for the first time in years. Everyone that was there, but me, knew the reason I was sent away. Then there was the new promotion.

I would be proud to say that I was a "Director" of something and not just an Administrator, which is a glorified clerk.

Author: Victoria E. Kain

It was almost strange in a spooky way that the two things had happened simultaneously. "Grandmother would be so proud of me," I thought as I looked around the crowded platform, this time making eye contact with the passengers and not holding my head down as I used to do.

"That's what I am going to do going forward," I said. "I will no longer look away when people look at me as if I have something to be ashamed of." Just as I had spoken the words, I glanced over and vaguely recognized the man in the light gray trench coat reading his paper. "It's Bradley," I thought, my heart began to race!

I turned away from him quickly just to look at the ad on the platform wall which gave a reflection from the black background. I was checking to see if my hair was in place. Once I determined that it was still flawless even with the light wind that had been blowing, I turned back around to face his direction hoping he would look up from his paper.

I was very excited to finally see him again. I didn't want to go up to him just in case he didn't remember me, which would have been mortifyingly embarrassing. I decided to make sure that I could be seen by him. Determined, I looked out of my peripheral vision to ensure that he could see me, but patiently waited until he looked up.

"Come on, come on," I whispered in my head, hoping he would get a glimpse of me and turn around to acknowledge my presence first. I knew if we got on the train at opposite doors we would never speak because of the distance and people.

Just when I was about to give up all together and chalk up my opportunity to ever speak to him again, a strong wind came up and blew his newspaper out of his hands onto the platform. In his effort to catch the flying papers, he frantically grabbed for them in midair to no avail.

Looking very silly to all the onlookers including me, there was something very special in the playful way he majestically reached for the pages. You could almost see the muscle structure in his arms as he reached above the heads of some of the people on the platform. There was something happening here as I secretly watched him.

Finally he looked up after picking up one page as if to see who else was looking. He slowly glanced around the platform and out of nowhere there were scores of other women trying to get the same attention I was trying to get. They pretended to pick up the same page of the paper that he reached for like chickens pecking for the same morsel of corn.

I was almost getting sick to my stomach watching the shameless fiasco of the women coming on to Bradley. I was agitated by now and was a little nervous, because one woman had almost accosted him.

She was all over him with cheap conversation about the earth, wind and fire. He even smiled and went along with it. It was as if it eased his embarrassment to have the silly conversation. This took all other eyes off his struggle to get the newspaper when some of the sheets were now on the train tracks.

I thought for a moment that perhaps he had been just as friendly with all women he met as he had been with me that first day on the train.

I began to doubt my feelings of attraction for the man on these final thoughts. Finally I resolved that I would let go of the thought of getting his attention and move on nurturing the wounded spirit of the loss of my Grandmother and the joy of the new promotion I had just received.

Even though I really didn't have anyone special waiting for me at home, except possibly Jared. I accepted that and looked away. Out of nowhere, Bradley caught sight of me and stopped talking to the woman mid-sentence. He was now desperately trying to get my attention.

The woman looked at Bradley as he now completely focused his attention on me from across the platform. The woman seemed to develop a very dismayed look on her face as if she were a summer cloud turning very dark waiting for a thunder storm to begin. She reluctantly followed his eyes to where they were clearly fixed and noticed that his attention was no longer on her at all.

He had dropped the papers in his hand altogether, leaving her holding them. The woman on the platform's final look was as if he were cheating on her and they didn't even know each other. She finally spoke where everyone could hear as if to further embarrass him.

"Oh, I see that something else has caught your eye." She looked over at her girlfriend and threw the paper on the platform floor and beaconed for them to move over for her. Once again, Bradley spoke up as if he were in a court setting.

"Have nice ride ladies."

"Humph!" they all said, turning up their noses. Bradley slowly made his way over to me and now he was standing directly in front of me.

I glanced up as if I hadn't seen him at all, knowing I had been an eyewitness to the whole fiasco. I tried to stay calm.

My heart was racing and I couldn't help it.

"Hello again, he said." A little nervousness in his voice. I looked around as if I was startled.

"Oh, well, hello yourself!"

"Fancy seeing you here!" I said, in my sweetest voice, hoping he noticed a difference in my voice compared to the women he had just been amused by.

"Well, I believe this is where we met before?" He said.

"You're right, it was right here." I lamented.

"How is your practice?"

"Going well," Bradley was now smiling with dimples showing. "That's right, you are a clerk with a local company, downtown, correct?

I now had my first opportunity to gloat about my new job and was happy to respond eagerly,

"Nooo, you must have me mixed up with someone else, I am China Stone, Executive Director for The Brief Publishing Company."

"Oh, great, he stated, then let me introduce myself."

"I don't see how I could have mixed up such a beautiful face, but I have been known to be forgetful when I am in the presence of such beauty." "I am Bradley Steinberg, Criminal Attorney with that firm on the billboard, behind you." I turned and saw his picture and smiled. "I am pleased to meet you Ms. Stone." Bradley said. Both of us were playing cat and mouse with our emotions.

If he had touched my chest he would have seen that my heart was literally skipping a beat with every word he uttered.

We both laughed about the phony new introductions and began talking until our train arrived. We walked onto the train and there were no seats available at all this time and we both had to stand. This seemed to be okay with Bradley as it gave him the opportunity to tower over me and be the protective guard dog that he appeared to want to be for me.

Being very tall gave Bradley an advantage over most people. He could hold the top strap in the center aisle. When the train took off, I was pushed into his arms. He gently stabilized me with his strong body to brace me. I quickly changed my stance and was back on a stable footing. We laughed and talked, but this time, he quickly asked me for my number and continued to talk to me face to face. He seemed relieved that I had willingly given it to him.

I was simply ecstatic that he asked for it. Wow, this man is a successful Attorney and he is of another race and seems very interested in me. I was very moved by the vibes I had where this man was concerned. Again, I kept getting the fragrance of his cologne. After all, I was right at his chest because of the packed train. I didn't want to ask the name of the cologne and spark yet another type of conversation. I even dared close my eyes for a moment fearing that I would be lost in his beautiful presence.

Once again, the stops were too short and his stop came up first. Before we reached the part of the platform for the massive doors to open, we could see the scores of people who would be trying to break into the train to find seats for their long rides home. Bradley looked down at me and stated, "I have an idea."

"What is it?" I asked. Trying to be as coy as I could while I raked my long hair off of my face.

"Why don't you get off on my stop and I drive you home?"

I was a bit nervous, but realized that I may not get this moment again to meet this man who I was clearly attracted to and could tell was attracted to me as well.

I thought for a moment and rationalized that Jared would not be at the station tonight because he was not aware that I actually had gone into work. I could have called him but didn't want to ruin this moment again. Go with your gut! I said to myself

"Well okay, if you agree to just a ride home," I said, smiling the kind of smile that denoted my feelings.

"You've got a deal." Bradley commented quickly, elated I had accepted his invitation this time.

It felt good to know that someone had taken an interest in me since my divorce.

When the train came to a full stop Bradley politely touched my shoulder as the door opened and grasped my hand and stepped in front of me to ensure that he would make a clear secure path for me. No one would ever be able to push, grope or unsteady me as long as he was in front.

It was as if people knew who he was…sure enough, the bill board had a legal ad that had his picture plastered all over it. Wow, no wonder people were moving aside and women were looking at me with envy in their eyes as they sneered.

"Excuse me", he said to all the passersby as they made their way down the platform steps. It felt good to have a man do this for me again.

Even in marriage, I realized it was not what I really expected it to be, but more than I imagined as to how good the right man could make a woman feel if he really wanted her for all the right reasons.

We finally got to the bottom of the train station steps and walked down into the corridor. The valet attendant apparently recognized Bradley and beaconed for him. Bradley reached into his pocket and pulled out a ticket and gave it to him. The attendant stated, "I'll be right back with your car Mr. Steinberg." I was impressed that we didn't have to walk in the snow which is what I would have had to do if taking the bus. I felt like a princess today and cherished each moment. People were still passing by us staring and it felt wonderful.

Bradley looked proud to have me with him. Finally the driver brought the car around. Bradley reached for my hand again. The warmth from his hands was almost overwhelming. There was something calming about how it felt just touching him. He held one of my hands and put his other hand around my waist to ensure I didn't slip on the ice.

The valet opened the door and Bradley ushered me in very gently and closed the door. I almost wanted to faint from sheer excitement. It had been a long time since a man had made me feel this special and I never wanted it to end. Before he came around to the driver's side, I saw him tip the guy. He must be very successful, I thought.

Bradley got into the car and took his scarf off and laid it on the back seat. His phone and fax and email automatically connected and began to tell him of messages he had.

He gave a voice command to forward all messages to his office and the system simply, shut down on his command.

"Now, where to, my lady?" he said. But, before I could answer, he asked very seductively,

"Have you had anything to eat?" I quickly answered,

"No I haven't."

"Well, that's settled, how about I take you to my favorite spot for Italian food, do you like Italian?"

"You look Italian, so that's why I suggested it hoping it is your favorite."

"I do love it," I said, smiling from the inside out. That was the first time he had made any inference to my nationality. We both seemed to like the same type of food which was good. I wondered why he thought that I was Italian. I had never thought that before now.

It was exciting to know what he thought about my nationality. Was I Italian? It made me more conscious about finding out about my heritage. I was actually starving because I hadn't eaten since I got the news about Grandmother the day before and breakfast was only a bagel and hot chocolate.

Bradley, turned onto the expressway and I settled into the soft leather seats that were heated. He had soft music playing and the car smelled very new.

We rode for about 20 minutes with small but interesting talk. Finally we arrived at the restaurant. Once we entered, the waiter came over to seat us and soon took our order. He called Bradley by name, apparently Bradley was a regular there. This was a very swank restaurant as well.

I must say that I did fit the part tonight and was glad about the dress I had chosen to wear in to work. It was very appropriate, even though I had no idea that this is where I would be this evening. It would be a nice ending to the new promotion I just received. Bradley ordered wine and special cheese. I love cheese and he had several different types that I liked. We talked about everything and laughed more than I had done in years. The wine made me warm but in a good way. I finally told him about my Grandmother and he grabbed my hand and held it tightly. It almost shocked me but I didn't pull away from his kind affection this time.

Was I changing and growing from my childhood inhibitions? Time would tell. He rubbed my hand as if it were a crystal ball and wanted to make a wish. He told me how sorry he was for my loss. I appreciated his concern. When I told him I would be leaving to go back for the funeral, what he said next was the strangest thing. "Would you like some company on your trip? I actually have family in the South somewhere and won't be in court for the next two weeks and have scores of time I can take off." He had a strange, unsure smile.

I didn't know what to say, knowing that Jared would explode into a thousand Jared pieces if he couldn't go with me. It would be like taking candy from a baby. Dinner yes, traveling now…I thought. Not yet.

"No, I couldn't let you do that Bradley." I said.

"That is kind of you, but I will be okay." Taking a sip of the most expensive wine my lips had ever touched.

"You sure now?" He said, raising a brow.

"I am sure". I said,

"Well, you will call me and let me know if you change your mind, right?"

"I will," I said.

"I can be on the next plane to come and get you."

Bradley completely changed the subject after that as if he had never said it. "What a man!!!" I thought. We had the most amazing dinner and conversation. He seemed so warm and kind and oh so amazingly intelligent. I was literally in seventh heaven and overwhelmed by his generosity, but cautioned myself thinking about Travis and his kind offers which landed me as a divorced woman at an early age.

For the first time, I felt that I could actually be falling in love with this guy. Was it possible? We finished our meal which was delicious. People stared the entire evening and a few waved at Bradley. As a gentleman, he accommodated with a professional nod, but never turning his full attention away from me. Then he finished his glass of wine and looked down at the table and held my hand again. I was a bit nervous. I knew it couldn't be a proposal, but wished it had been enough time between us for that. He looked me square in the eyes and quietly said, "China, I don't know how to say this, except there is something very special about you and I don't know why I am feeling this way."

"What do you mean Bradley?" I asked.

"Well, you make me feel something I have never felt before."

"For the first time in eight years, I have been riding this train, I have never prolonged a conversation with any woman I met until I met you. It is something about being in your presence." He paused and looked away for a moment.

"You have done something to me in my heart and I don't know where this is going, but I will not let you go before I find out what this feeling is. I told you I was an attorney, and I am accustomed to analyzing people and their motives. I want to ask you one question and need a straight answer. I promise I will accept and respect whatever the answer is."

"What is the question Bradley?" I said, now trembling as he held my hand even tighter. With extreme hesitation, he asked, "Do you have the same feeling about me that I just expressed to you about how I feel?"

"Do you want to know where this relationship can go as well?" Before I could think any further, the words came out of my mouth.

"I do." I said calmly. We both looked at each other and smiled. Bradley gently kissed my hand and said,

"If everything goes the way I feel right now, the next time you say I do…it will be at the altar." This was a most tender moment I had ever experienced with a man. Knowing that there was something special in this person I sat quietly and took it all in.

We finished our meal and Bradley took me home as agreed. The snow was coming down hard now and it had gotten colder outside, but I was warm and cozy sitting next to him in the car. He didn't try to come up for a night cap or anything, but I must say that the goodnight kiss would become the stamp of approval to our future relationship.

After I walked into my Condo and closed my door. I watched Bradley pull off slowly into the night. I lightly touched my lips as a remembrance of him having kissed them.

Could this really be true? Is it possible that love and a promotion could really come at such an awkward time in my life? I didn't know and didn't care, but I was determined to give everything a chance.

The evening with Bradley had been more memorable than I had ever expected. I wasn't sure where the relationship was going but felt good knowing there was someone interested in me at this time of my life with so much negative history behind me.

I briefly wondered if Bradley really was seriously interested in me or if it was like most men, just a physical thing. I decided to make better decisions this time around in the guy category and would take one baby step at a time. I would see how often he called and what he would do to truly pursue me.

For now, I had to come back to reality and prepare to travel with my faithful companion Jared who had packed up the trunk with the two suitcases we agreed to take. We did not want to lug all kinds of baggage around so we had limited it to only two. This was a short trip and besides, no one wanted to think about having fun on this type of trip. The day seemed to drag on before it was time to leave for the airport.

I had booked a night flight because I did not want to deal with the traffic once we arrived. We left the car at the airport so we wouldn't need anyone to pick us up when we returned. I hated using the transportation services because the buses were crowded and the drivers all seemed to be mentally challenged and they drove way too fast.

Author: Victoria E. Kain

The trip to the airport was long and arduous. Traffic was horrible as usual because it was rush hour and everyone was on the road. It was actually only an hour and a half to get to the airport, but it seemed like forever. As I looked at my phone to see if the flights were still leaving on time, I confirmed that they were.

We would have about forty five minutes before our plane departed which was plenty of time for us to get to our gate. I hated rushing but knew that Jared would carry the two bags.

The porters took our bags out of the vehicle and Jared wanted to feel like the big guy and tipped the guy ten dollars. He was actually broke until his parents gave him his next stipend for the quarter but he wanted to impress me and the porters. My mind quietly slipped back to Bradley tipping the valet and the man almost tripped over himself because of the large tip.

We got to our boarding gate and I never did like flying, but would do it if I had to. We arrived at the gate and watched people old and young moving about mechanically in the boarding area. Everyone was pretending to be busy like they really weren't hoping their flight got to its destination safely. That is on everyone's mind when they fly.

I sat wondering why people were more nervous flying than bungee jumping. It was the fact that you are off the ground longer which is not normal for humans…that's all I could think of. Finally the attendant called for our flight to board. I began to pick up my things and get ready to get in line. It seemed that everyone in the place got up and I immediately thought, "no way!"

All of these people cannot be getting on that one plane! Sure enough, all of the people were getting on the plane. Over 300 people!

I was a bit nervous and thought, "What kind of plane can this be?" As I turned to look out of the window, my mouth dropped. The plane was HUGE!!!

Jared loved to fly and would get on anything with wings, so the bigger the better for him. This plane was coming from Hawaii and it was a 747 and was massive. We began to board and fortunately we were in first class so they let us on first. This was nice. I felt almost sorry for the people in coach. It was like riding on the tire of a motorcycle. Jared and I took our seats and the stewardess gave us special pillows and headsets for the movie. The stewardess came on the intercom and let the passengers know that we would be taking off in 15 minutes.

They gave the routine information and closed the door to first class. The music began which was very soothing. Jared was gearing himself up for a cocktail. I could see the gleam in his eye. Humph! That's probably the only time I will ever see a gleam in his eyes. Finally the doors closed to the plane and the pilot came over the loudspeaker and confirmed that we were preparing to taxi the runway.

He lets the stewardesses know they were to take their seats, for takeoff. I listened to the sound of the pilot's voice and it was soothing. I was tired from the day's activities and only heard them say that the weather in South Carolina was sunny and 77 degrees with a cool breeze. I leaned back in my seat and closed my eyes. I did not care to fly but I would if I had to… and today, I had to. The plane taxied the runway and I could feel the heaviness of the plane as it lifted off the ground.

It took off very smooth and almost felt as if it would never get up high enough…but thankfully, it did.

I was very thankful that the plane was so large because it is a smoother ride when the planes are bigger. They seem to absorb a lot of friction. I closed my eyes again as we lifted off the ground and continued to climb higher and higher.

Finally we were high enough for them to turn the no smoking signs off. I felt comfortable. I tried not to think about Grandmother but I couldn't. I just wanted to sleep, even though my night had been great with Bradley…all the way there, I thought about our dinner and what he said to me. I went into a deep sleep and did not wake up until we arrived in South Carolina.

The landing was almost perfect and there is always a sense of accomplishment when a plane lands and you are safely on the ground. It is as if you have cheated the odds and made it. I wonder sometimes why we don't feel that way when we take a bus or train, they all are equally as risky, nevertheless. As the humongous plane rolls up to the gate, I couldn't believe we were back on southern soil. Driving from the airport was a miracle... as usual, the airport was crowded and busy.

We got our rental car and Jared was a bit agitated because they did not have the size car we requested. He was mumbling about what he paid for and what he was going to get and it was making us later and later. I was tired and wanted to get to wherever we were going so I could go to bed. I had napped but was not rested.

"Who cares" I said…it's only two of us and why do we need to have any more room in our vehicle than this. Sometimes this man is crazy... He finally settled down and we put our things in the trunk of the car and took off. Leaving the South Carolina airport was a mess.

There was construction everywhere! It seemed as if we were all turned around but we finally got on the right highway. It was getting late and I was irritable and Jared was tired as well. He tried to be patient because he knew I was edgy. It seemed we had driven for hours but it had only been an hour. We stopped to get something to eat at this little roadside café.

We walked in and there was a mangy looking cat running behind the counter to the kitchen. I almost was sick to my stomach. The waitress that seated us had stains on her dingy apron. She had stringy hair and her skirt was extremely short. She seated us at a back table and the cloth was visibly torn from wear and tear of years of customers eating on it.

We placed our order and thought, maybe the food would be better than the place looked. We determined we would get something fried all though it was against Jared's religion to eat anything fried but today he was eating it. We prayed it wouldn't give us diarrhea. We ordered French fries and a burger. The burger was horrible but the fries were perfect. A carb was all we needed.

We asked for directions and finally got back on the road. If Jared had not forgotten to get a GPS for our rental… then we would not have had a problem. We had gotten turned around and had been driving for about an hour or so and it shouldn't have taken us so long to get to Grandmothers from the airport. We finally stopped at the intersection of the highway.

It was already getting dark and I was so tired and cranky that I could not even see straight. I got the map out and tried to find out where we were. I knew he didn't know since he had never been South in his life. I was hungry and my bladder was full.

Author: Victoria E. Kain

With no place to relieve myself but in an open field, I was almost in tears as I turned the overhead light on in the car to look at the map. "We are lost!!!" I yelled. We kept looking at each other and the map trying to see where we had gone wrong. Jared was frustrated and was beginning to blame me for his taking a wrong turn and making the trip.

This is one of the reasons I knew that Jared was not the man for me. If Bradley were here, he would know exactly what to do, I thought. Just as I began to tear up, thinking that we would be lost forever, I looked up and straight ahead in front of us was the little store that we use to go to when we were kids out at my Grandmothers.

I screamed! And startled Jared.

"I know where we are now!" Striking Jared on the shoulder and grabbing his shirt.

"Easy, now, girl, okay, we know where we are," he said.

"I know exactly where we are!" I kept yelling. I told Jared to keep straight across the intersection and turn right at the next road. I knew exactly where I was when we came down the lonely dark road that I now recalled so well. As we rode slowly towards the old house, my eyes searched from side to side, looking out of the window for anything I could remember..." where is the old pond?" I said in a whisper, looking closer.

Finally I spotted the pond by looking at the moons reflection on the water… "Aaaah, there it is" I quietly whispered again…as if satisfied that the body of water was still there. We moved closer and closer to the gate towards the house. We slowly pulled into Grandmother's yard. Her tiny house was dark and still as I had never seen it before.

I remembered the house as being full of light and life, but this night…it was silent. This was a realization that all of the life that was in the house was gone out of it and it reminded me of the reason why I was here…to bury Grandmother.

As we sat in the car silent for a moment gaining our composure, there was a feeling of solace for me as I looked up in the night sky. Could this be the same moon that had shown so brightly when I was only a girl? Still shining its brilliant light even though everything around it was dark? There was now another house behind my Grandmothers' house that I did not recognize. The dim light shone from the inside and I could not move for a moment.

Tears welled up in my eyes... my chest was tight and my heart was filling with emotions that I didn't even realized I had anymore. I began sobbing so hard, that I could barely catch my breath. My emotional state shocked Jared, and this time he did not know what to do or say, but I knew that I was finally home again. Every thought, feeling and emotion I ever had, came back to me at that moment.

The place I had been torn away from many years ago as a child and to never return, was here before me with bittersweet memories. Standing again in the lonely place of my beginning and not knowing any more about myself or my family now than I did then troubled me. I wanted to be more in control of my life and vowed to make better decisions than what were made for me by others. It was time to make decisions that benefited me and what I wanted out of life. I would learn to never let anyone else hold the key to my future.

~ **CHAPTER 5** ~

SKELETONS IN THE CLOSET

Skeletons In The Closet

Uncle Jimmy had been so gracious as to get us all back together for Grandmothers' farewell. He knew there was a lot for me to know before the services but wanted to school me first so I wouldn't be shocked about how things had changed.

It seemed that when someone died who had a lot of information like Grandmother, other family members would sit and reminisce about the past and accidentally tell things they wouldn't tell when the person was alive. People tended to talk more. I decided to listen carefully because I would only have a window of opportunity to gather any information I could. It would be these tiny pieces that I would use to piece my life back together.

We sat down after we were inside and Uncle Jimmy told me things I had never heard before. He filled many gaps in my life history that I had no knowledge about. I couldn't hold back some of my emotions about some things he told me about Grandmother.

He also talked to me about Ed, who now lived a stone's throw away from Uncle Jimmy and he said he would take me there whenever I was ready. I couldn't believe that Ed was that close to me. My heart was on fire thinking I would faint when I saw him. I didn't know how to feel.

At last I had some information I needed to begin my search for my family. He also told me that Ed had another daughter that had been killed years earlier. Ed had killed the man in self-defense and was still serving time in prison. That was why he wanted to protect me. This is what Uncle Jimmy had heard and eagerly shared.

I wondered how much of this could be true since Jimmy had an eighty percent hearing loss and he was legally blind. I had nothing else to go on. All I needed now was corroboration. After talking for a while, Uncle Jimmy finally asked me in a kind voice,

"China, you want to take the walk to your daddys' with me?" I took a deep breath and answered him. "Yes sir, I do." I felt like I was taking vows again.

Jared got up to accompany me while Uncle Jimmy and I spoke in unison.

"Not this time Jared!"

I needed to see Ed alone. Jared sat down as quickly as he got up. He understood. Uncle Jimmy and I walked out of the door and down the street. It was a short walk and finally we came to the front door. The yard was very neatly trimmed and there were flowers in a flower bed out front. In the back to the side of the house there was a small garden. I could see tomatoes and squash and other vegetables. It was clear that Ed or someone had a green thumb.

Uncle Jimmy knocked only once and the door flew open as if it had no hinges. Ed opened the door to the double wide mobile home and slowly looked out. He had salt and pepper hair that was wavy like mine and I felt comfortable again. He was slightly leaning forward almost as if he would fall flat on his face if he leaned any further.

He adjusted his thin framed eye glasses and squinted as if they were doing him no good at all being on his face. Then he looked hard to see who the images were that were standing at his front door.

The Blanket of Southern Heat

The light on the front porch was barely lighting our feet as we slowly opened the screen door to the mobile home. The closer we got to the door, the less Ed squinted over his glasses and a slight grin began to form on his smooth but weathered face as a way of approving who was finally clear in his vison!

Finally, when we were face to face, Ed let out a hearty grin and laughed out loud... "I don't believe it's you!" I just don't believe it's you!" Ed continued to chant the words.

I finally reached up and gave him a big hug. It felt strange hugging him after all these years. Part of me wanted to punch him and the other part wanted to continue hugging him. After all, it had been almost two decades since I had last seen him.

Ed still looked as youthful as he always did on his pictures. I had not seen him in a very long time so I probably wouldn't pick up all the little changes that had taken place with him since the last time I saw him when I was a child.

The only difference I noticed was the gray on his temples and a little belly fat. After all, I had only seen him up to my 8th birthday and back then, all his hair was black. He looked to be Italian and very tanned with a salt and pepper mustache. As I looked over his shoulder, I could see why he hadn't contacted me.

His new wife Trudy was very graciously working in the kitchen as if she dared not come and greet us at the door for fear of stealing Ed's thunder of having "his" family coming to see him. She waited until he invited her to come meet me.

He seemed proud to have someone visit him and invited us into his cozy little home and I gave his wife a hug as well. With the large amounts of money he sent me throughout my life, it was odd to see him living so modestly.

Author: Victoria E. Kain

I guess it was what he wanted having been in prison so long. I was always taught to be polite… and so I did what I knew I was expected to do. Ed and I talked for a short while and it was getting late. I wanted to know so many things but it wasn't the time to get all of this information from him.

I was the first of the children to arrive at Uncle Jimmy's and Ed's back in the South. The house was cozy and they had three bedrooms and two bathrooms. Ed and I looked at each other but we did not talk much. It was a little chill in the air because of the forest and the lake behind us, but the fireplace kept us cozy. It was odd seeing Ed after all these years but there was something familiar about it.

I began to look around the house and then went to the window to get another look at Grandmother's old house outside. You could see it real clear from the small window even though it was getting dark now. I kept looking at the silhouette of the old house. It was quiet and nothing stirred outside, not even a breeze. It seemed eerie to look at the house knowing my Grandmother was no longer there. Sometimes when you think about your loved ones that are gone on, you wonder why it is so sad when you are in their home and they are not there anymore.

This thought made me remember a song Grandmother used to sing when someone died. "You can look all around and somebody's gone." Now, someone would sing that song on their front porch for Grandmother like she did for others. I couldn't help thinking about Ed and his new wife.

I sat looking out the window like a kid who couldn't go out to play. Ed had some medical issues and had gone to lie down after we had visited for a while.

I agreed for me and Jared to stay with Ed. Uncle Jimmy said it was okay. Finally Jared came over to Ed's and he began to chat with Ed's wife. I slowly blocked out all the chatter in the other room and closed my eyes from exhaustion as I was taken back to another time in my life.

In my mind, I could feel the morning sun beaming through the eyelet curtains in the tiny room I used to sleep in. I sat there for a moment remembering how long it had been since I was a kid. I thought about Grandmother and wanted to remember the good things about her.

Everything was very quiet finally and I was about to drift off to sleep when my cell phone rang. Of all people, it was Bradley! "Wow," I thought, my heart now racing as I checked in the living room to see if anyone was paying attention to my phone having rung, no one had.

"Hello," I said.

"China, this is Bradley, how are you doing?"

 "I am great," I said, examining my emotions after hearing his voice.

"I wanted to check to see if you got into your family's safely?"

"I did…thank you." I said. My heart still racing from the sound of his voice.

"Well, it looks like a snow storm is coming your way in New York," I said, making small talk.

"Bummer, huh." he said.

"Yeah, it is!"

"I drove to work today because I didn't want to be on the train and not see you." Bradley said, leaving a quiet pause for my response.

Author: Victoria E. Kain

I was stunned, but elated about the confession of his heart. I felt good and wished he was here with me.

"Aaw, that is sweet." I said, not knowing how to appropriately respond.

"The flight here was amazing."

"We did get lost though," I said before realizing I let the cat out of the bag that I wasn't alone.

"We?" Bradley asked in an inquisitive voice.

I gulped, and regrouped realizing I was not married to anyone.

"Yes," I said, boldly," regaining my composure with no guilt.

"My friend from college came with me," I said, wondering why I even needed to give him an answer at all but wanted to be respectful. I hoped he didn't ask for a gender.

"Oh, okay, I don't mean to sound so bossy, but you did refuse my company so I wanted to know that no one else is taking my place," he said jokingly, "no one is taking your place."

"I promise," I said.

"Well, I am still in traffic so I will check on you after services on Saturday, unless you want to call and talk to me. I am always available for you. Take care!"

"I will, and thank you Bradley." I said, still looking in the living room, now noticing Jared fidgeting, coming towards me.

"Bye."

"Hey come on back in with us!" Jared demanded.

I thought it only proper for me to get back to the rest of the family, since Ed had come back in to join Trudy and Jared.

We quietly waited for the other family to come down to Ed's. I really wasn't hungry but Ed insisted that I eat something. We sat and talked about many things but being that this was my stepmother who I had only met just now, I really did not have a lot to say but tried to make idle conversation. I thought about how sweet it was for Bradley to call me! Wow! That was a nice feeling. Then I heard my text message beep.

"Just wanted to send you a photo so you won't forget me," the message said from Bradley.

"OMG!" I said, looking at the gorgeous photo…what a looker! I had almost forgotten how handsome he was before this photo. I didn't have one to send him and was careful not to because I still needed to get to know him a little better, just in case. I didn't want my picture floating out there, in case there were others picking up his newspaper pages on the train platform.

Ed called the other kids to see how far out they were and what time everyone was getting in, but I was so tired that I wanted to turn in for the night. The short power nap earlier was only the tip of the iceberg of what I wanted to do in bed. Sleep was still hitting me very hard. I never knew how quickly life could change and how drastic the measures would be when I understood the need to make immediate changes in my life. My poor Grandmother had already gone on and now we had to bury her.

Her old house was still and dark like nothing I had ever seen before. I wanted to ask many questions about Grandmother, but was afraid that I would awaken the old Ed I heard about when I was a kid. We were not allowed to ask too many grown folk questions and I did not want to break his good demeanor.

I really didn't want to see the Ed portrayed in some of the letters he sent Aunt Paoli. I never liked much of what I heard, but I loved him because he was all I thought I had.

Pearl and Gem finally got there before I went to sleep. Pearl was staying with Uncle Jimmy. She had gotten very fat and she had her little boy with her. He was cute in his own way but looked nothing like Travis. For a moment, I wondered if it actually was Travis's child but dared not think it. We spoke to each other cordially and I had an opportunity to hug Gem. I noticed that Ed did not say much to Pearl but laughed that side grin he always had and I knew he was happy to see us all.

The night went well, but everybody was tired and we all went our separate ways after dinner to crash and burn…the bed was comfortable, but the room was cold. Jared slept on the couch and me and Gem slept in the big room. Pearl went next door to Uncle Jimmy's. It was nothing like Grandmothers house. Before I went to sleep, I rolled over to the window, which was very close to the bed, and peeked out through the blinds to look at the silhouette of the old house one last time before sleeping.

I was like a kid again, anxiously waiting for the sun to rise in order to feast my eyes on the place that I once called "home." Sleep now took over.

The next few days would change my life drastically. All of my family would be there for the services for Grandmother. People from all over were piling in. Even Brendalyn and Aunt Paoli came even though she really didn't get along with Grandmother. We all had changed a lot since we last saw each other. This seems to be the only time black people visit or see each other, when someone dies.

Everybody comes out of the woodwork to see the children that moved away and those they had only heard about from the stories that were told in the front of many fireplaces during the winter.

After all, what could children do out in the country but eavesdrop? Some skanky neighbor women look for any loose men at the funerals who might have a little money to show them a good time for a few days and they give them the works.

It is a way to get the latest gossip and a big mac and some fries on the side. The conversation would go something like, "Who is that boy?" Somebody might say. The response would mimic "Oh, that's so-and-so's boy."

"Hush your mouth," The person would reply...eyeing the boy longingly as if they had X-ray vision. In their minds they reminisced about when he was a boy and start this cheap conversation.

"I remember when you were knee high to a duck's tail, just a little something." Giggle, giggle, grin, and grin! It would be sickening. The next thing you know, they would disappear down behind something…anything that was tall enough to conceal them for a moment or two.

Believe it or not, people dredged up your life history in one fail swoop of a stare. It seemed as if they would go into a trance of sorts and freeze for a moment to gather all the thoughts of when you were a child.

Bringing back a memory moment and maybe have the guts to come up to you and speak, depending on how much you had changed. Everyone seemed to file in the next day and I was able to see people in the family I had never seen and they had never seen me. But everyone had heard about me.

"You Cassandra's girl aren't you?" It went on like that all day. Everyone tried to make jokes and keep a light humor, but we all were sad. Pearl finally drove up and got out of the limo. I didn't know how I would feel but knew that I couldn't take anything out on the innocent child.

The chauffeur got out and opened the door for her. I knew she wanted to make an entrance like the worm she was. I couldn't take my eyes off the door to see what would emerge from the vehicle. Slowly the man reached in to offer assistance to the woman and out comes Pearl weighing three times what she weighed before she had the baby. It was sad to see her so large, but I had warned her before she confessed to cheating with Travis.

Still, when she looked at me, she almost cried. I could see the look in her eyes. I was still a size 7. Then her little boy got out of the vehicle behind her. He was obese too, as if she stuffed him to keep from being fat alone. Sadness came over me for her plight and I turned so as not to let her see me looking at her.

She dodged me for a while until it was inevitable that I would see her. The funeral was getting crowded, all the neighbor folks were there. The crowd seemed to be staring at us all when we entered the little parlor for the services. They put the family in the first row and I didn't want to be there because I didn't fit in anywhere. I hated seeing Grandmother as she lay there sleeping.

I wanted to be able to call her name and have her answer me, but I knew that would not happen. Remembering her from childhood was the only way I could get through this. There was no hollering and whooping, and the service was quiet and dignified.

The Blanket of Southern Heat

The ceremony ended and I left the building but as I walked out, I saw a man out of the corner of my eye that was very familiar to me. It looked like the same man I saw across from the Library one day in New York. He looked familiar, but when I took off my sunglasses to get a better look, he went out of the opposite door.

I tried to look for him outside but he was nowhere in sight. The day had been long and I wanted to get home and rest. Jared was there by my side and was just as out of place as I was. They opened up Grandmother's old house and it had been remodeled with the money Ed sent every month. I sat and thought for a moment.

There were rumors that Grandmother was rich because she lived well. If you had a T.V. in this place you were considered rich. It was amazing how you could sit in the window and smell the fragrance of watermelon in the air. There was a mystical feeling that came over me as I was seduced by the haunting smells that came out of nowhere. You could hear laughter and see porch lights from a distance and hear people walking down the dark lonely roads at night. Now I understand how the old folk could tell their stories and look off into the sky and smile…it was a good feeling just remembering that and I am still young and have my life ahead of me. Those fragrances still haunt me to this day. There was something mysterious about certain aromas and events that caused you to visit your past as I had done today.

It was a strange but wonderful feeling that you would get when you experienced this. It was like instant time travel back to a place that was peaceful and calm.

With the services finally over, I kept thinking about all the people I had gotten to see. I hoped that Grandmother would be remembered by all her friends.

I would find out later how some of these people really felt about Grandmother, even though she was always sweet to them. After the services, the ladies in the area came down to the house brought all kinds of food and drinks.

It was customary that this took place with most families, regardless of their religion. Everyone brought food and set up a table outside in the yard during the afternoon. If it was later in the day, they would take everything inside. Some people would even go home and change clothes after the funeral and come back to the family home of the deceased as if it was a time for rejoicing and getting to visit everyone that had come home.

I really didn't feel much like eating so I just nibbled on chips and drank a little sweet tea. Jared ate like a wolf and the girls were all over him and he loved it. They knew he was soon to be a doctor and someone wanted to have his baby. I steered clear of him, not wanting to give the wrong impression. Everything went very orderly and Ed seemed to ensure that all went well. People respected Ed.

He looked very nice today and I was proud to have him as my dad. I noticed he didn't cry at all and I wondered why he never shed a tear. I realized it was time to mingle. Everyone always try to tell stories about when we were kids or when they remembered seeing us last.

I looked around the small group of people looking for Ed again and caught sight of him across the yard talking to the man I saw in the parlor that disappeared. I tried to get a closer look and started walking towards them and the man saw me coming and got in his vehicle and drove off.

The guys all went off in a corner of the front yard and compared who had started losing their hair. The women sized each other up as far as their figures for the last 20 years to see who looked best. Trenton, the son of my Grandmother's best friend was there!

They were like family. He married his wife when he had just come back from the military. He and his wife came down to the house in the evening after the sun was going down.

I was nine years younger than Trent. He was such a hot commodity back in the country and all the girls wanted him. He was tall and tanned and had nice hair and his mother was well known. He and his brothers were the lovers on the old back roads in the country.

They could probably have any girl they wanted except for the city girls who were a little bit slicker or too young for them. I think Pearl may have given them some time as well, from what I heard.

As everybody in the room were laughing and finally Trent and his wife Janise came into Ed's living room since the dining room was full. The small double wide was filled to the max with people. I think it was making Ed nervous, but he didn't care, he just liked having us all there.

Trent's wife was always very jealous of Pearl because she always knew Pearl was easy. She kept asking, "where is Pearl?"

"Where is China?" I got so sick of her asking and finally came out of the other room and looked her in the face and said, "Pearl is outside!" Janise ran outside like she was on fire trying to get a look at her.

Author: Victoria E. Kain

Trent was happy that he could now look at me uninterrupted. I brushed my long hair out of my face and flicked it up off of my shoulders. I looked over at Trent, who was literally starring with his mouth open as I walked over to him and gave him a hug.

Hugging this way in a crowd made it easier to hug the guy without the wife being offended…besides, it was the aftermath of a funeral, what was she going to do, scratch my eyes out?! She probably wanted to, because Trent seemed to hug me as tight as he could as she walked in and caught him. Janise still was silent as I let Trent go and smiled and all the guys were going, "Ooooooo, you in trouble Trent!" Trent quickly spoke up,

"China is family! It's good to see her all grown up." Trent said to his wife who was now seething. She ushered Trent out. "Thanks for coming," Ed said.

They all knew not to start any mess in Ed's house. Janise was standing there with her short haircut, rolling her eyes at me when Ed spoke to her again, this time with more authority in his voice, "I said, thanks for coming! Gone home now". He said.

It seemed to get very quiet and Trent was grinning from ear to ear as they left. I walked over to the table and picked up a chip, and then walked over to Jared and fed it to him. I had finally silenced Janise once and for all. I will never understand why that was an issue for everyone.

My goodness! It seemed as if the drama would never end. Even with all of that going on around me. Everyone was just milling around and some people were beginning to leave.

After seeing everyone and going through the way back when time, there was a strange sort of peace about everything. I seemed to feel a sense of belonging here in this old town. I couldn't figure out why I felt the strange urge to stay, but I wanted to leave at the same time. The most amazing thing was that all of this was taking place in the South where I had not resided for many years.

It was nice being here and realizing there was much I missed. The hot sweltering days and the cold winters. The most important thing now was that I wanted to be there with Ed to get to know him again. It had been so long since I had seen Ed and I thought this would be a wonderful reunion.

But little did I know that the skeletons in the closet of our family's life was about to come alive and many of them I would be able to call by name. This closet of my life was in this small country town that I had come to know so well in the short time that I visited. All of the anxieties were hitting me at once.

This was beginning to be too much for me to bear. I even longed to go back to New York. I looked around the room and saw many faces that had grown old. Some were even older than I remembered them being and some were still the same. Eventually, everyone started going home.

They realized that the day was over and my Grandmother had been laid to rest forever. Now it was time for us to get some rest with the hope of rising to see another day…It was really hard for me to keep thinking about her not being here anymore. An even sadder thing was that I actually had someone else on my mind at the same time as well.

Bradley still kept coming up in my head.

He had sent the largest flower arrangement and a separate bouquet to me personally. It was beautiful. I took a sneak peak as often as I could of the text he sent me with his picture. It got me through the day. After everyone had finally left and my stepmother Trudy was cleaning up after all the guest that had stopped by. I hurriedly did the dishes and helped her by sweeping the floor. She seemed very happy that we all were there.

Of course, Ed sat back like the king of the roost as he always did and Trudy waited on him like she always had. Jared had gone in to get ready for bed but I stayed up with Gem and Trudy. Gem told me all about Pearl and what happened to her before the baby was born. She had a difficult time and I felt sorry for her.

I was asking Ed to find out who owned the land next to his. I figured if I would buy it, we could have the entire 400 acres back that his grandfather had bought and paid for. That is why he was there in the South. Ed had worked so hard to keep that land. I found out that he put the land in Grandmother's name while he was in prison so no one would kill him and forge the deed. That was the reason he continued to take care of her and send her money.

I kept asking Ed for this man's telephone number that owned the land next to him and he had given it to me reluctantly. He reassured me that if anything happened to him, I would get the land, all of it. I didn't ask any more after that.

But the more I thought about coming back, the stronger the desire was for me to get back to my Condo in New York. The next day seemed to go by very quickly. Watching the family and their kids enjoy being at Ed's for the first time in many years seemed to have him sticking his chest out for a moment.

We had stayed up late the night before talking and laughing. Ed seemed to enjoy that time with us. Everyone would be getting ready to go to the airport and leave while Jared and I would be the last to depart. We had a couple extra days. Jared installed a motion detector on Ed's front porch because it was so dark when we first came up.

Ed felt grateful and ranted and raved about Jared's accomplishments. Jared was good with anything electronic. "Boy, you know what you doing?" Ed and Trudy literally begged us to stay longer.

"Don't go, China Doll," Ed said, he called me that when he wanted to show his closeness to me. He was almost begging. I never thought I would hear him begging me to stay with him.

"I have to go Ed," I said.

"Jared and I both have to get back to school and work. I just received a promotion at work and need to get to the training."

I forgot that Jared had not heard about the promotion.

"Really, China!" Jared exclaimed.

"When did this happen?"

"The day before we left. I had called in about my leave and the V.P. offered me the position. I will be the new Executive Director of Marketing at the Publishing Company." Ed, Jared and Trudy cheered for me.

"Well, China," Ed, said," I guess I understand. Maybe another time you and Jared can come back to see us."

"We will Ed. For sure!" I said.

"And, besides, Ed, you have Trudy now, I know you guys have a lot to do together."

Ed, had a strange look on his face. It felt like Trudy was someone that kept him warm at night, and she may not have been the love of his life, but still she was there for him and a sweet person, exactly what he needed.

Our flight was leaving at 4pm and it was already 1pm in the afternoon. As I finished packing, I looked out of the window at my Grandmother's house. I threw my blouse on the bed and told Jared I would be right back. I ran up on the porch and opened the door to my Grandmother's house slowly.

As I walked in the front bedroom of the old house, my eyes searched the rooms as if I were looking for gold. A flood of memories came back to me in an instant. I looked down on the fireplace hearth. I could visualize Grandmother sitting there in front of the fire combing our hair, while telling us a story before bedtime.

I looked around frantically through each of the rooms that brought back fond memories. My heart raced as I searched to find something to take back with me as a memento of happier days with Grandmother. The old house didn't seem so big now that I was an adult and my views had changed.

Tears streamed down my face as my eyes desperately scanned the rooms only to be left with visions of old worn out shoes, costume jewelry that had already begun tarnishing and tattered clothing worn for many years due to abject poverty.

There were things scattered about and a few pieces of furniture that I could never take with me. Pearl and the other family members had done their worst and did what people do best in the South when someone dies that they know.

They come over and grab anything they think they want, even if it doesn't mean anything to them and leave it behind in their remains for someone else to do the same. It was a vicious cycle.

I continued to cry silently because I couldn't find anything that I felt would satisfy the hole in my heart. I finally rationalized for a moment and stopped grieving and sat on an old crate that was in the small kitchen. As I quietly rested there frozen and unsure as to whether I wanted to rise up and walk out of the house once and for all, a calmness came over me as if something had touched my heart. It was such a strange feeling that I could hear my own heart beating.

As I took one last look around and resolved that I would leave and never return, I smiled when I thought about how Grandmother used to kiss me on my nose when she thought I did something funny. I then realized that the simple memories of her smile and emotions was something that I would take with me. The thing I was looking for I already had in my heart, which was love.

In my heart was all the love and laughter that I had been given. All the hugs and kisses she planted on my cheeks. It gave me a free spirit to love others and know how to make a home for my family someday. I knew that I could walk out of the old house now feeling satisfied that what I have can never be lost or stolen. It could only be handed down to those I love.

I said my goodbyes to Ed and his wife, and Jared and I left the South that day sad but satisfied. Knowing that I had learned what love really felt like. Knowing this was only the beginning. I would soon duplicate this feeling in my life and would stop at nothing to keep it.

Author: Victoria E. Kain

~ **CHAPTER 6** ~

A TIME OF REFLECTION

A Time of Reflection

It had been weeks since we had been South and came back to New York and there was much to digest from the trip and meeting so many relatives that I never knew about. The most unreal part was that there was still no one there that remotely resembled me. It was the same as when I was a little girl and this thought saddened me.

I had to give credence to the fact that while I was back home for the funeral, I did feel a sense of belonging. There was something about the southern lifestyle that was different as night and day to living in New York, now, all of my adult life. I had grown accustomed to the liberal attitudes of the people in the big city and had to almost dumb my mindset down to keep up with some of the southern folks antics.

I always knew that I didn't think I was better than them, just a bit ahead in some ways now because of a change in my environment for so many years. That is what had changed much about my way of thinking.

There were many things I still enjoyed about living there. The hospitality of the people was one thing that always made me feel welcomed. I missed the feeling of people wanting to be in your life, even if they were nosey sometimes and asked a million questions just for the sake of knowing things about you. It was an innocence about the way southern people approached you.

They still made you feel as if you were a part of something special. Food was another area of their way of showing affection. If they liked you, they fed you, and it was evident that most people were liked because they were always eating in the South.

Author: Victoria E. Kain

Southerners paid close attention to people. The men watched their women walking, coming and going. There was something sensual about it. For some it was down-right weird. If it were a close relationship, you felt special, like your guy was really into you. He probably was into others as well, but he never let his woman go lacking for that attention if he wanted her.

You could also put on a few pounds and the men thought that was just peachy! They watched their women's butt roll around under their dresses and in their pants like two basketballs being dribbled by Magic Johnson. They didn't mind a little meat on their woman's bones. Everyone in New York wants to be a skeleton. Maybe that's why the closets were so full of them.

It seemed that if you could get a good education in the South and have more freedoms it might not be so bad to live there. In New York, people didn't even look at you unless they knew you or wanted to know you. They really didn't care about you as a person unless they could get something from you. That's the only way you got ahead. I had mixed feelings about the only home I knew and finding out about my heritage.

The next weeks were back to the grind stone. I immediately had to catch up on my homework and was so terribly behind. My mind was foggy since the trip down South as if I were conflicted about what I wanted to do with my life now.

Up to now, everything seemed so crystal clear about my schooling and moving forward. Jared was amped about the trip but was also behind in his studying and really had to catch himself up with the biology he was studying. I didn't see him for weeks after the trip.

Going back to work was even more challenging with only a week off and a new promotion. Once back, the department head Mr. Pemberton called a division meeting and everyone was there. They made an official announcement with all the department heads and everyone now knew that I had gotten the promotion as Executive Director of Marketing.

Brigitte, my prior nemesis now turned work friend, was ecstatic about my promotion and was very congratulatory. We always kept our close friendship on the down low because we saw how horrid the rules were for the employees and thought it best to keep it secret. I could also get information that the fifth floor big wigs, as they were called, didn't leak to them.

I would sneak information to Brigitte to keep her from being sabotaged out of her job like some were. They never suspected me and our friendship grew. Now a year and a half later, I am promoted to the fifth floor.

"Way to go, Ms. Stone," Brigitte said. This time with sincerity. She had calmed herself down quite a bit since our first meeting and was a totally different person. She found that the man she was so concerned with being her man on the 5th floor had other interests with quite a few others on the 5th floor.

She came to me and apologized about her initial behavior when we first met and told me that no one had ever spoken to her like that before and it really opened her eyes to see why she may not have been promoted yet after 10 years with the company.

After leaving the meeting, Brigitte came to my new office and wanted to assist me getting moved in.

"Knock, knock," Brigitte said. The door was wide open.

"Hey, come on in," I responded.

"So, how does it feel to be on the fifth floor now with the big wigs?" she asked.

"Well, we all know that I don't wear a wig," I said, flicking my hair like I had done when we had our first encounter, now smiling.

"Just kidding, I know what you meant, and it feels great." I replied.

"I wanted to see if you needed any assistance getting settled, lady." Brigitte asked.

"Well, maybe help with moving some of the things from my drawers downstairs, but my new Admin already got everything set up for me before I got back." I said. Now sitting down slightly twirling in my leather chair that I had waited so long to occupy.

"I wanted you to know that if there is anything I can do to assist you China, please don't hesitate to call on me," she said continuing her conversation.

"Over the years now, we have worked closely together and I appreciate your help in showing me by way of your own conduct, what it really takes to get ahead."

"You have worked hard Brigitte, your time will come for you like the rest of us, I know it will," I told my secret friend.

"There are many positions opening up here at the company and I encourage you to keep working on moving up. As a matter of fact, there may be one or two positions in my department that may come up in the future, so keep your resume ready."

I smiled and winked at Brigitte. It seemed that this was what she wanted to hear.

"Thank you China for your kind words! I know that is not a promise, but I appreciate you giving me hope."

I have worked here for over ten years and now realize what I have been missing in my work ethic." Brigitte said.

"You know, I am from the South too, and it seemed to me that it's really difficult for some to get promoted in companies like this unless you are very friendly or look like you," Bridgette said, raising a brow.

I was concerned about the statement made and was careful how I responded. I knew it was a loaded statement and I didn't want to get caught up already in anything H.R. related. I had learned not to always take everything people say for fact, so I responded honestly, but cautiously.

"Well, Brigitte, all I can say is that working hard and getting your degree really helps for getting many of these positions."

"Do you have a degree?" I asked Brigitte.

"Well, no," Brigitte said.

"I wanted to go to school but my two kids needed everything and I just didn't have time or money because of work and taking care of them. Do you have your degree?" Brigitte asked.

"Yes, I am finishing my Masters this year."

Brigitte was shocked. She looked very dejected and stood up to leave.

"Wow, you seem to have it going on."

"I am going back to school this year too," Brigitte said.

"You are right, this is important. I never thought about it like that."

"Thank you though, and let me know if I can assist you in any way."

"I will Brigitte. Thank you!" I said.

Brigitte left my office and Mr. Pemberton walked in behind her and turned up his nose. I wasn't sure what that was for, but welcomed him in. He congratulated me again on my new position. He was very polite, almost to the extent of being fresh.

He talked some business about the firm, but I was more concerned about some of the statements he made concerning our first meeting. He referred back to my first day working and stated how he was smitten by my beauty. Mr. Pemberton further stated that he had never seen such a beautiful woman until I graced the firm with my presence. He boasted about being the one that gave me the large raise the first year I was with the company. He wanted all the credit for what was done. His final nail in his coffin was that he said that he pulled all the strings to get me in the new Directors position. I was floored!

It was as if he was already trying to get his dibs in first for a date before the other Executives, thinking that by letting me know what he had done for me, I somehow would owe him. I had also noticed how all of the men on the fifth floor had made similar statements about how they had supported me. By the time Mr. Pemberton left my office, I was now clearly aware of why I got the job. It was like most of the men that approached me. They all wanted something from me for whatever they would give me. Again, it was a "Trophy" syndrome, which is what I called it.

I was deeply concerned and disappointed about the conversation. I knew I had to be careful because these type of men were very crafty. They could promote you one minute and destroy you the next with the stroke of their ball point pens. I decided it was time to play the game that these men played.

They wanted to put beautiful women near them which gave them the eye candy they desired, but they always wanted to control. That scenario might not be so bad if they would be faithful to one piece of eye candy, but it was common knowledge that men like these wanted a candy "Bowl."

They wanted lots of choices of candy. Chocolate, vanilla, caramel and even nuts. I knew I needed the salary and the job with the condo and finishing my last year of graduate school.

I would figure things out to make this work for me. Everyone coming by the door for the first week smiled and winked and did all kinds of special things for me. I received a key to the Executive wash room for the ladies and my own parking space, next to Mr. Pemberton in the garage. I began calling him Bob as a measure of control. I was now becoming fearless with men and it felt great.

I was sure now of what Brigitte was saying. These men would use the women for their own personal use and then discard them or never promote them at all. Keeping their job was the prize they received. I was thoroughly disgusted. But I would not be beaten in this man's game ever again.

Days went on and I did well skirting around the advances from the sorry men in the suits on the fifth floor. I decided to do something I had never done before. I figured out a way to stop the madness. I was very disappointed that I had received the promotion thinking it was on my own merit only to see that there were strings attached.

Time went on and I only had six months left for my graduate degree. I was really excited about it.

My relationship was flourishing with Bradley and I felt that things were going well until he took on a very prominent client that lived abroad. Now he had to travel to Brazil to represent him.

Because of this man's wealth and position, they required that Bradley stay there until the case was tried. This put Bradley and me on a long distance relationship. I was okay with it at first but didn't think Bradley would last. His client had four beautiful daughters. That was like putting a snake in the henhouse. Someone was going to get bit.

There was a lot of publicity about the trial and Bradley was all over the news and the client and his daughter were all seen by the world holding onto Bradley's arm, as he escorted their father out of the court room. I became furious about what I saw.

I saw Bradley smiling and holding one of the daughters around the waist. Was that really necessary? This case went on until his client set up a Villa in Brazil for Bradley to live in. Bradley was required to reside there in Brazil during the trial and was not able to come home until it was completed.

I communicated with my love over the phone and skype for months. I had freed Jared of our quasi relationship so that he could begin his life with whomever. We still kept in touch as friends. I dealt with the long distance relationship until one night Bradley called and halfway through the conversation, a woman walked up to him and asked him if he was ready for dinner. He tried to mute but was not quick enough.

He spoke to me as if I were another client, telling me he would get back to me the next day with an update and hung up. Furious was not the word to describe my anger, but I refused to call back.

I knew that things were changing with this long distance love with Bradley. Ed was doing well that year but his wife took ill and passed away. He was very lonely afterwards and Uncle Jimmy said that he was really going downhill and they wanted me to come back to South Carolina to help him for a while but it was just not feasible at this time.

The job and finishing school was just too much to handle along with a long distance love relationship with Bradley that seemed to become more and more bizarre as time went on.

Lately he spent more time abroad and didn't get home to New York at all. The man he was defending was said to like him as a son and they all fell in love with him. He was like the son the man never had and he wanted him there.

It didn't help that his daughters were as drop dead gorgeous as I was. Not that I couldn't hold my own, but I knew that with that much tail around, it would be difficult for Brad to hold his own. Any man for that matter.

Two months, turned into three and four and then he didn't know when he would come home even when he did not have to be in court for weeks. I was clear where this was heading and realized it was only a matter of time left for the relationship. I determined that I would not waste too much time worrying about it.

I had kept myself to myself and that was probably why he stayed so long. He was being fed on Brazilian soil, but I had other fish to fry in New York. Each day I came to my office at work, I received calls from Ed asking me to come back South. I was always glad to hear from him, but was not ready to leave New York. I still had unfinished business.

There were still questions I had about my own heritage and life and was still wondering where my family was. Since everyone had a family, I wanted to know about mine. Even when I talked to Ed about some things, he didn't seem to have many answers either. It was getting very ridiculous and I was getting tired of the same lame answers. I wanted to know more and would soon decide to go to an agency with what I had.

I was doing well with my classes and my job. Brigitte had enrolled in a local college and was very excited about her progress. She worked hard and when my department had a position open, Brigitte applied for it again. She was a good candidate for the position, but Mr. Pemberton denied her request for the interview stating she was not suitable for the position.

I was concerned because I knew that Brigitte had all of the qualifications and it did not require a degree. I got information from other men on the fifth that Mr. Pemberton was prejudiced and didn't like Brigitte. They thought that by giving me this information they might have a shoe in for dinner or such. I continued to use the men to get what I needed.

My group was hitting all the department targets and Mr. Pemberton went back and had Human Resources put a degree requirement on the job description which would make Brigitte officially unqualified. Another candidate got the job. I was clear now with what was happening at the firm. I was very frustrated with the procedures there and realized what I wanted to do. Brigitte looked very forlorn each day and didn't speak much to anyone, but just came to work and went home. I felt bad for her because she had worked hard and deserved a second chance.

This was an opportunity for me to help someone else, so I devised a plan but I had to be careful. Weeks would go by and I had calls each day from Ed. I was beginning to miss being there with him for the short while I was there almost a year ago. I felt bad for him and called him often to check on him. One evening I called and talked for a while.

In the conversation, I asked him about the man I saw at my Grandmother's services and at the gathering afterwards. He avoided the topic all together. This concerned me, but I didn't insist. He started coughing and pretended he had to go.

I would try again another time. Things were going well and Bradley and I had fewer and fewer conversations. I finally heard on the news that Bradley was opening a new firm in Brazil as a result of clearing his wealthy client of all criminal charges. There was talk also that his firm was in cahoots with the verdict of not guilty and that was how he opened the new law firm from money funded by his wealthy client.

I knew something was going on, and hoped that Bradley would at least come back to let me know if he was staying for good or not. Well, sure enough, Bradley called one evening to let me know that he had decided to stay in Brazil since he had opened his new law firm and was getting things set up.

He claimed that he wanted me to come there to be with him, and I knew he really was not sincere, but I agreed to come anyway. I made the arrangement to travel to Brazil for a week. Mr. Pemberton approved my time off. He wanted me to be happy thinking he would be paid at a later date, but in reality, I knew he'd never get a dime.

Several days before I was to travel to Brazil, Brad called and told me that he was coming back to the states and to cancel my trip. He had paid for it and when I didn't cancel it, he did. I didn't hear from him for weeks after that. Finally, I received an invitation in the mail which stated that he was getting married to his client's younger daughter. They were to be married the week after I was supposed to be there.

I wasn't really shocked having so much drama of my own here in Ney York, but I was mad as hell! Why couldn't he just tell me he had fallen in love with someone and wanted to get married? Why do men feel the need to lie to a woman? That is the very reason I gave him nothing more than the phone calls and dinner. It is the best way to see what a man is all about.

If he is serious, he will wait for you. If not, he will jump for the first open door. The relationship was officially over. For me, it was war on slick men! I was sick of men thinking they could use beautiful women any way they chose. I decided to entertain the thought of going back South. Now, I was tired of New York and all the trashy people in it.

There were no tears in this break up and I told Ed in our next conversation that I was considering moving back. I expressed that I would need to get a place there and Ed was so excited that he told me he would buy a new house if necessary. I didn't require that but told him that I had some loose ends to tie up the next few months. I had a trip to take and would not miss it for the world.

I booked a first class ticket to Brazil to attend Bradley Steinberg's Wedding. I felt that if someone had the audacity to send me an invitation, I should attend and flex a few muscles of my own.

I checked into the Brazilian Court Hotel for one day and then stayed in a private villa owned by Mr. Pemberton. Not only did he have frequent flyer miles, he owned other land and properties in Brazil. I was brought to the wedding ceremony like royalty and was escorted in as a special guest of Bradleys.

When the wedding was beginning and Bradley walked out and took his place at the altar, the first face he saw before his bride walked in was mine. He looked as if he would faint, but he didn't. He smiled a sheepish smile and I waved a coy waive. I couldn't help feeling a bit nauseous. He looked sweet in his tux, but I was waiting for the bride to come in, wishing it was me.

I made sure that I was able to be seen by Bradley. I was dressed to the nines and everything was in place. The Bride's father stood next to me and I told him I was part of Bradley's family. He then, grabbed me and kissed me and held my hand and then walked to the back to escort his daughter in for the ceremony. Bradley could see it all and seemed very nervous.

His face was red. I was waiting for the bride to enter and here she was. The music started and the doors opened. My heart was racing as I looked around to see some beautiful girl walk through the door and what emerged was traumatizing.

The woman on the man's arm was extremely obese, she still had acne and was a mess. She looked nervous but happy and while everyone was watching her come down the aisle, I watched Bradley. Funny thing though, he had a look in his eye that actually spelled, L.O.V.E. It seemed that he was really happy to see her and I can imagine that.

When she got to him, he just stared at her like she was a piece of cake. OMG!!! He was actually in love with her. Not that he shouldn't be, but for that reason alone, I couldn't be mad anymore.

I went through the long drawn out ceremony and skipped the reception and got the next plane out back to New York. I put my headset on and slept all the way home. I only spent one night in the beautiful Villa, and without a man… Bummer! That was the end of that chapter with me and Bradley. I gave him a card but no gift. He tried to call but I blocked his number from my phone.

The next week at work was tedious. I decided that I would have H.R. post the Assistant Manager position for my department. Sure enough, Mr. Pemberton came to my office to discuss the candidates that had applied.

I called off many of the names but did not call Brigitte's name. I knew that he would have blocked her application. He made his usual advances towards me and this time, I played along with him because I wanted something from him. I knew that if I pretended to like him, I would be able to get Brigitte in the position this time.

It was crystal clear now, that only certain people got to the 5th floor at the firm. Once you got there, you were private property and passed around like a cheap blunt. I knew all too well what this was about. They did not realize that some of what they didn't want to see on the 5th floor was in my blood and already there, you just couldn't see it.

I had prepped Brigitte about what was going on here and asked her if she was ready to fight for what she wanted, and Brigitte was.

Mr. Pemberton asked me out to dinner again and this time I accepted the invitation. I knew that I needed to get him in a public setting to control him and dinner was the best way to discuss business related things.

Naturally he invited me to his private place and I declined, because of deadlines I had at work of course. He accepted the decline because he felt that there would be another time. Before we left, I asked him a question.

"Bob, I am really in need of someone strong to take on this new workload for this Management position coming up in my department. Most of these applicants are people who are just too weak," I said.

"They don't want to work, and are more fluff and no substance, I need someone that can work and do whatever I need done. I need someone that is hungry!"

"Who else do you have in mind?" Mr. Pemberton asked, eager to hear my suggestions.

"Well, I had other resumes come in today…well, let's see, Brigitte from the first floor applied, she is a hard worker."

"She is just too Ghetto for this firm. I really want to get rid of her because she is too opinionated!" he said, not even blinking to hide his true feelings or taking into account Brigitte's excellent skills.

"In order for me to be able to be free to come and go at will, I need someone that will work hard, otherwise, these deadlines will keep me tied up forever and will never be met," I said, shrugging my shoulders and flicking my hair in a coy way. I even looked down at my nails which really was ghetto but Bob thought it was cute with me doing it.

Author: *Victoria E. Kain*

"I see your point," he said. Squirming in his seat like he had hemorrhoids, but smiling the "I will give you whatever you want grin. "Well, if she gets the position, reduce the amount of salary she receives so it will take her longer to move up the ladder and we can get more out of her."

"We can always get rid of her later if she doesn't do what you want her to." he said. I was thoroughly disgusted but agreed. I had seen this all too often and felt horrible about the conversation. I agreed with Pemberton to hire Brigitte and put a lower pay in other than the 60,000 per year. He suggested 40,000 to start. It still would be an increase for her, but it was a horrible cut. The dinner ended.

I submitted Brigitte's resume to H.R. and the next day, Brigitte began her interview process. We kept the plot secret. H.R. put all the data through for Brigitte and she got the job. Brigitte and I met that evening at her home and she was very excited.

She was so happy she would make 40,000 dollars a year, but when I told her that I left the amount at the original 60,000, she broke down and cried. To help my friend, I would let Bob take me out to dinner again and pretend I forgot to change it in H.R., knowing he couldn't take it back. I told Brigitte to keep the job for two years, make her mark and go to another company. Mr. Pemberton would be out of the country in Japan for a week and everything would be done by the time he returned.

Brigitte got the job and had two direct reports supporting her on all projects. She did an excellent job. No one but Brigitte knew I was planning to leave. I gave her time to learn her job and become strong before I requested a leave of absence because my father was ill.

Ed actually was ill and this was perfect timing. Brigitte was coached by me before I left and had been given the authority to bring on two other clerks under her. I explained to her that these people had to be hard workers or she could lose her job.

Brigitte found two other hard workers on the 1st floor that were as loyal to her as she was to me. She recommended them for the new positions and they began the process. When they were brought on board on the 5th floor, the culture was beginning to change. I was very excited and pleased with what I was able to do. I helped Brigitte to see that in order for her to survive, she had to learn to help others as well and not put them down.

I explained that we never know where our next helping hand would come from. I let her lease my Condo to get her out of the Ghetto, which was why I kept her salary at 60,000 a year. I had my old Realty Estate Company I had worked for, manage the property. I then prepared to take the leave of absence. Mr. Pemberton was not initially concerned, but did raise a brow every time he saw Brigitte in the hallway.

Now Brigitte knew how to play the game and keep quiet about things she knew. Doing so had landed her the promotion. She was my friend for life. She also knew that I was leaving New York for good and that if it ever leaked out, she would probably be railroaded out of her position. I had set it up beautifully. I prepared to take the leave and Ed was patiently waiting for me.

My love life was a flop again and apparently Bradley was happy. They announced that he was going to be a father. His wife must have already been pregnant when they married. This might have been why he was in a hurry and her father insisted on helping him set up his business.

Author: Victoria E. Kain

My love life was still a wreck! I still had no clue who or where I was from and who my family was, but I was trying to make the best decisions I could. I had found two new friends, Jared and Brigitte, an unlikely pair, but it showed that I was open to all races of people.

That was a good thing. What is it about men who try to bed every woman down they see? I still was young and learning things, but I was learning them fast. Oh, well, Bradley got what he asked for. I was moving back to the life I remembered.

This was my last year in school and I wanted to savor the moment. It was my last chance to find out about my own heritage. New York had actually been good to me.

~ CHAPTER 7 ~

BREAKING THE CHAIN OF SILENCE

Breaking the Chain of Silence

Months had passed by and there was no job at this point for several reasons. I had ended the leave of absence from my job in New York for taking care of Ed and finally tendered my resignation. Before that time, I had made one trip back to New York to visit with my old boss, Mr. Pemberton, and gave him my sob story and he understood.

That way when I resigned, he would agree to give me a great referral. Through my trusted friend Brigitte, I also found that a new catch was on board and Pemberton wanted her on the 5th floor. I called it perfect timing. I began wondering if I had made the right decision about leaving to come back to the South since neither Grandmother nor my mother was there anymore.

Being a woman in a divorced status in the family was a negative stigma, especially for a woman of color. For me, even more so because I was bi-racial. People seemed to think that women should not divorce a man, but it is okay for a man to divorce a woman. What difference did it really make if either of the parties were the wrongdoers?

Besides, in this case, Travis was already gone from my life. Being married too young and for all the wrong reasons didn't help either. Now I had to finish what I started with completing my Graduate degree. I would be the first in my family to complete this level of education which would set a new standard for the children coming up in that impoverished area.

Finishing college would be talked about for a long time. I would then become the "story" they would tell the children sitting around the fireplaces as an inspiration to their hopes and dreams. Maybe there would be no more slavery stories told to the young listeners to frighten them into unnecessary submission which handicaps their minds and take away their creativity. This was a good reason to be back home.

Helping people learn how to educate themselves was important to me and I wanted to do more positive things to show young men and women how to survive, the right way. I would tell my story of hope and pray that it helped someone else. There had been enough negative things talked about here in the South for a lifetime.

Coming back to the South brought many old memories to me as well. Some were good and some were bad. The strange thing is, there are some memories that I am still fuzzy on as far as what really happened during my childhood.

 Either way, I did what I did to satisfy Ed, Grandmother and my mother's wishes of finishing college and being who I wanted to be. Some of this is becoming a bit much to swallow but I will continue to do it all by taking one step at a time.

Ed was alone now and since I had not seen him since I left before Grandmother passed, a major factor in coming back was to finish living the life I was torn from as a child. The stark reality is that now, as an adult, I can take care of myself. I decided to go back to selling real estate. It was not what I wanted to do, but I had to do it.

Author: Victoria E. Kain

The laws are different here in the South and tuition is very high. So I had to get started right away if I was to finish on time. On Wednesday, I immediately got a paper and began looking for real estate offices and finally found one located not far from where Ed lived.   Days went by after putting the request and resume in for the real estate offices and I had not heard a thing.

Finally one Friday, I received a call from a real estate agency for an interview. Elated about the call, I forgot that Ed didn't like me going into town without telling him or he worried about me. He was still protective and a bit chauvinistic and would be until the day he died or I got married.   I didn't mind because Grandmother was gone now so Ed was all I had.

It was strange calling my dad Ed, but he felt comfortable with that since it had been that way all my life. I still accepted him as daddy though. Either way I was going on this interview today because I needed the job really bad. I finally found the location of the agency. It was a little surprising that the building looked so run down, but I remembered where it was.

I found a parking spot and gathered my portfolio and made my way to the door.

I was greeted by this southern woman about 50 or so, and extremely overweight, who looked me up and down.

"You here for the interview?" The overweight woman asked. I can only call her that because she didn't think it necessary to give me the courtesy of telling me her name.

I guess I was not worthy. "Yes," I said, and gave my name.

The Blanket of Southern Heat

"Billy is the manager and will be right with you," she said in a snide tone. Still looking at me like she wanted to chop me and eat me up, literally. In an effort to keep from appearing rude, I amused myself by mentally estimating her weight so I didn't have to look at her. She was very rude.

I sat quietly brushing my hair from my face...and another woman came from the back and this one was the opposite of the first. She was all of 90 lbs.

"What is this," I thought!

Is there anyone between 100 and 400 lbs. around here?" I said to myself, pretending to be looking at the magazine while both women were whispering just loud enough for me to hear them.

"What is she?" The first woman asked the other.

"She don't look black or Mexican, what is it?" the skinny woman lamented.

"Oh no!" They both looked at each other and laughed at me. I thought... they must know that I can hear them... it really didn't matter, I am used to the stares and snide remarks about my race and besides, I needed this job. That was the order of the day. I didn't care if Attila the Hun came from behind the door. I was prepared to speak "gorilla," if that is what was needed.

My tuition was coming due and if I wanted to stay in school I had to find a job and fast! Finally a man emerged out of the other office.

"How you doing little lady?" The man asked. I smiled and greeted him.

"I am fine, thank you sir."

"I am China Stone," I said. At least he was closer to 175 pounds. He told me his name was Billy and he seemed really nice.

"Come on back." he said....a typical southern greeting for a typical white man...with a white crisp shirt on, black slacks and rugged face, nice smile and he smelled like shaving cream....I don't remember the name of it, but one of my uncle's wore it my entire childhood... I will never forget that smell!

Billy was really nice and the interview went well. He told me all about the big girl at the front desk and the little one and gave me their names. The bigger lady was named June and the smaller one was Mae Ruth. Typical names, I thought, but with a name like China, I didn't have too much room to say anything on that note.

Looks like they might have been a couple according to some things he alluded too... either way, I was not interested in anyone's love life, but wanted him to say those four words, "you got the job." And before I left that day, he said the words, "you got the job."

It really turned out to be pretty effortless but if everything was this easy, I was home free and would deal with anything that came up. I needed to hurry and get home before Ed got there or he would be worried. It didn't take long to get there. He always was suspicious of any woman in his household and I chalked it up to his prison days and understood.

I loved the attention from him anyway since I had no man in my life. Ed would always say to me, "China, you are a beautiful young woman and men know this." He would pause for a moment and scratch his head like he had to get the rest of the statement from his brain. Finally he would continue, "You know what most men are looking for from a woman, so don't be out there selling yourself short," he'd say, looking off in a distance.

"Your mama was a beautiful woman and every man wanted her." "But she only chose one." He concluded, looking down in his lap as if he had lost something.

"I believe that's why we lost her so early."

I had learned to read into what was said to me, and wondered why he didn't name himself as the one she chose and what did he mean about how we lost her. Time would answer these questions. We talked about something else.

I picked up all of the real estate leads and brochures for the area and received my passwords to get into the real estate system... I decided to set up my system to begin receiving leads on selling houses as soon as possible. I was always good at real estate, but Travis never liked me showing men properties.

He used to say I made sales because I was pretty. I hated when people thought I had no talent. Beauty is not a talent. Since the job was commission based, I had to hustle to get paid, but I was not afraid of work. I paid attention to the road as I hurried looking at the areas, still new on these country roads could be confusing and you could end up lost in the middle of nowhere.

A couple of weeks went by and I was getting to know the strange crew at the real estate office. A few leads were coming in, but they were going nowhere. It seemed that with all of my real estate savvy in the north, I didn't do well here in the South.

Everyone was selling houses and letting me know in no uncertain terms that I wasn't doing it right. No one seemed to have any money unless it was for commercial property and I had no leads.

"Shoot, I am so sick of them with their country attitudes, thinking I don't know what I am doing," I said. I was getting nervous with no leads. I had made up my mind that my tuition was coming due in two months and I really needed a closing on the books in order to make the tuition payment. Since I had not paid since I left New York.

I decided to go in early the next morning to be the early bird, as they had suggested I do. But when I arrived, the parking lot was full of cars as if no one had even gone home the night before. "Seriously," I lamented in my car before opening the door.

"Doggone-it!"

"I can't ever beat these folks here!"

"Even as country as they are!"

"Do I have to live here to get first dibs?" I said, talking to myself.

First dibs is when a call comes in, whoever gets there first gets to take the lead....I really needed this lead today... I slowly opened the door of my vehicle…trying to act as if I had not planned to get there early…I didn't want the team to make fun of the fact that I was early but still was too late to get the worm.

I slowly walked into the office and pretended to be the perky city girl. I knew that it would irk the women in the office to come in all dainty like and give Billy a big smile. I gave them all my biggest smile and showed off my perfectly straight teeth and greeted everyone... "How's everyone this morning," I asked, raking my hands through my long hair as I put my briefcase down on the desk. My dimple on my right cheek was deep and looked ever so cute when I smiled.

Billy was the first to speak. "How you doing lil' lady bug?" that's what he had started calling me because my car was a VW beetle. But the woman June at the front desk just grimaced and said "good mo'ning," in a Sahara Desert dry voice. I had figured that every time I said hi to everyone, she would say good mo'ning and if I said good morning, she would say, "Hey." She always wanted to say the opposite of what I said as if it made her different in some way.

I really didn't care because I knew they all did not like me and I didn't like them either. It was a job.

Katie was the nice girl in the office and she called me over to her office and told me that we were meeting in the conference room for the leads for the day because they delayed it due to a new way they were going to be distributing them in order to give everyone a fair shake.

"Hey now," I thought, this could be a benefit for me... I was excited and didn't know what to expect. I didn't care but was the first in the meeting room. Everyone came in and Billy left and Trisha was leading this meeting today for some reason...

That made me nervous since she hated me for a hundred reasons. She smiled more than she had ever smiled and this made me suspicious. I rolled over to the head of the table and everyone piled in. Brandon, Scotty, Trisha, Beverly and Ellen Ann...Beverly was really nice to me and she opened the meeting, Trisha pulled out a list and a small basket.

"Well, today we are doing something different per Billy."

"We have a new lead that came in and will now draw for the lead and whoever's name is picked they will work with the client." This sounded strange, but there were names on the pieces of paper neatly folded in the tiny basket... all the sidebar conversation distracted us as Trisha carefully placed the basket in the middle of the table.

Finally she abruptly said, "Ok, we want to have Beverly pick a name out of the basket. Once selected, they had Brandon do a drum roll on the desk and everyone chimed in beating the drum beat of a sacrificial ritual. Not ever thinking I would win, Brandon opened the paper and read the name.

We all sat quiet for a moment... then Brandon said, "the winner of this lead is, China Stone!!!!" Everyone started clapping and I jumped up and did the yes!!!!! Sign and a victory dance. They all laughed and congratulated me since I was the new girl and had won the lead. "So, who is the client?" Trisha handed me the folder and I hurriedly opened it. Mr. Vladimir Francisca was his name.

Who in the world is this, with a name like Vladimir, in the Deep South? "Can someone tell me anything about this man?" I asked.

Trisha mumbled and said "All I have heard from other realtors is that he is a rich old greedy geezer." Everyone started laughing and got up to leave the room...I thanked them and they congratulated again on my win and continued laughing and looking at each other strangely.

Excited about my win, I began reading the address to see where the property was located. I googled it and saw an old huge estate deep out in the country... "Wow what a win this is!" I mumbled under my breath trying not to sound ungrateful. After all I had just been praying for a lead, and Grandmother always taught me to be thankful for what I had.

Who will want to buy this house? I again whispered in an undertone.

"Well," I thought, I don't have time to fuss over it now. So I made my way to the parking lot to try to get home before Ed got there. I was excited about having someone to share my day's win with. As I started up the VW Beetle, I turned the music up loud and took off for home.

The next day began with the sun beaming through the window of my bedroom in the upstairs part of Ed's house he had bought. The mobile home had got too small to live in with all my stuff from New York. I loved waking up to the smell of the honeysuckle that grew up alongside the fence line and every time the wind blew the sweet fragrance on the blossoms came through my window.

I had never experienced this in New York. I lay in the bed for a moment stretched out in pink pajamas feeling the slight breeze coming in through the window.

I wanted desperately to stay in bed and daydream today about my childhood on the old road, but hurried and jumped up and got dressed. I had planned to preview the property today that I had won in the office pool... Ed had already left for work so I didn't have to explain much to him.

I locked the front door and jumped in my car and took a shortcut to the highway. I had time to think about the life I had left behind in New York and all the experiences I had from the time I was taken there at nine years old.

Before I could get into my commute daydream on the boring road, my cell phone rang. I clicked my Bluetooth and began speaking.

"Hello, China Stone," the voice on the other end was feeble and raspy and hard to hear.

"Hello? Hello?" I said. Finally I was about to hang up and a man's voice was heard!

"This is Vladimir!

"Who?" I asked.

"Vladimir!!! The man screams.

"You deaf?" A sickening feeling was in the pit of my stomach and I quickly realized that this was my new client.

I recoiled from my strike mode for what I thought was a prankster and said, "Oh yes, Mr. Francisca how are you?"

"Just call me Vladimir, you haven't sold my property yet!" he stated in a gruff voice,

I realized at that moment that just as I thought, my winning this lead was no accident...

"Yes sir," I said, in a suspicious tone, now seething from the joke played on me.

"I am on my way to your property now, I can meet you in an hour."

"Can you come now?" he said.

"I'm old and have better things to do with my time."

I looked at my watch and rolled my eyes and you could only see the whites of them. In a calm voice I responded kindly.

"Yes sir, I am on my way. Can I get anything for you, Mr. Vladimir?"

I said, trying to butter him up. But before I could finish my statement, "Buzzzzzzzzzz." Mr. Vladimir had hung up on me while I was still speaking.

"How rude is this guy?" I said making a quick turn in the Starbucks drive-through to pick up my expresso latte.

I needed as much caffeine as I could handle. I really did not want to do anything to stop the sale but it sounded as if he was a geezer and very rude. I really needed to make this work for me. I drove for one hour and finally made the turn on the old dusty road.

I looked back and forth to make sure it was the right direction and I went down the road and continued looking right and left and there were no other houses nearby, only miles and miles of land.

I couldn't see anything until finally through the tall pine trees, way off the road I saw a huge old Victorian plantation type home with three levels.

"Well, I'll be John Brown." I am not sure I really want this lead anymore, but after looking at the house, it was majestically beautiful.

As I drove up, there was something strange about how it felt coming up the tree lined road. It was like a scene from Gone With The Wind.

I attempted to make a telephone call back to the office to let them know that I had already made it to the old Vladimir house but there was no signal to be found. That worried me a little realizing that no one knew that I was on my way there but Vladimir and he had just hung up. I was not used to these old roads but knew that I should be able to pick up a signal when I passed the trees.

I drove slowly up the long winding driveway with trees covering both sides of the road. Looking to the right and to the left and as far as the eye could see there was land for miles and miles. I wondered if he owned all the land or if he just owned the house. I parked the car almost in the middle of the yard so that it could be seen from the roadway in case of an emergency.

I looked down at my cell phone to see if it had picked up a signal yet and it had. Great! I thought. So I called the office and left a message letting them know where I was. I reluctantly called and left Ed a message, just in case. I sat in the car making notes on the paper waiting for Vladimir.

I picked up one of my law books for school and began to read. I kept looking back from the rear view mirror to see if Vladimir was approaching but did not see anyone for the next 35 minutes.

"What in the world could be keeping him?" I thought.

"He said he was on his way."

"He's probably so old he forgot and went back to sleep." I thought. There are thousands of things I could've been doing but I guess I can't complain.

I sat there for another 15 minutes past the hour. I was getting a little worried as it was beginning to cloud up and looked like rain coming in. That is all that I needed today being in the middle of nowhere.

The wind started picking up and the trees started blowing in the wind very hard... this was a summer storm that came out of nowhere. Suddenly, the wind rocked the VW beetle just a little and I wasn't sure what the weather was doing because I could no longer get a signal. I looked around and still did not see Vladimir and decided to run up on the porch before the weather got worse to get inside the house before it began raining. I didn't want to be a target for lightening sitting in the car with all those tall trees around.

As soon as I walked on the porch it began to pour down rain. I looked in through the window to see what I could see. The wind picked up more and was blowing rain onto the porch so I used my lock box key and unlocked the door. I opened the door, looking back out towards the road to see if old man Vladimir was approaching.

When I didn't see him, I gently closed the door behind me. I looked out of the huge window, then turned towards the winding staircase that graced the old dusty room. I wondered who had lived here, guessing that they must have had money at one time or another to have owned such a large house.

"Well I guess as old as this man is said to be, it was probably his family's home," I thought. I began to peek into each of the rooms.

During the course of my inspection, I noticed that the weather was getting really bad outside. The clouds became black almost instantly which was indicative of a summer thunder storm. It was beginning to lightning and thunder in the distance and it always frightened me ever since I was a little girl.

I looked into the big oversized living room and saw an old roll top desk with a chair that was amazing. Walking over to the desk, I ran my hands over the ridges and carved emblems on the top. Finally I pulled the chair out and flipped the cushion to see if anything was under it.

You can't be too careful in these houses because of brown recluse spiders, scorpions, snakes, you name it. Seeing it was clear, I made myself comfortable. I could look right out of the window across the yard onto the roadway. "Wow this is nice," I thought. I wondered what memories this old chair may have had. I rolled the chair over to the side of the desk so as not to be in way of lightening that could easily come through the glass.

I was concerned that the old man had not showed. I realized that the other realtors may have played a cruel game on me and I was almost brought to tears thinking that once again I had trusted the integrity of people only to be made of fool. I won't let this happen again, I said. I looked down at my phone… still no signal! I began fidgeting with the old roll top desk.

Deciding to leave when it stopped raining, I busied myself with examining the old desk. Having always been fascinated with antiques, I ran my hands across the back edge of the desk and felt a piece of paper through one of the drawers sticking out from behind.

I lifted up the roll top desk to peek inside and see what the paper was... Looking over my shoulder to ensure that Vladimir had not crept up on the property, or pulled up from behind the house and entered in from the back, I continued my examination.

Pulling open the drawer, several packages were exposed. It looked like envelopes… large manila envelopes. I was nervous wondering what this could be. "Could this be something important?" He is selling the house, but why is the desk still here? Does he know it is here? Or, as a final thought, I wondered if it was another trick from the office staff to see if I would be snooping around.

I didn't know if I should do this, but was so inquisitive that my instincts kept nudging me to open the first envelope. I began flipping through the pages going back to the first page. "What in the world is this?" After careful examination, it appeared to be a manuscript of sorts. Quietly I read the title, "The Masters' House." I mouthed the words as a way to digest what I read. My eyes were racing across the pages to glean any reality of what was in my possession.

The title was interestingly strange and I couldn't understand it. My desire was to read the pages and quickly looked out of the window searching the sky hoping the rain clouds would perhaps blow over altogether. Being more nervous now than before, my heart was beating so loud that I could hear each beat, thumping on the front of my shirt.

Even with the adrenaline rush that was present, I began reading the pages in an undertone. It was as if I were stealing from someone's memories.

Flipping through the first page, I noticed that the writer deliberately omitted putting their name to the pages to conceal who they were. It may have been that they did not want their intimate thoughts found out and kept it anonymous.

I was completely intrigued by the invisible personality of the writer. I begin to read more. Little did I know that what was written on these pages would ultimately change my life forever. I sat quietly and began reading…

THE MASTERS' HOUSE
(Manuscript)

Inside the masters' plantation house or the "Big House" as it was aptly called in that time, there were many secret places. Many of these places only the master was permitted to enter. The masters of the old plantations were privileged to do the selling and buying of land, livestock and other goods on the market. This also included the buying and selling of human souls. Slaves were used to further the masters' revenue to live the best lifestyle he and his family could live. The masters owned large houses and had many slaves they owned to work and harvest their crops they took to the market for payment.

The slaves lived mainly in shantys or lean-tos on the Masters' property, as they were aptly called. The houses were made of wood with rocks or brick mortar for the foundation and were called "lean to," because of the slanted positioning of the dwelling that the slaves lived in. Most of these shanty's were very simple and provided the basics of what an animal would need to protect themselves from the elements to stay alive to continue working for the Master.

Now, the Masters fed and clothed all of their slaves and livestock, thereby giving them the right to be called owners. During that time, it was a way to "claim" them as yearly tax exemptions, if you will. You could say they were owned by the masters and treated as property in that they were given medical attention when they were sick the same as a horse or a cow which the master needed for the advancement of his own family's wealth.

Author: Victoria E. Kain

Also, the slaves were disciplined or reprimanded as needed if they tried to run away or if they were found purposefully stalling the workload because of the hard labor they were exposed to. The slaves and their families, on the other hand, had no rights at all and were brought from different plantations like cattle. Sometimes, the slaves were bought or won by way of a poker game when the masters were having their night out with the locals...so to speak.

Some of these slaves that were bought may have even been related biologically to one another and never knew it because they all were kept away from bonding with each other long enough to find out if they were kinfolk. It was thought by the master that they needed to keep the slaves separated, to keep them from joining forces to possibly come up against them. Although the Master did not consider the slave as being as intelligent as he considered himself, there was always that little something in the back of his mind that cautioned him that underneath that subservient attitude, there was a fire burning.

After all, even though the slaves were not educated, they were not stupid either. The male slaves worked the fields and the cattle, and the women cooked and cleaned the masters' houses and tended their children. While they all worked in the field, there was a class distinction between the slaves. Some were darker or lighter than others for various reasons. The lighter slaves might not work in the fields the same as the more pigmented slaves.

The Blanket of Southern Heat

The female slaves were allowed to have babies in order to grow the masters' field hands and house slaves who would cook and clean and raise the few children the masters wives might have. These house slave girls were also taken by the master and at some point were impregnated with his children.

The slaves were very intelligent and realized that they did not want to bring a baby into the slavery life and would sometimes have an abortion. They had their way of doing this. Many of the old Mammys' knew how to do this but they had to be very careful because if the master found that they were hindering the advancement of his field hands, they could be put to death.

There were not many abortions because among the slave group they valued life even though it was wretched. If the female slaves were acceptable to the master, after a short period of time the master might become fond of some of the slave girls and found them pleasing to the eye.

They would then allow them to work and sleep in the masters' house which would give the slave girls an unwanted but sometimes advantageous opportunity to stay indoors of the "big" house and out of the fields where true hard labor was taking place. The young women were given to the mistresses as her helpers in the big house under the auspices of serving the slave masters wives and keeping her company when the master was away.

The fact was that the young women were being allowed to cook the masters' food, clean his house, eat some of the food and wear clean aprons and bathe regularly. Much of these exemptions were due to what the master wanted for himself. He was free to take any that he wanted before other male slaves could.

Author: Victoria E. Kain

The masters always kept the slaves separated because they did not want them to bond as a family. This may account for the mentality of the history of black men not taking the initial responsibility for their families as they should, though they wanted to. Most masters' never allowed their male slaves to marry at all as well, until much later.

The younger female slaves would tend to the children of the master and the older mammy's would care for the little ones and the overall house chores. They would always shoo the black male slave away that came around the big house looking at the pretty female slaves. There were little ones who were selected to sleep at the foot of the masters' bed as "bed warmers." The master would warm his feet on the tiny bodies of these little Black children in order to make himself more comfortable during the cold nights.

Sometimes, the master began to look at the slave girls, and would take them as they chose. When the masters would bed down the young slave girls and impregnate them, the masters' wife would not be happy about this arrangement, but was silent. When the wife would see that the slave girls were pregnant, they would not say where that baby came from for fear of being ostracized herself by her own husband.

When the babies were born, they were pretty little pecan colored girls or boy babies. Curly hair, sometimes kinky with a slight hint of straightness in it with full perky lips and big brown and sometimes "lord forbid" blue eyes. When all of this was taking place, the master would allow the slave and his baby to stay in the house or they would allow them subtle special privileges.

*The slave girl would continue to work and live in the masters'
house and sometimes would be allowed special things because of
the intimate relationship with the masters. They had to be very
careful not to let on that the master was fond of them behind closed
doors. She had to always remember her place.*

*The fact was that the slave girls were not always attracted to
the masters. Rather, the masters were attracted to the slave girls.
In the masters' house it seemed that he was the only one that was
able to do whatever he pleased.*

*He had many children born in this manner by the slave girls,
yet many of them never would be acknowledged as his children,
only the ones the masters' wife bore, which were few and far apart.
The children continued to be populated by the master with the
slave girls who were fertile. When they were finished bearing
children, they were allowed to go back with the male slaves.*

*What a horrible feeling this must have been to be known to
have been taken by someone that you did not choose. It is said that
in some masters' houses, bedding down their slave girls became
the norm and would get out of hand to the point that the masters'
wives were almost being forgotten.*

*It was thought that it was often enough to the point that many
of the masters' wives became unsettled and jealous and would beat
the slave girls for having the masters' children. When the master
was with the slave girls, the mistress of the plantation was in her
room, soothing herself with the best scotch or brandy that the
sweat off the backs of the slaves could buy.*

*Trying to forget what her ears heard and what her eyes might
see if she dared peak through the key hole of the masters' private
room.*

Author: Victoria E. Kain

She was a witness and sometimes a prisoner in her own home. Many times the way the master compensated for this was by taking her out on Sundays and parading her around like a prize bull only to be put back up on the shelf at night while the master takes care of his business that kept the Masters' Wife clothed in the best linen hats and shawls.

She was not allowed to ask questions of her husband's business because his "Business" took care of them and bought them the finest dresses and carriages and homes and trips and jewelry, and scotch. It still left them empty handed and empty nested for many years.

The masters' wives did not have many babies, but the slave girls did. The male slaves were not permitted to have the slave women that the masters wanted for themselves. They would be considered tainted. The master had to be the first to integrate the slave girls into their sexual orientation. If it was thought that there were two slaves, male and female that showed an interest in one another, the master would quickly sell off one so that they could not mate. They would never see each other again.

Shortly afterwards, the master would impregnate the slave to claim her and settle her down adding her to his conquest, leaving the male slave feeling helpless and lost and the masters' wife lonely and frustrated. The children of the master and the slave girl were almost misfits in another way.

With the two bloodlines being so different, the children that resulted were not as rugged as the babies born to two slaves and this was because they had the masters' blood flowing through their veins as well. They could not stay in the sun all day and pick cotton.

The Blanket of Southern Heat

They bruised easily and did not fare well behind a plow. The slave women did not like being taken by the masters any more than the Masters' wives' liked knowing they were being taken. Either way, it was a bone of contention for both.

The masters' wives resented the slave girls for centuries because they received the attention from the masters which was unsolicited by them. Yet the wives might not see their husbands in a way that was supposed to be only for husbands and wives. The slave girls learned to cope with their plight in life and at times were silly enough to think that they had a position of authority because they had laid down with the master.

When they forgot their place, the mistress would quickly bring them back in line by beating them to solidify their position as head of the household, and sometimes would scar the slave girls beautiful brown bodies as a way to deter the masters' interest to bed down with them any longer. This too would become a trait in history to show how Black women would be hated and abused verbally and told that they were nappy headed or black with big lips…well, we will know a very different story in the future.

The masters' wives would quickly beat down the slave girls and let them know who was in charge, keeping the slave in place and trying to soothe some of their own humiliation. It really did not matter because the children of these masters would never be able to inherit anything that he had. Only the children by the masters' wife would gain anything from their father's inheritance. The mixed children would only beget sorrow and pain and confusion as to where they belonged. Longing for clarity of what they felt inside from two races of blood flowing through their veins.

Author: Victoria E. Kain

These words would echo in the post slave women's heads for centuries. The slave masters wives resented the slave girls and resented that "they", the slave masters' wives, were not permitted to enjoy the same union with the male slaves, as the master was able to do with the virgin slave girls. Could it be that the master knew how much more of a mess there would be if the masters' wives were permitted to lie down and mate with the burly strong male slaves at that time?

What strength would this union have brought to their plantation home and where would the loyalty have been from the children of these male slaves?

Could it be that the master knew that it would destroy his kingdom if this union were permitted for the masters' wives and male slaves to mate as they did with the slave girls? Yes, he knew. He knew well that there was a curiosity that was ablaze in the masters' wives to find out what was behind the loin cloth the big male slaves wore. Their arms bulging from their shirts and trousers too small for their hideously large anatomy. They could only look out of the window and long for the justice and freedom they wanted to take for themselves, but knew that if they dared cross that line, their lives would be in danger.

Some did cross the line and were sent away. Babies were killed at birth and the women committed to asylums. Gone forever. The masters could buy and sell anyone they wanted. He could also have sex with and father children by the slave women if he chose to.

They could beat or kill the slaves if they chose to. In short, the masters were powerful and could do whatever they wanted.

The Blanket of Southern Heat

During that era the female slaves did not necessarily want to have babies by the master because at that time, there really was no benefit to having a baby by the master since the times were difficult enough to be in bondage and for those who truly hated the slaves would become the enemies to the women and children they bore the master.

Many of these haters would seek to kill the mother and their child if they could to cut off the bloodline. It was thought to be a sacrilege to have such a mixing of bloodlines with slaves and the masters' blood. Either way, the female slaves learned to do what they were told to do and for those that did, most of them were allowed to live in the masters' house and sometimes become more educated than the other field hands.

Even though, the masters' wives got to wear the pretty dresses and shop in town, the female slaves that were bedded down on numerous occasions were allowed to stay clean and were "kept", so to speak, under the Masters' roof for a number of reasons.

Even though the Masters' wives lived in the big house with the servants, the slave women were equally molested by the Master to his pleasing. This fiasco took a toll on many Masters' wives over the centuries. Although the Masters' wives felt special being put on a pedestal as a possession, what they soon found was that they may have sat high up above the other women, but their husbands were down low where the rest of the women were and was having his fill of all the carnal pleasures as she sat perched on a fine limb of a tree she was dangled from, totally out of reach of any other man, but not out of ear shot of the goings on in her household.

Author: Victoria E. Kain

It seemed that the only ones that had any fun was the Master! For hundreds of years the masters' wives were viewed by others as being flawless and untouchable, and that is what they were…"untouched!" Everyone seemed to forget that even a trophy needs to be taken down off the shelf every now and then and dusted off.

The Masters' wives were human too and deserved to have exclusive rights to their husband, yet they had to share them with the women who were supposed to be beneath them.

This is what drove some of the Masters' wives and the male slaves insane down through the centuries. They also wanted to know the mystery of why the master feared the male slaves so. When humans are deprived of their needs, it drives them to animalistic behavior.

Down through those centuries, the Masters' wives fantasized about many of their male slaves but dared not cross the line or the Master. Even the Masters could not take knowing what they would know and would even kill the male slaves and send the wives away to asylums or some would mysteriously disappear. Why was this so prevalent? No one can really answer this question…or can they?

(End manuscript)

I was stunned at the content of this manuscript. They were well written but some parts made no sense to me. I could not tell how old the manuscripts were because of the modern envelope they were in. It appeared that someone else may have read them and put them in this new container. I was glad the rain continued and I wanted to keep reading as long as the rain was coming down.

I reasoned that if old man Vladimir came, I would be able to explain that the rain had forced me into the property. I really didn't have to give a reason because I was his realtor, and once you get to the property, the house is opened for the client. There was something disturbingly familiar about the information I had just read.

I remembered a history course during my first years of college and information about slavery, but I could not believe what I had found or understand why that information was left in this roll-top desk...

"Where did this information come from?" I thought.

"This is crazy!" I wanted to continue reading but was in a state of shock and realized that the rain had stopped. I wouldn't want to blow my cover on this new "find" and be caught trespassing on someone's property as a realtor so I hurriedly put the manuscript back in the envelope and closed the drawer carefully.

I decided to call Mr. Vladimir to cover my tracks and left a message that I had waited for him for over an hour and had gotten caught in a storm while there. I knew he never picked up the phone calls and I was glad that he didn't.

I closed the front door, locking it just the way I found it, as if I had never been there.

Author: Victoria E. Kain

Looking over my shoulder hoping no one was spying on the house from the massive trees that surrounded the property.

As old as Vladimir was, who was to say he didn't have surveillance cameras on the property? I was getting nervous as I drove back to the city. No music today, just thoughts blazing through my mind, wanting to know more about what I was reading. I wanted to know who wrote these words as I tapped on my steering wheel trying to keep my mind on the road. Even though Mr. Vladimir didn't show, what I discovered made the trip worth it. What intrigue!

Before arriving at my destination, I pondered whether to tell anyone about what I had found. Common sense kicked in and I realized that those foolish women would have a fit if they knew.

I wouldn't even tell Ed. Some things you simply keep to yourself. I really shouldn't have been in there without the owner on the first visit, I thought, but I was there legally and no one knows that I know the manuscripts are there.

I went back to the office very perplexed and did not say much about my adventure except that I went to meet Vladimir and he did not show. No one said much to me because they knew that they had tricked me into winning this client so they did not want to engage in a conversation with me and blew me off.

They thought that I was being aloof because of realizing what they had done but in fact it was because of what I had found in the old desk. I drove home back to Ed's house thinking of how I could get back to Vladimir's property to continue reading the manuscripts. Now there was a burning desire to finish reading the manuscripts.

I ate quickly and quietly and didn't talk much to Ed this evening but he had loads of conversation that I just wasn't in the mood to talk about. I took a shower, washed my hair, went to bed and snuggled under the warm blanket Grandmother had made for me. It was the only thing I had left from Grandmother. I thought about what I had read and wondered about "The Masters' House."

"Could this really be information from the time of slavery from the slave masters' wives point of view?" I thought. I became very nervous and intrigued all at the same time but nestled into the pillow and realized I heard more raindrops starting to fall on the old roof and I finally dozed off to sleep...

The next day, I couldn't wait to get back out to the old house...I had to make sure that someone knew I was going back there. After all, I was his legal representative from the agency, even though they gave me this lemon. I wanted to get something out of the deal and reading those manuscripts gave me the payment I needed.

This time, before going to Mr. Francisca's, I stopped by the office first. My attitude was positive realizing what had happened and knowing that everyone was extremely nice to me because they thought I was stupid. I figured I might as well make the best of this. I asked the Admin if Vladimir had called knowing that the old geezer had not. I shared with them how I had been waiting all day yesterday and how I had gotten caught in the rain storm.

I asked Billy if he thought it was okay for me to go back out to put the signs up on the property... Billy wanted an opportunity to go with me so he insisted.

"Well little lady bug, I can go out there with you, because that's a long drive and it's boring." The lady at the desk made a comment to him about his schedule.

"Billy," she said,

"You have an appointment in one hour, with the mayor."

I was glad that I spoke up.

"That's okay Billy, I can go ahead and put those signs out it won't take me long."

"Besides, the mayor is more important."

"Well okay, but if you need anything you call me." I snatched the signs out of the back area and tossed them in the back of my car and was on my way. I was almost giddy when about halfway there and the phone rang again... I looked at the caller ID and saw that it was Mr. Vladimir.

"Oh shoot, I didn't want to talk to him today." I answered anyway. "Hello Mr. Vladimir how are you sir?" I said, rolling my eyes towards the top of the car.

"That's none of your business, Miss," He said abruptly.

"Really!!!" I though. How rude this geezer was!

"Are you going to be able to meet me out there at the property today or not?" he growled. What is wrong with this old man? I thought. He doesn't even remember I went there yesterday? He probably didn't remember anything for that matter. I hurried and answered before I got snappy with him,

"Yes Mr. Vladimir, I'm on my way there now!" I said in my cheeriest voice, if there was such a word.

"Great I will meet you there in an hour...

I could not wait to get there, but what he didn't know was that I was already halfway there as we spoke. My friend Bev in the office had given me a short cut that kept me on a busy road so I was not completely in the rural until I reached the road that lead up to the sprawling estate.

I pulled into the driveway once again and this time the property felt very familiar to me. Not at all like the first time I came here before reading the manuscripts. It was a strange feeling that came over me as I looked at the trees lining the road this time. I did a once around the property as usual to make sure no one was there and put the signs out and held one for last, in case the owner actually showed up.

I opened the front door slowly and checked the inside to see that no one was there and went straight for the roll-top desk. Carefully sitting down in the chair, positioning myself so that anyone approaching the property could be seen. I couldn't wait to read the rest of the manuscripts.

I flipped through the pages to exactly where I left off and anxiously searched for the next page. The second set of papers held the same mystery in its title, I thought, with much intrigue this time.

It was becoming very evident that these manuscripts were about the slave era written by someone who had direct access with the process. This new title would shed more light on the mystery of the masters' house and what happened with the male slaves specifically.

I wasn't sure how I would feel about this information but found it oddly satisfying to have access to it. It would soon make sense about what I saw happening in the South where Grandmother and other family lived. I examined the title and shook my head in disbelief... "Black Man's Britches?" Once again I began reading.

BLACK MAN'S BRITCHES
(Manuscript)

As we have come full circle from the goings on in the masters' house and are past the slavery era, there are laws in place within our society to enforce the human rights of "all" peoples. We come to a part where we can see why there may have been those mentalities that have festered for so long. The curiosity is about to be exposed. But why must it be this way?

The masters of old created a two-headed monster when he put his (wife) on a pedestal for the world to see giving her everything materially but leaving her empty on the inside, needing everything. He did the same for his male slaves. He exposed them and paraded the burly men naked at human auctions with his wife peering from the balconies behind their delicate fans they used to cool their warm skin from the perspiration that appeared.

But, mostly from their internal temperatures that had arisen from the sight of these men that they were forbidden to mingle with in any way. The thoughts of what they saw would never go away.

The Master did not pay as much attention to his wife's needs as he did his own slave girls.

The masters basically bribed the slave women to breed children and they could buy their way out of working the fields. This was the excuse the masters' used for acquiring the pleasure of their personal property. It didn't look as bad if they could boast that they had new fields to be picked and were doing what any shrewd businessman would do.... "humph," the ole mammy's would say...

The Blanket of Southern Heat

The male slaves on the other hand could not buy their way out of a burlap sack... which was a tightly woven wool that was almost impossible to cut with a sling blade, which is what they used to cut tall weeds when clearing a new field.

The male slave had to suffer through the misery, time after time and wait for an opportunity to strike back. To hit the Master, hard.   Now, that was not to say that the male slaves are at fault for what they have been given as a lot in life.

They all, or most, have had a curiosity about the masters' wives and now they are able to do what they have wanted to do which was to "be in the masters' shoes. The masters' wives saw that the masters controlled the male slaves, so the masters' wives thoughts may have been, "why can't I have that same authority along with other authorities as the master has?

Why not have that same desire? It would be like having your cake and eating it too. To be able to be with a slave man and he take care of me, this would be a plus. Most slaves had a wild curiosity about the masters' wives.

It was not as if they all wanted the Masters wives for their own, but the majority wanted to feel the pleasure of avenging those who were forced to watch their women being taken from them and used for the masters' pleasure and benefits for centuries. It was more of "an eye for an eye."

They wanted to see if there really was a difference. The masters' wives possessed a syndrome that may have caused them to feel the same way. Desiring to see what it was like to be with the thing that the "Master" forbade so vehemently.

Author: Victoria E. Kain

The only down side to this was that they would be ostracized by their families if they aligned themselves with these men and would have nowhere to go.

Once the alignment was made, the masters' wives would no longer be welcome in the masters' bed. That premise would never change down through the centuries.

To be had by the male slaves meant that the women would become outcasts in their own race and would be taken in by the Male slaves families who were ever so eager to bring them in because they were accustomed to taking care of the masters' children, and accepted that lot in life. Did the masters' realize what he had created centuries ago in those fields?

Yes, he knew. He knew well that there was a curiosity that was ablaze in the masters' wives, to find out what was behind the loin cloths the big male slaves wore.

Their arms bulging from their shirts and trousers too small for their hideously large anatomy. The masters' wives could only look out of the window and long for the justice they wanted to take for themselves, but knew that if she dared cross that line, her life too would be in danger. Many did cross it and were met with many tragedies. Babies were killed at birth and the women committed to asylums.

This fiasco took a toll on many Masters' wives over the centuries. Although the Masters' wives felt special being put on those pedestals as a rite of passage as the sole possession of the master but what they soon found out was that while they may have sat high above all other women, their husbands were down below where the rest of the women were and was having his fill of all the carnal pleasures as she sat perched on a shelf...

alone and totally out of reach of all men, but not out of ear shot of the goings on in the masters chambers late at night and early in the morning.

It seemed that the only one that had any pleasure was the "Master himself." For hundreds of years the masters' wives were viewed by others as being flawless and untouchable and that is what they were…"untouched!"

The seemed to forget that even a trophy needs to be taken down from the shelf every now and then and dusted off. The wives of the slave masters began to resent the slave girls when they realized that the masters enjoyed the intimacy with the slaves. She realized that this is what "He" wanted. She also realized it was "Not" always for the sake of having more field hands because the children of the masters by the slave girls were thought to be misfits.

They could not stay in the fields and work the same as the others. This is what drove the Masters' wives insane down through the centuries to want to know the mystery about the male slaves and why the masters feared them so. Why did the Masters want to degrade the male slaves so? When humans are deprived of certain needs, it drives them to an animalistic behavior. Down through those centuries, the Masters' wives fantasized about many of their male slaves.

Some even dared to cross the line. Even then, the Masters could not take knowing what they knew about that union and would kill the male slaves and send the wives away or some would simply mysteriously disappear. Why was this so prevalent?

No one can really answer this question…or can they? As time would move forward, the masters' wives would take no more!

They would no longer want to live under the chains of restrictions handed down by the masters', where the male slaves were concerned. Their lives would take a turn for the worst in their own culture to experience the forbidden pleasure of being in the company of "The Black Man's Britches."

(End Manuscript)

I had become so obsessed in my reading. Enchanted by the manuscripts I continued reading until I was interrupted by a miraculous phone signal. My phone began ringing out of the blue which startled me. It had never gotten a strong signal before at the Vladimir Estate.   I dropped the pages in my lap as if they were engulfed in flames. Answering quickly, I thought it might be Vladimir. With my mouth open, unable to speak about what I had just witnessed on paper I didn't know whether to laugh or to cry, realizing clearly what I was reading.

"Hello. This is China Stone."

"Yes, China, this is Beverly from the office. Billy will need you to come back to the office for a meeting by 3pm. Okaaaaay? Thanks Hun," she said.

I ended the call and thought it was ridiculous that my reading was interrupted by such triviality. But I thought about the reading and had never had anyone to talk to me about life as I grew up and not being privy to the information about slaves during that era, I had no clue about how people really were treated back then, but these pages were shedding light on many things.

Now I understand what Grandmother was saying about her grandparents and how these pages mimicked many things that I now remember hearing her talk about, while sitting on the front porch on Saturday evening after supper. The things that happened back then were hard to forget for those who experienced it personally or indirectly. Could these be pages from the history books that never reached the print? I thought.

I was stunned about this information… Not understanding why there was such a bad blood between Blacks and Whites in the first place. Why was it necessary for one race to be richer than all other races? I wondered. The children of the Masters were treated differently making them stand out in a bad way. Many were hated by their own brothers and sisters because they were given special treatment, but they were shunned because of the better treatment they received and this has trickled down through the centuries.

I realized now that this is why I may have been treated so differently, because of my complexion. If you don't look completely Black in the Black community, many times you are ostracized. It may have been why Pearl hated me so because she was dark in complexion and she could not get past the color of her skin.

She believed if you were dark, you were ugly, but in my eyes, she was beautiful. She had smooth skin and beautiful eyes. Pearl could do more styles with her hair texture than I could, but she never seemed to believe that she was as beautiful as she was. But the Slave Masters' saw the Black slave girl's beauty. The mindset had been handed down from slavery that if you were dark in complexion and your hair was coarse and not curly or straight, it was nappy and ugly.

The thought came to me and I recalled what my attacker had said to me that night right before he tried to violate me and kill me, "You are a white man's baby, you don't belong here!" I never told anyone what he said. That was it! I thought, now trembling.

Stroking my long curly hair, looking at the ends of it as if to examine whether I could be part of the race issue because of who had possibly fathered me. Finally accepting that I could have been a white man's child, it might explain why I had to be sent away and was treated with such dismay.

I recalled hearing Grandmother's brother's talk about the "man," but never understood. What was more important to me now was finishing reading the manuscripts. What was it about the "Black Man's Britches?" Such an interesting title. What if Vladimir came and took the desk away? I realized I might never know the end to these writings. I looked out of the window to see if anyone was approaching the house and no one was. I left that day locking the door behind me as if it was a secret place, and that the old house belonged to me. It almost felt like home. I could not understand why Mr. Vladimir never showed again so I went back to the real estate office to meet with Billy.

Billy was always nice to me. Not like the ladies in the office who stared at me and talked amongst themselves about my olive skin color and long curly hair. Billy seemed to like me quite a bit and always was a gentleman. He came in the office and I talked to him about my situation with Mr. Vladimir.

He had me pause my conversation with him and when he got up to leave the room, I looked at the basket on the desk that had held the winner's name and realized it all was a trick. I instinctively opened up one piece of paper and saw my name and my name was on all the other pieces as well. I hurriedly put them back in the basket very neatly and realized I had been tricked once again.

Author: Victoria E. Kain

Why was it that people thought that I couldn't see what they were doing? All of my life people hid things from me and lied to me. They teased me about being high yellow, as they called it in the South. That is when you look almost white and you are lighter than everyone else in your family. I had a small nose, having long curly hair and having beautiful skin and hazel eyes. Why was that such a bad thing?

I thought I was Black just like everyone else around me. I just didn't look the same, or that is what I was always told. I simply didn't understand. I realized that I was in a place now that I wasn't sure what race I was, so they didn't know what category I fit in. I just wanted to be treated like everybody else that didn't belong. Billy came back in the room and I just stared at him.

I remembered some of the things that I had read in the manuscripts and began to realize that I felt something different for the first time in my life. I wanted to bolt out of the door screaming but I knew that I could not give away the secret, not yet. My eyes were finally beginning to open. After that day, I became obsessed with wanting to read more and prayed that I would be able to go back to the old estate.

I was beginning to realize that that there were things that were being said in those manuscripts that had special meaning to me and may even affect my future. For the first time I began to question my heritage and where I had come from after reading the manuscripts.

Up until now I had accepted what everyone told me, that I was black, my father was black, and my mother was black despite mama looking white on all of the pictures I saw of her.

Everyone had different looks because of the genes in the family. Now I really wanted to know the truth.

I left the office that day and drove home slowly. On the way I rationalized that I did not have the right to pry into the manuscripts and read anymore but I would go one last time and close it out forever. I was debating whether I would tell the people in the office that I knew what they had done as a way of gaining power and strength to stand up for what I felt was right in my mind and heart.

Should I tell them I did not appreciate it and for a moment had considered resigning, even though I really needed the job? How serious is this? I thought.

When I arrived home, dinner was not on my mind and I could not eat a bite that evening. It was strange, but Ed did not even say two words to me…he must have had something on his mind as well. Either way, he just looked at me as if he did not know me, but wanted to. It could have been because he knew I was not his daughter but he couldn't tell me. That is what people did in the South.

They took care of the babies that they knew were not theirs. They kept the secrets and took them to their graves. Even though they knew the truth, they just lived with it and fought with their wives on Saturday nights after getting drunk. This was a lot to think about.

I tossed and turned that night thinking, and rationalizing about all of the things that happened in my life. What was it about these manuscripts that made me feel as if I had been missing something in my life? Who was my real father? Who is this man who seems not to know anything about me and is so strangely suspicious of everything I do?

Who are these people that I call family?

No one looks like me, but old Mr. Moody would say, we all are God's children... They say we can take after many generations of people....is that what the manuscripts are talking about?

I knew if I didn't shut my brain down now, I never would. Rest was all I needed. It had been a long week and I was off for the weekend which should prove to be relaxing…after all, I had been tricked by the staff members in the office and my first client.

It seemed to be the norm for someone like me batting a consistent zero. I closed my eyes and slept.

The weekend sped by swiftly and Monday converged upon me like a thief in the night. I decided I would make my last return to the old house today, vowing never to come back, regardless of what I read. I was ready to let the manuscripts go from my thoughts. Besides, I knew that Grandmother would not approve of me snooping around in folk's personal affairs or their private possessions. I got dressed and left for the office.

Deciding not to physically go into the office today, I boldly left a message for Billy, purposely omitting any of the old women that didn't like me. This would give them something to hang their fangs on while they ate their biscuits and syrup or whatever it took to keep them fat and juicy for their menfolk.

I was really sick of them now and didn't seem to care anymore about how they felt about me. I was beginning to feel different every time I read something from the manuscripts as if the words were changing me internally.

I even added on the voice message to the office that I had other prospects of my own for a real estate sale and would be in the office later.

With the trick they had played on me about winning old man Vladimir's account to sell his millions of acres in real estate, I really didn't care what they thought at this point...I wanted revenge!

There seemed to be a fire in my gut that was never there before. I was simply tired of being the scapegoat. I remembered something I read in the manuscript and wondered if this was the reason I had the spitfire attitude. Had I been inspired somehow about how these pages were written? Or by the person that had the tenacity to write these things down?

When I pulled up on the old Vladimir's estate in the country this time, the air seemed fresher to me for some reason." It must be the recent storm we had," I concluded. That always makes everything smell fresh and clean. This time, I didn't look back at the road to see if anyone was there. I really didn't care.

I boldly walked up to the steps of the house and opened the door as if I had been invited in. I went straight over to the old roll top desk and stood for a moment making up my mind that when I returned to the city this day, I would call Mr. Vladimir and decline his offer to represent him. This would be a third no-shown which gave me the right to cancel the contract.

I sat down to read and picked up the manuscripts and held them to my chest. This time, my mind was open and ready to receive any information the manuscripts had to give. Would I find out who wrote these things today? I flipped the pages to where I left off and began reading the next set of papers.

Since I knew this would be my last reading, I stopped to think before I began. I wondered for a moment if my new found strength was coming from some of the things I read.

Author: Victoria E. Kain

I understood that what we take into our mind feeds our entire body. Little did I know, what I would read next would be a lot to digest. I want to know more…

I slowly read a new heading entitled, A Letter to My Father. I frantically searched for a name to put with these words and realized that this was someone's intimate feelings I was about to read. Unfortunately, I did not see a name.

It did not stop me from making the decision that I would read it anyway. "Besides," I thought, it's not like I am stealing it. I am just reading." Now that I had purged my own shaky conscience I began to read…

The Blanket of Southern Heat

A Letter "To my Father"

My life seemed to start off very slowly like a silent movie playing in slow motion. At some point it began to speed up taking off into thin air like a stealth fighter jet, hovering and then disappearing in the night. In the transition of these many years, I learned something very true but sad about myself, my life, my family and friends and which actually encompasses the entire human race.

Some parts of my life were good, bad and some very ugly. Only the beautiful part is what I chose to cling to, which has prompted me to write down my memories and make them come alive for the world to see how "similar" we all are. Not that the world is really interested in knowing anything special about me, or who I really am, but knowing that I "CAN" tell you what I feel and what I know, whether you want to hear it or not. It's the American way, right?

Our lives are simply our own books written in our own heads and we create this instant replay movie of ourselves, our lives and what has happened to us, over and over and over again. If we all could publish our lives, and divulge something about ourselves to the world that they didn't know, many of us would have best sellers.

How sad, though, that the majority of us go unpublished in many ways and simply fade away reducing our memory of us to a mere sigh or tear from those you believed cared about you for the brief moment you were here. Well, unlike many others, I chose to write it down.

Author: Victoria E. Kain

Besides, isn't that the way you keep things remembered? Most of us leave this world never saying what we wanted to say. Our true voices never heard. Our goals, never achieved, and our dreams, never coming to fruition and that ship we so often talk about coming in, we let it come in and dock right before our very eyes and we never recognize that it had come and gone, yet we hold on to an empty dream, never waking up to the reality of true life.

All of this begets never doing what we wanted to do, going through life envying others, isolating ourselves only because we did not have the guts or the tenacity to take that chance and climb Mount Everest, or ski the alps, or for some, get an education or change the way you look at yourself and stop being a "Victim" of society.

I decided to start writing down the many stories of my life that I told others and shared what I remembered from as far back as I could, which would be about three years of age. You probably don't think I could remember things from that early in my life, but I found that if those memories were important enough, our marvelous brain will hold on to every event in full color detail as mine did.

These memories were so vivid that I can remember sounds and smells in the air that were associated with that time and place. Yes, it is that serious.

I remember it all and hope this information reaches the hands of someone from a new generation of people in this world. My life might be long gone, but maybe, just maybe it would not have been wasted.

Whoever reads these words, I hope you will do something about what you have read in your life in order to change the lives of others. You may realize that my life was and is, in many ways, much like yours. You must now "Break the chain of silence."

(End Letter)

Author: Victoria E. Kain

The letter I read was unbelievable. I was stunned for a moment trying to digest the letter I had just read. Puzzled at how the writer had made the letter personal but then made it public and to the reader as if they knew someone would read the letter because they may never have given this to the person they originally wrote it for.

"Oh My word! This letter is written for me?" I did not quite understand the letter. Was it from a son to a father? Or maybe to a grandfather? Since there were no names it could have been from anyone. Finally, I realized that I had omitted a gender, naturally assuming that females were not as open and direct as most males. I thought once again, and realized that my classes in history were paying off.

"It could have been from a "daughter!" I exclaimed. Once again, putting the writings down in my lap, rationalizing that the writings could be from a female who would have to hide their thoughts depending on the timeline that it was written. "It could have been a girl writing to her father," I said aloud.

The supposed writer could have been sharing deep seated expressions of what they felt about their own life and what they witnessed growing up in a house of a father who owned slaves. It could have been that she too witnessed the atrocities that took place with the male and female slaves and the masters' at that time and was compelled to write down her thoughts.

Once I reasoned that this was the case, I referred to the writer as "She." Needing to feel the writer was a woman and was in need of leaving her own legacy.

The writer must have known that because of the era she lived in, she would not have been permitted to divulge her inner thoughts and feelings and had no other way to express them.

I wondered if these could be some of the answers I was looking for in my own life? A thousand things fled through my mind from the words written on the pages of the manuscripts. It made me think about what I really wanted out of life. I didn't want to leave the earth never having said or done the things I wanted to say or do. I wanted real love from someone who loved me and to know who my family was and to make a difference in my lifetime.

Why was it that I could feel a truism from what someone else wrote about their life? Could it be because it mimicked my own? Why was I so moved and connected by these words? I finally stopped thinking and tossed out all logical answers and accepted that these words were written for me. I was sure of it.

I accepted that I would never know the writer except in the words they wrote, yet I received something valuable in the answers it gave me. Where did this old information come from about slave masters, the feelings and thoughts of their wives about slave men and young slave women? What was this? It wasn't that I was not clearly aware of the Civil Rights movements and MLK and JFK, but some things are kept from us until we get to this point in life where we feel strong enough to hear our own voices and refuse to accept the secrets and lies from anyone else anymore.

Today, I stumbled upon a part of history. "My history?" I added. I began to reflect on how I came about the client. "Who was this wealthy old man Vladimir Francisca that no one wanted to deal with to the extent that he would be raffled off as a way to discard him?

Author: Victoria E. Kain

How did he come to own so much land when so many around him owned so little? Why was the old roll top desk left in his house? I believed that the desk was left for me to find the information which would tie my very existence back to centuries ago. But, I didn't know what to do about the information I had.

"Oh, my word. What if?" I said. "What if?" Now, stunned and speechless, I sat quietly in the old chair, rubbing the arm of it, as if it would somehow give me all the answers to my life's questions, knowing this was only the beginning of my magnificent find. How ironic that the answers I sought would come from the silenced voices of someone from the past. These words had been penned long before I was born.

Something special had come over me and I refused to leave the house feeling unsatisfied. I tried to busy myself with jotting down notes for a paper I needed for class. I used excuses that the information I was reading would help me reflect on a paper about American history and had decided to choose the topic of slavery. "Yes, these pages in the manuscripts are perfect to use as a point of reference in my own words," I mumbled to myself, still trying to justify being in the house a little longer.

I did not have an author to cite, which would be disastrous if not cited appropriately. These pages made too much sense to use and let it lay dormant. In my entire life, confusion had been a personal bedfellow as if I were enslaved to an invisible foe.

Reflecting back on my life, I feel that what I read fits how I have lived. I deduced that the writer spoke in a feminine voice. I began to reflect on my own childhood, remembering how I had been treated as an outcast at times because of the difference in the way I looked.

The Blanket of Southern Heat

Reflecting back on the old manuscripts of the masters' house, I remembered what was said about the children of the slave masters. They were kept inside the house out of the heat and never really beaten as much because of their frailty and pigmentation of their skin and bloodline.

"Could it be?" I lamented. I wondered much that day about this new information that seemed to piece parts of the missing links to my history. Maybe this is why Grandmother never whipped me and even when she slapped me that one time, she was visibly shaken thinking someone would see the hand print on my face. I stayed indoors all that day because of it as a way to hide the evidence of her anger against me.

I quickly realized that I could not stay in the old house any longer fawning over the manuscripts that left me with a sense of closeness to the memories of the once inhabited abode of the souls that resided there. Feeling right at home, I leaned back once again, for the last time in the old chair, and gently rocked away all of the hurtful memories from my mind and body. The old house began to feel safe to me. I was no longer a stranger, but a resident of this new heritage that lived in the walls surrounding me.

Although the rooms had only dated wallpaper and worn floors and windows lacking weather stripping and panes that were dingy from years of being unoccupied, my eyes still fed on each room as I searched desperately sucking up the vision to store in my memory. I would take the image with me forever, down to the cracked bricks on the old fireplace.

I could tell that the fireplace had been well used by the accumulation of creosol on its walls.

Author: Victoria E. Kain

Imagining what must have happened in that very room where I sat intrigued me and brought thoughts back to what the writer of the manuscripts must have felt coming down the long staircase every morning for breakfast.

Even the old kitchen with its oversized bay windows were unheard of back then. The mammys and young slave women must have stood on those very floors preparing breakfast for the masters and their families while the young slave girls had warmed the masters bed all night only to awaken and be required to wash his floors in the morning before he could walk on them to meet his family for a meal.

I continued wondering how the bi-racial slaves fared during the time of oppression. Why were slave girls forced to be had by those who wanted them only for selfish pleasure and to be put in a position of authority with the man that would lie down with her, only to get up still a slave? When would she have the right to feel complete? I was beginning to realize that meeting guys from all nationalities was the norm for me.

I had married a black man who loved me, but he too wanted a trophy wife, placed on the proverbial pedestal along with being serviced daily, but having no real life or control outside of his needs, only to mimic the actions of the slave Masters of old.

Then, there were successful White men who wanted the same type of trophy but showered their women with gifts in order to be free to wander the countryside filling their quiver with whatever they desired with no consequences at all. Still carrying on the masters' desires for complete control.

Holding a man's attention was nothing more than being in his presence for me. Understanding why men seemed to only want me for show was like being a prisoner wanting to go home but you couldn't. Now, rocking back and forth in the old chair, I began twirling my long brown hair like a teenage girl waiting to be asked to the prom.

It was something I had not done for a long time. There was such a calm that came over me that day as if I were drugged from the tranquility of the house. I fought the inclination to stay and realized that it was time to go. "Where is my soul mate?" I asked myself quietly. Gathering myself to leave Mr. Vladimir's home forever.

I had gotten so comfortable that I had let time slip away from me again. I looked at my watch and then the manuscripts debating whether I should try to read more or not, I reluctantly held onto the papers before putting them back in the envelope as if I rightfully owned them. Knowing this was the last time I would visit the old house, I was glad Vladimir never showed.

I had found myself in the walls of the old house and was thankful to him for not being there to let me roam freely. I would remove my Real Estate signs from the property and accept the chiding from the other rat realtors about not selling the property and move on.

Once the manuscripts were almost back in their rightful place, I softly patted the desk one last time as if to say goodbye to an old friend that I would sorely miss. I got up slowly from the seat. I accepted that I would never know who wrote the letters I read or find out what happened in the "Black Man's Britches" manuscript.

As I turned to pull the desk top down, I saw in the distance a vehicle coming up the long roadway between the tall trees. I leaned forward towards the window pane, frantically wiping the dust off in a circular motion for a clearer view. I desperately tried to make out the vehicle coming up. It was strange to see anyone come up this road since no one had since I had been coming here.

For a brief moment, I felt as if someone was coming to visit me, and not that I was simply at work. I thought for a moment that maybe someone was lost, or maybe it was another buyer coming to look at the old house. Now I could see the truck clearly coming towards the house.

"Holy cow!!!" I said, rushing towards the front door.

"It's got to be Mr. Vladimir!!!" I almost dropped all of the pages of the manuscripts on the dusty wood floor but quickly captured them and stuffed them back in their secret place. Fluffing out my hair I realized I had not put on any makeup that day knowing Vladimir was never going to show up.

Besides, he was close to a hundred years old and had never showed up before, so I really didn't care how I looked. Then I realized I never really wore any makeup anyway and stopped fussing over myself.

After straightening up my clothes even though I knew this was an old man, I still didn't want to appear too casual because I was his realtor. I grabbed the sign and began to walk out of the door as if I was just leaving.

The car stopped next to my V.W. Beetle and the driver hesitated exiting the truck. I tried to make out a face and was shocked that such an old man would be driving alone at this age, and in a King Ranch F150 at that.

At least I knew he had good taste. "Wouldn't he have someone drive him at a hundred years old?" I thought. Then, slowly, the door opened. The windows were tinted very dark and I couldn't see anyone inside because of the angle of the vehicle in the driveway. I also did not know how many people may have been in the back seat of the vehicle either.

My anticipation had gotten the best of me with the expectation that an old man would emerge, but to my surprise, the door swings open wide and an amazing creature emerges. My eyes enveloped a young, handsome man. Completely tanned, with dark brown hair and wearing a stylish cap shielding the now beaming sun from his expensive sunglasses.

As he stepped down from the running board of his vehicle brandishing a white collared shirt and black jeans, with creases, I even noticed the buckle on his belt had an "F" which could have stood for anything and I didn't care.

I could tell that his entire ensemble probably cost more than my V.W. Beetle. While living in New York, I window shopped often at Saks Fifth Avenue and had bought something from there only once and knew the brands.

The man was about 6'4 and unreasonably handsome, carrying about 190 pounds of twisted masculinity. I almost went into a self-induced coma. Totally forgetting that though this man was drop dead gorgeous, I was every bit his match. I was single, but not dead, and if this was Vladimir, then he was "A-Okay" with me! It almost put Bradley to shame and he was an amazing specimen of a man.

Obviously, not letting outer facial expressions show that all sorts of bells and whistles had gone off in my head simultaneously, the man walked up to the porch to greet me with a smile before I could get to the end of the steps. I quickly counted all of the beautiful teeth he had exposed in his smile. "My, my," I said to myself. "If this is Mr. Vladimir, I will keep this lead and the joke is on those wacked out women who thought they were tricking me into this deal."

It was apparent that the man was making his own assessment of me. He slowly adjusted his cap and took off his sunglasses as if to get a clearer look at me and not have his vision impaired. The sun had appeared out of nowhere as if he had brought it with him. When he gave an approving smile from what he had taken in of my beauty, he introduced himself.

"Hello, I'm Nicholas, are you the owner?" he asked, still smiling and his eyes searching everything in its path not nailed down or covered. He knew I was not the owner but it got my attention completely.

"Right," I said, smugly pointing to my real estate name tag…" I am Ms. Stone, your realtor Mr. Francisca.

It's a pleasure to finally meet you." I said, knowing this man was way too young to be old man Vladimir.

Before he could answer, I recanted, "You are Mr. Vladimir, right?"

"Wrong," Nicholas said.

"I am actually the new owner of Mr. Francisca's estate, Ms. Stone." he said, nodding his head in a downward motion of his eyes, indicating that he knew a play when he saw one.

"So, are you related to Mr. Francisca or have recently purchased his estate and want me to remove my signs?"

"You are right to the first question," he said.'

"He actually was my grandfather."

"Was?" I asked sarcastically.

"Yes," was, we lost my grandfather over the weekend." Nicholas said in a solemn voice…

I felt horrible.

"I am so sorry to hear that Mr. Francisca."

"I was representing your grandfather in the sale of this estate… and I had never had the pleasure of meeting him. I have come out here several weeks now when he said he'd meet me, but he never did."

"That doesn't surprise me about Grandfather." He said.

"I am sorry that he stood such a lovely young lady up for so long, but glad I am the one that met you first." He again, smiled that devilish smile and winked at me, of all things.

Naturally, I was flushed at that moment, not believing I could be meeting yet another beautiful man when one had just slipped through my fingers in New York.

"Well, thank you Mr. Francisca, I guess you will be taking it off the market now?" I asked with a disappointed look.

"Actually, no," Nicholas said, "I still want to sell it."

"My Grandfather already had a buyer before he passed."

"My half-brother and I own all of his property now, but I have the majority interest. He really has no legal interest in it and will be turning his share over to me for a small stipend."

"Well, if you still would like for me to represent your family Mr…," Nicholas interrupted me mid-sentence.

"Please call me Nicholas." Smiling a magnificent smile…and looking me dead in the eye…

"Great, Nicholas," I said, in my most official woman voice.

Now that all the basic formalities had been covered, Nicholas seemed more at ease.

"So, have you seen the entire house?" He asked.

"Well, no," I lied, looking up to the heavens hoping God would forgive me for the lie I just told this complete stranger.

"Let me show you around."

"That would be nice," I said, thanking God for the opportunity to spend another moment with this wonderful creature. I realized that my biological clock was ticking fast and there was something about this man that made me feel different. I was really stunned, since I really didn't know anyone much in the South yet but felt that I knew this stranger better than I expected I would for a first meeting.

Nicholas began showing me around and took me through all the secret parts of the house that I actually had not seen…There was a hidden cellar in the house that I never would have found. I wanted to explore it but felt I had invaded more than my share of the home already by reading documents in their home.

Nicholas gave some history about the property and his fifth generation heritage...We stopped in the old country kitchen and looked out of the big window overlooking the estate.

"Your grandfather said that he wanted to sell the house and 250 acres." Towering over her, Nicholas, looked down at me with an adoring look. The softness in his eyes made me feel something special. I wanted to melt when he spoke my name. I had never felt this before. When he spoke, I could see the dimple that graced his right cheek.

"How far can you see property?" he asked.

I thought he was trying to be funny, and responded,

"I see nothing but property for miles."

"Then that his how much land he owns, over two thousand acres."

I was stunned with the numbers....

"This is only one area," Nicholas said, turning abruptly and walking back in the living room as if he had a moment of sadness for the memories of his grandfather. He stopped near the old desk and I was nervous, hoping he did not say anything about the papers I had been reading. He looked at the desk and chuckled.

"I always hated this old desk," he said. I was stunned by his statement.

"Why is that?" I asked, trying not to show any interest in the desk, knowing I had molested its contents.

"Bad memories?" I asked.

"When you sell the house, you can dump it or sell it with the house," Nicholas recanted.

I felt elated, but didn't know how to ask if I could take the desk. I decided to try an indirect approach.

"Wow, I rather liked the old desk."

"I have been out here so many times, the house would look empty without it." I said, hoping to evoke a right answer from him. He had already said I could dump it but I didn't want to seem as if I would take it from the garbage and needed to find a way to entice him into giving it to me.

"I am in school and could sure use one. I currently use the kitchen table at Ed's, my dad's." I quickly corrected myself.

"Which is it? Ed's or your dads?" he asked as if to clarify if I had a guy of my own.

"No, it's my dad's place. I have called him Ed since my mother died and I wasn't raised by him but by my Grandmother. I am not married."

Nicholas had a relieved look on his face as if he would have been crushed if I had been spoken for.

Nicholas looked at me and said, "Congratulations, this is your first gift of many from me."

"You are now the proud owner of this old desk, compliments of me." He said and did a gentleman's bow to me.

I was stunned that my plan had worked.

"You're kidding, right?"

"No."

"Were you kidding when you said you needed a desk?" he asked me.

"No." I stated.

"Then take it." "It's yours, from me!"

"I can have it delivered to you if you'd like. Where do you live? It certainly won't fit in that Bug of yours." He laughed.

"I will have our guys bring it to you." He said, picking up his cell phone to make the arrangements.

I thought fast before he could set up a delivery.

I was so happy but knew I needed to get it moved as soon as possible. Where was I going to put this thing? Ed would have a fit bringing in another piece of furniture in the house that was already overcrowded with my stuff from New York, but he wouldn't fuss too much. I had to move it fast before Nicholas examined it and found the papers.

"Well, I will need something in writing since I technically work for you." I said.

He smiled again and conceded.

"I understand. I will give your agency a note."

I didn't want him to examine the desk and made idle talk. I immediately called a friend of mine from the school and asked if they could meet me at the Vladimir estate to pick up the desk today…I didn't want to take any chances of him coming back out and examining it. My friend Manny was on his way after my call. I told Nicholas and he cancelled his arrangements with the professional movers.

Manny was sweet on me and would have carried it on his back for me, but like Jared back in New York, I vowed never to get in a relationship that I really didn't want for keeps.

I was excited knowing I would be able to read the entire manuscript if I could get the desk out of the old house. We both walked out of the house together. Since we were waiting for Manny, we stood at the back of Nicholas's truck at the tailgate. Nicholas unlocked the gate and let it fall.

He turned around and without warning gently lifted me up by my waist with both hands and placed me on the back of the tailgate as if I were weightless. Instinctively I held onto his shoulders as he picked me up. I could smell the light fragrance of his cologne and it wasn't old spice. "Mmmm," I thought, he smells wonderful. Not over powering like most of the folk that lived in this town.

The tailgate of his King Ranch had a custom soft lining on the back of it and it was more comfortable than sitting in my little bug. Nicholas leaned back against the truck as if I wasn't there. I wondered why he turned to face the road after such a Gone with The Wind Rhett Butler move of him picking me up and placing me on the back of his truck.

I remembered that he had just lost his grandfather and must have been grieving. Here was a man who had just lost someone dear to him and he gave away an antique without thinking about it. He must have a kind spirit. I liked that feeling. I felt it was necessary and the right thing to do to console him.

"Are you okay Nicholas?" I asked.

"Yeah, I'm going to miss the old geezer." He said, chuckling a bit of light humor. He began talking about his grandfather and what his plans were. We laughed about the fact that his grandfather was in a nursing home when he called me and was never coming out there.

"It was what he did to stay active. People would come to see him when they thought he was selling property. They knew he was filthy rich and no one else came to see him but me. He knew people could keep running there for nothing more than the money they thought they would get from their greed."

Nicholas continued to purge himself with his grief. I had learned from my psychology class about the grieving process. This was an important part. So I was a good listener today. It wasn't hard to listen to someone like Nicholas. He seemed kind and generous. He continued to purge himself and I listened.

"The truth was, Grandfather had never sold an acre of land since he acquired it from his Great, Great, Great grandfather." Nicholas said, finally looking back towards the house. He looked for his keys and found some music in his glove compartment and took his key pressed a button and the CD player began to play. He opened a cooler on the back of the truck and pulled out two flavored waters and gave me one.

"Wow, you have everything in this truck."

"Not quite," he said with a twinkle in his eye.

"It's hot here in the South and if you are not from here, you'd better learn to BYOD."

"I have never heard of BYOD." I said.

"It means Bring Your Own Drink." He began laughing breaking the solemn mood.

"I got it," I said, pulling my hair up in a pony-tail. Nicholas stared at me as I twirled my long thick hair up on the top of my head, making me look even younger than 24.

"What?" I asked, watching him glare at me.

"You're very pretty," He stated in a serious tone.

"Don't get me wrong, I am not making a move, just an observation."

"Well, you have good eyesight!" I said, laughing.

"Ed, my dad, used to say that when people complimented him."

"Your dad must be a good looking man."

"I can only imagine what your mother must look like to have produced you." For the first time, I proudly reached in my purse to show off a photo of the only family member that I really knew.

"Here is a picture of my dad Ed." I said, eagerly waiting for his response.

Nicholas looked at the picture, and his face went cold.

"Nice looking guy, but, you must look like your mother." I was stunned! That was the first time anyone had said that to me. I was proud to say I had a dad, but I had always thought that I didn't look like Ed. But since everyone else always said I did, once again I believed them. And here this man, a stranger, was telling me a truth I had never heard.

I had always wanted the truth but didn't realize how the truth would feel and saw that it hurts when you have been lied to for so long. I was quiet for a moment, and then there was dead silence. The kind you don't want when you are initially attracted to someone.

Finally Manny was coming down the road with two of his friends to move the desk. It broke the silence between me and Nicholas. When Nicholas saw the vehicle approaching, he reached for me to lift me down from the tailgate and I quickly jumped down on my own, showing my independence while pulling the band from my hair and letting it all cascade down to my backside.

I playfully pranced to the truck where Manny and his friends were as if Nicholas didn't exist. It seemed to evoke a different reaction from him than I thought my actions would.

I was puzzled and wondered why I reacted that way towards a man that had just been very polite and generous towards me. The old desk was definitely an antique and I knew it and so did he.

"What a fool I am," I thought, trying to figure out a way to fix the mess I was making. Before I could come up with anything, Nicholas went inside the house and brought out the chair for the desk and lifted it effortlessly up on the truck. Manny and his friends went inside the house after drooling over me like star struck kids. They yelled like kids would yell trying to show off in front of me.

It was embarrassing. I looked over at Nicholas and he smiled and raised a brow and walked over to me and whispered in my ear,

"Why don't you move out of their sight so they don't kill themselves trying to impress you with lifting this desk? It is very heavy and could ruin a man forever, if you know what I mean." He winked at me and I instinctively moved aside as he had kindly suggested.

It was my chance to regain some credibility.

"They are freshmen at the University and are nice guys," I said, smiling.

I moved over to the back of Nicholas's truck again to get out of sight. He walked over and opened the door. He started up the vehicle and turned on the air conditioning for her. He didn't ask, but told me to sit in the front and stay cool. I gladly accepted his invitation because I was very hot and was beginning to perspire. That wasn't cool at all.

This time he let me get in on my own but held the door open for me. The truck smelled new and everything was nice.

I sat in the truck feeling like Scarlet O'Hara in Gone with the wind when Rhett took the reins and took her home on their buggy to Tara. I secretly watched him work through the tinted windows of his King Ranch.

It felt great to be looked after again. The guys struggled to get the desk down the two steps but they made it. Nicholas did more orchestrating than lifting. He had rolled up his sleeve and ensured that the doors on the desk were taped so they didn't open and crack in the move.

Once the desk was safely on the truck, he took a cord and tied it down. Once secured, Manny and the guys got back in the truck and took off. I got out of the cool vehicle and thanked Nicholas again for the generous deed and gift. I reminded Nicholas to give the note to the Real estate office about the desk. He immediately walked over to his truck and pulled out his phone and sent a message stating:

To whom it may concern. I am the new owner of the Vladimir Francisca Estate and have met with Ms. Stone, his agent at the property and asked her to personally dispose of one antique roll top desk any way she chooses. It is being put in her possession at my request and is being removed as we speak. No further communication is needed on this matter.

Nicholas V. Francisca

He asked me for my phone number and sent me a message to the same effect.

"Is that satisfactory, Ms. Stone? I certainly do not want to upset you any further," he stated.

"I always want to see a smile on your face."

"Yes, it is satisfactory," I said, smiling nicely and for the first time was unable to look at Nicholas. I realized that his middle initial was V. which must have been his grandfather's name, "Vladimir." How nice, I thought, to be named after a grandparent. I only wished I knew who I was named after, or if I was named after anyone.

"Great! Then it's settled," Nicholas said.

"Well, I guess I best be getting along since Manny has left." I said.

"Well, before you go, I really have one other questions about the sale of the property and would like to discuss it further if you are free this evening?" he said, very sure of himself.

"Would you like to have dinner with me?"

"Just dinner," he added, with a raised brow.

I thought quickly about my response. I didn't want to make the same mistake twice from earlier with the picture incident. I wanted to say yes but was a bit conflicted because I didn't know if I should accept on the first request. I had done everything wrong where Travis, my Ex, was concerned and wanted to be careful. The same with Bradley, I didn't accept his first invitation, but almost missed the second chance to see where the relationship would go.

But, there was something different about this man. He seemed sure of himself and what he is doing and is very patient. I am no longer a child and know what I want. I reflected on what I had gleaned from the manuscripts and sensed a new person emerging from within me.

I threw the idea out of my head as quickly as I thought it and realized I was not getting any younger and there were no other guys that even came close to matching this man's seeming character and background.

"Yes!" I said, that will be fine. Now, preparing to put my hair back in the pony tail and wrap it up. Nicholas leaned over and gently pulled the tie out of my hair and it cascaded down my backside again.

"I rather like it down," he said, smiling.

I stood facing him staring him in his hazel eyes, stunned at his boldness but intrigued that he did what he wanted to do and it was no secret that he liked what he saw in me. I searched his eyes and slowly plucked the tie from his hand and held it up to his face and shook it gently and smiled. Then I put it in my pocket.

"What time tonight?" I asked in an authoritative voice. No longer feeling like the girl I used to be, but the woman I was becoming.

"I can pick you up at 7 o'clock," he said.

"I need to go by the real estate office and pick up some papers that my Grandfather left with them for me to sign."

"Well, I can meet you at the office if you'd like," I offered.

"Sounds great!"

"And it makes it look really legitimate," he added, now in full laughter. He looked off in the sunset and adjusted his hat. He rolled his sleeves down and opened my car door and secured me inside. With his strong hands still on the door, he winked and said goodbye.

I smiled and slowly drove off feeling as if all the days I came out to the house for Mr. Francisca were finally paying off.

The women in the office are going to crap their pants when they see the sale I will get. I wanted to speed back to the office but knew that Manny drove like an old lady. He had the key to the side door at Ed's, but I called him to let him know I would be there later so would not wait for me.

Daddy knew Manny and was okay with him coming by the house. I couldn't wait until I saw Nicholas again. "Could this be true?" I thought. Two great guys in the same year? It was almost a miracle. Now what? I thought. I had to stop at the real estate office and was gloating all the way there. I couldn't wait to see their faces. I drove for about 30 minutes and could see Nicholas in her rearview mirror. He turned off somewhere else and I arrived at the office before he did.

Today, I would feel a hundred times better when they chided me about the account and not having a sale. I parked in my usual spot and got out with my signs. I walked in the almost hot office. The manager was cheap and didn't want to turn the air on because he said it saved money, so we were scorching. I hated it but dealt with it as long as I could.

"Hey, Chiney" the office worker said, slandering my name. I spoke and then the manager called me into his office. I wasn't sure what he wanted but went in and waited. The office worker popped her head in and said, "Oh, your client Mr. Vladimir Francisca, well, he's dead, so you don't have a client no more." She walked out. Another jab. But I didn't care to respond. They would know soon enough. As I sat there at the table waiting for the manager to come in. I looked in the basket again that held the names of the staff that had participated in the fake drawing. As I opened each piece of paper that was neatly folded, all the names were mine.

Author: Victoria E. Kain

I was still furious and wanted to scream! I was sick of people trying to trick me thinking that because I was kind, that meant I was stupid. "What is this ignorant attitude of people thinking they are smarter than I am?

"Well I am going to show them." Just when I was madder than a hornets nest, the manager walked in.

"How's your day going little lady," he asked.

"Great," I said, perturbed.

"Well, I have some bad and good news."

"Okay" I said, not really caring because I had news as well.

"Your client Mr. Vladimir Francisca passed this weekend," he was stunned that I didn't respond.

"I hope that was the bad news, so what is the good news?"

"Well, Vernise will take over the account since Vladimir's grandson is coming in to take over his estate. He will be in shortly to sign some papers. Vernise is from the other location and she wanted to personally work with him since you are new here and not accustomed to our area and you did not do so well with Mr. Francisca. We heard nothing from you on that lead little lady. I am sorry," he said, "I want you to meet her."

Before I could say, Jack rabbit, in comes this bleached windblown blonde. Two pounds and six ounces.

"Hey Sugar! I'm Vernise Fryer and it's a pleasure meeting you," "I'm going to be taking over the account. I know you don't mind since you never got a chance to meet Mr. Francisca, but I have met his grandson Nicholas before and am sure he will want to work with me." "Kaay?" she ended the statement.

I was dumbfounded about the skeleton standing before me and how they had railroaded the account. I thought they ran a fair real estate office. I was mad and was about to speak when I heard Nicholas's voice in the lobby asking for the manager.

He had come by to pick up the papers. He stormed into the manager's office and Vernise attacked him.

"Nicholas how are you?"

"We are so sorry about your loss. I'm Vernise, remember me?"

"I will be your agent for the Francisca estaaaaate," she said in her most southern drawl. Finally Nicholas had a chance to speak.

"Actually, I don't remember you ma'am. And I am Mr. Francisca" he said, never taking his eyes off me.

"I already have a realtor, Ms. Stone."

"As a matter of fact, I am here to pick up the papers and Ms. Stone to finish discussing the 400 acres we will be selling tomorrow. We are meeting with the buyer this evening to write up the contract," he stated, never wavering.

The manager and Vernise were literally speechless. They were nervous and staring me down with anger in their eyes. Vernise tried one fail attempt to get the account.

"Well now Nicholas, I have been in the business for over 28 years and I know the market and the data and can serve you better. Ms. Stone is new to real estate and I must admit she is a looker, but won't you reconsider experience over beauty?" Trying to make a joke, but no one laughed but her.

"Well, let me see," Nicholas said. "Ms. Stone is blindingly beautiful," winking at me, then responding,

"I gave it some deep thought Ms. Vernise and the answer is No!" Ms. Stone will do just fine.

She came out every week and my grandfather never showed. You all knew he wouldn't, but she showed persistence and loyalty to her client. She deserves the sale."

"Are you ready to go Ms. Stone?"

"Yes, Mr. Francisca" I said.

"Oh, you can call me Nicholas," he said.

The office manager was elated to know that his office would get the sale.

"You take your time, Ms. Stone" the manager said, sucking up big time!

The two of us walked out of the office looking at each other and exploded in a viral laughter. We almost couldn't catch our breath remembering the look on Vernise face. It was a day to remember for me. I never had to divulge the trick they played on me.   Nicholas knew they had done it from knowing his grandfather's feelings about greedy people. He had protected me and spoke on my behalf. The shoe was finally on the other foot. They got what they deserved.

"Are you hungry?" Nicholas asked.

"I am starving," I replied. We walked toward his truck and I got to the door. This time, he again opened the door and assisted me up. I looked back towards the office and saw all three of the ladies watching us from the dingy window.

They almost had their noses pressed to the window pane. I smiled and Nicholas closed my door and looked back and waved at the faces of the sad looking women at the window trying to get a closer look.

As we pulled off, still laughing, Nicholas said something that took my breath away.

"You know, Ms. Stone."

"I was with my grandfather before he passed and he said something to me and I wasn't sure why he said it."

"Well, are you going to keep me in suspense forever?" I asked, elated that it was me in the vehicle with this wonderful man.

"He told me that when he was gone, I was to go out to the estate as soon as possible because there would be something waiting for me in the house."

"What did he mean?" Showing concern now, hoping I had not been seen by some video camera.

As we pulled onto the next street, his music came on a very soft volume. His Bose speakers picked up every beat in the song playing Ray Charles singing the Long and Winding Road, which was a favorite of my Grandmothers.

Completely stunned by the statement and his frankness, we stopped at the last red light before getting to our freeway entrance. Sitting at the light, Nicholas turned and looked deep into my eyes.

"I didn't know what my grandfather meant by what he had instructed me to do until I pulled up to the house on the estate and saw you walk out of the front door. It was as if you were at home coming out to meet someone you already knew was coming."

Nicholas stopped smiling for a moment and had a solemn look on his face. It was the kind of look that you see in the eyes of a man that was falling in love.

I now understood that look. I remember seeing it once before in my life but couldn't believe I would see it again. I sat quiet for a moment.

Author: Victoria E. Kain

"Could it be? Could it really be?" I thought, my heart racing. I had thought that love would never come my way again, but for some reason, this moment felt right to me. There was something that touched my soul as I sat next to Nicholas. It was as if I truly belonged here with him. It was not like anything else I had experienced. I knew that only time would tell.

The days went by very quickly and I knew that school was about to end and graduation was around the corner and would be a thing of the past in only two weeks. Nicholas had become the love of my life from that moment on. He never left my side and had been instrumental in strengthening the relationship I had with Ed. I was looking forward to graduating with my Master's Degree in Psychology, but had to concentrate on studying for my final exam in order to receive my certifications for this degree.

I thought about Nicholas and me going back to New York to visit Jared but really had not talked to him much since I left. I missed my old friend and wanted to know how he was getting along. The weekend finally came for my graduation. All of my classmates were amped up and I felt the same class spirit. Ed was ready and so was Nicholas and Uncle Buddy and Uncle Shane. It would be the first time there would be someone there in the audience to cheer me on at a graduation ceremony.

I had graduated high school, and my first four years of college with no one in the audience to be proud of me. It felt as if I had brought myself into the world sometimes, but I got by. This night would be different. Nicholas picked me up and we rode together to the ceremony. I had wanted Ed to go with us, but he had not been well lately and would be coming with Uncle Buddy and Uncle Shane. Those three were inseparable.

I climbed in the truck with Nicholas, the man I knew I loved more than life itself.

"Well, this is the day you have been waiting for," Nicholas said.

"I know, I can't believe it is finally here," I said, adjusting my cap on my head ensuring it was on straight.

"How does it feel to be completing this monumental task?" he asked.

"Going to school was not a problem for me. I think it was having to graduate each time with no one there to represent my family, but me," I said, looking out the window as he pulled out of the driveway.

"Well, you never have to worry about that again, China doll. Today, is a very special day for you. It will be one you will never forget, I promise you," he said, with a serious look on his face. I knew that look, and didn't question it at all. Besides, I knew I would never forget it. I had waited for two years to finish this degree with so many disappointments along the way.

I loved it when he called me his "China Doll." It meant something special for Ed to say it, and now the man I loved had the same endearment for me. It was all I had of family sentiments to remember.

I settled back in the seat and listened to the soft music as we rode to the auditorium. This night, I would not be alone. I would have my family with me. The thought of that warmed my heart. We arrived at the auditorium and all the graduates looked like penguins with the tuxedos on and special garb with their regalia all pressed and colorful representing the different degrees.

Author: Victoria E. Kain

Family members piled in to get the best seats. Nicholas let me out at the door so I did not have to walk far at all.

I was practical with the shoes I wore so that I did not stumble. Before I left the truck, Nicholas gave me a big kiss.

"That's for how proud I am of you," he said.

I smiled and blushed as I noticed some of my classmates making faces at me outside the window beaconing for me to hurry and walk in with them and take a few group selfies. Excitement came over me as I opened the door and looked back and the wonderful man I had fallen in love with.

I blew him a kiss and adjusted my dress and ran off in the crowd with the other graduates like I was a high school student all over again. The time went by fast and about an hour later, we all were lined up ready to go into the auditorium. All the families were seated and they began the pomp and circumstance music.

It was something about this music that brought chills to your bones. I felt as if I was on top of the world. I still looked frantically in the crowded room for Nicholas and my dad and Uncles. Finally as I came to the end of the row before going up near the stage, there they were, all sitting in the front V.I.P. section. They all waved and my heart was pounding with a joyous feeling. I was so excited to have family here tonight.

They went through the level of degrees and finally came to the master's. There were not as many of those graduates so it went by very fast. They soon came to my name and I walked on stage to receive my degree for my years of study.

I only wished Grandmother and mother had been there to see me. As I graced the stage and positioned myself to receive my scroll, I was happy that my dad and uncles and the man I loved were there.

I was very proud when they called my name for the first time, "China Stone," Master of Psychology, *Magna Cum Laude.* There was a pause and soon I saw Ed being escorted on stage. I was nervous and was wondering why he was coming up. "Is he alright?" I thought. Searching the room looking for Nicholas to reassure me that everything was alright, I finally made eye contact with him in the front row.

He nodded an affirmative "yes" as if to answer the question in my head soothing my fears. Ed approached me and the Dean handed him my hood. Ed was permitted to hood me for this degree and I burst into tears. The photographer took a picture of us and the room was cheering and gave a standing ovation for my father hooding me.

Camera flashes went crazy in the room. Everyone including the newspaper reporters were there. I could hear Nicholas and Uncle Shane and Buddy yelling and whistling in the front row as we both walked off the stage.

It was the happiest day of my life and I couldn't think of anything that could make this day any better. After the ceremony and all the festivities were over, scores of family members and graduates were taking myriads of photographs in the front of the lobby. Ed was sitting on the sidelines from exhaustion. Buddy and Shane were there too chatting with each other as I took photographs with classmates I would probably never see again.

Author: Victoria E. Kain

Finally, Nicholas was taking pictures with me and someone walked up behind me and tapped me on the shoulder. I turned quickly, thinking it was a classmate wanting a picture and my mouth flew open in shock!

Lo and behold, it was Jared, my quasi fiancé from New York. I was in tears as I grabbed him and gave him a big hug before realizing that Nicholas was standing there. I quickly let go of him and was amazed how much he had changed.

"What are you doing here you crazy guy?" I shouted.

"I couldn't miss this for the world," Jared replied, looking confident.

"I can't believe you are here!" I screamed.

"Thank you for coming!" I said. Before Jared could say anything else, I turned to Nicholas, who was patiently waiting his introduction to this man that had almost accosted his woman.

"I have someone I want you to meet," I said.

"This is my boyfriend, Nicholas."

"How are you, I'm Dr. Jared Alexandra."

"Nice to meet you Jared," Nicholas said.

"Congrats on your medical degree."

"China told me a lot about you."

"Well, I have been out of pocket for a while with finishing school."

"I would like for you both to meet my wife Mitzi."

I was looking around frantically for his wife and there she was sitting over near Ed on one of the benches. She was at least seven months pregnant and couldn't stand up much.

I rushed over and hugged her gently.

"It is a pleasure meeting you!" I said.

"Same here," Mitzi replied. Leaning back on her hands trying to get comfortable.

"Well, this is my father Edmondo"

"How are you Sir?" Jared replied. Ed spoke cordially and moved on quietly. I introduced my uncles as well and felt that this was what I had missed all these years.

Everyone at the graduation had someone there for them and now it was my turn. We all laughed about old times and realized that Jared's wife was one of the medical students who was in love with him from their first year. She waited for him and me to break up although we really were never officially together. I assured her of that which was a relief to his wife.

Jared and Mitzi had a flight to catch so they left for the airport. It was the most wonderful evening of my life. That evening, Ed took us all out for dinner. He wanted to talk to us about something important.

Too much had gone wrong in my life from the time I was conceived until now. I wanted to have more honest days like this in my life. I wanted to let all of the men in my life know how important this day was for me. It was a first and I wanted more of these firsts. Ed wanted to talk to me about something but said he would talk to me later. This was my night.

We arrived at the restaurant and were seated. Nicholas gave me a big hug and kiss again and we took a selfie.

"I am so proud of you China," he said.

"I guess there is nothing much that I could do to top what you have done today," he said, looking serious again.

"Well, it was a pretty big accomplishment." I said, winking at Ed as he smiled and held my hand.

Author: Victoria E. Kain

"Well, I think I want to try anyway," Nicholas said, reaching in his pocket and pulling out a ring box.

I saw the box and was in shock. I slowly shook my head in disbelief. I had waited to hear special words from him, but would it be today, I thought.

"China, I was in love with you the first day I met you on my Grandfather's estate. I don't want to live another day without you being by my side."

"Will you be my wife?"

I was stunned as he opened the box and pulled out the most beautiful ring that had belonged to his Grandmother. His Grandfather had given it to him before he died.

"Well, will you marry me?" he asked again.

Now with tears in my eyes and trembling, I mouthed the words slowly, thinking only for a fleeting second praying that Nicholas was the right one. I realized that life was not going to get any better than this and it was my second chance at loving someone.

"Yes, yes, I will marry you!" I said.

Nicholas put the ring on my finger and kissed me again. This time, I knew this was for real. How much better can this get for me? I thought.

Ed finally spoke…

"I have waited a long time to hear those words!" He said with a quiet chuckle as if he was talking to himself, but wanted us all to hear him. I reached over and hugged him and whispered,

"I love you Daddy."

There was a strange look that came over Ed's face and he held his head down for a moment and tears came to his eyes…he could not speak and got up and excused himself from the table. I was confused as to why my statement of "I love you" had touched him so.

After a moment of contemplating my statement, I realized in all the years I had known him, I had never called him "daddy" before now.

It was as if this day was the first day for many things that had happened in my life since I was a child. I had never experienced anyone being there for the special moments in my life to hold as memories. I knew that giving money to support a child was different than being in that child's life.

Although I appreciated what he did for me, which helped me get through it all, I knew I loved him for all those years he was away, but was not permitted to bond with him.

It just seemed like the right time and it was natural. I wanted to follow him out of the restaurant, but Nicholas gently took my hand and told me to let him have his father moment.'

"After all, he is losing you to me," he said, with a smile and gave me another big kiss. Those seemed to come more often tonight, but I wasn't fussing about it at all. I welcomed his affection, always.

Uncle Shane and Uncle Buddy congratulated us both and gave us a hug and we soon left the restaurant after our meal.

My graduation day and Nicholas's proposal was the most precious day of my life. We dropped Uncle Buddy off and Uncle Shane and Ed went out for drinks. Daddy didn't want to come home right away. Me and Nicholas went to the park and made plans for our wedding. We talked and hugged and cried.

He didn't want to wait long to marry me so we agreed on a small wedding and said we would go to Italy on our honeymoon to visit the rest of his family that might be too old to travel to the wedding. It was the happiest night of my life.

I couldn't wait to become his wife. He talked about his plans and wanted to know how I felt about having lots of babies. I was ecstatic! I always wanted a large family and agreed without any hesitation. He said that's why he wanted to marry me soon. He didn't want to wait any longer.

This day, his hugs were very tender and he held me close to his heart. I could actually hear it beating in his chest. To feel his face on mine was something I had longed for since my marriage to Travis. I had conducted myself according to what I had agreed to do which was to abstain until I married. I believe this was another reason Nicholas didn't want to wait much longer, but I believe love had truly captured him.

There was much to do to prepare for the simple ceremony in the next three months. Most brides-to-be would be scurrying around fussing over what kind of wedding gown to wear or who would be their bride's maid. I was not concerned about that. I was clear what type of dress I would wear.

I knew that Ed would walk me down the aisle and that was all I needed to know. We left the park that night and he took me home.

Nicholas and I stayed on the phone all night. Neither one of us could help ourselves. We were simply two people madly in love. The following days were a blur for me. It seemed that school was over and now another project was on the table. The next morning I went to Dads bedroom door and knocked and got no answer. I knocked again and finally the door opened slightly and I could see Dad lying on the bed.

"Daddy, are you awake?" I said. No answer was heard.

"Daddy, rise and shine, we need to get your tux ordered today." I said.

Still no answer… I was very worried now and was bold and needed to see why he was not answering me. He never slept this sound.

"Daddy, I'm coming in backwards, not looking, but I am coming in." Finally I looked at my dad and he was still.

"Oh, my Lord." I screamed.

I ran to the phone and called 911. The ambulance got there and took Ed to the hospital. I called Nicholas and he came right away.

Ed had had a heart attack and it had been caught in time. It was a miracle that I went in to check on him.

I was glad I had been there for him. He would be doing better after two weeks in the hospital. I had almost worried myself sick and realized that I had to stop thinking about it and believe that all I needed was Nicholas to love me and my dad would be alright.

Nicholas was there for me and Dad. We looked for an apartment closer to the hospital just to be near him.

Author: Victoria E. Kain

He did well and was recovering. One day I went to see him and down the hall from his room I saw the same man that was at Grandmother's funeral coming out of his room. I could see now that he was the same man I saw across from the library in New York. Before I could get to Ed's room the man had gotten on the elevator. I talked to Ed and asked him about the man and he pretended not to know what I was talking about.

I played it off because of his condition but knew something was strange. I did not discuss it further and talked to Nicholas later about it.

He agreed to look into it for me. We began talking about other disturbing things I had seen and I discussed much of my past with him. I had vowed that I would keep nothing from my husband to be. We put some data together about the only past I knew and found papers on Ed in the house to send in for a history family tree research. I wanted to find out about my past. There was too much that had happened that was a secret about me. I needed to know so that my children would not be in the dark about their past...

Nicholas was totally with me on my quest to know about my family. He had become my best friend and I believed that everything else would fall in place. After all, I had Ed and my Uncles and that was all I needed. Nicholas contacted his family attorney and they began a family history search with the sketchy data I had. I had so little that it was difficult to even begin.

"I don't know what to think about my life," I said.

"We will find out as much as we can about you," Nicholas said, rubbing my back to soothe me. He would do anything for me and this was only the first of many things he wanted to do.

It was evident that he wanted to spoil me by the size of the ring he had placed on my finger when he asked me to marry him. I knew now, for once in my life, money was no object. But it never had been an object for me anyway.

I was reared in a household where we were fairly poor and although my dad, Ed had provided well for me, his prison term hindered him from being able to bond with me. I was moved around and did not get to feel the effects of being cared for by a parent since I lost my mother at a young age. I learned to deal with people who were filled with greed or some form of selfishness. Because of this, I became more of a giver than a taker.

Nicholas and I grew to love each other more and more. We spent most of our waking hours together planning for our big day and it was evident that we were in love by the way we treated each other. I continued to work at the real estate office and closed on large houses after I closed the deal with Nicholas's Grandfather's estate since his brother had bought the first 400 acres. Many large land owners came to me after that sale and with the support of Nicholas, I did very well in the business.

Many of the other realtors left the company because they could not sell anything and soon I received my notice that they no longer needed my services with the agency. They seemed to hate that I had made more commissions than any of them in the year I had been with the company verses the years they had been there.

Author: Victoria E. Kain

I would have looked for another job, but Ed had taken ill again and wasn't doing well. I was worried about him and wanted to be there for him so I spent as much time with him as possible. I knew I could feasibly lose him and the thought stifled my inner being. We temporarily stayed in an apartment Nicholas got for us to be closer to Ed's doctor for his treatment. Nicholas spent much of his time with us even with only weeks before the wedding.

Everything was in order for the wedding and Ed seemed to be getting stronger each day. They had fitted him for his Tux and he was feeling a bit better. I felt relieved at this time. A week before the wedding, Ed disappeared for a whole day and no one knew where he had gone. We were worried he had gotten ill somewhere and couldn't get home.

The authorities were called and said there was nothing they could do for at least twenty four hours. Within that time Ed came home as chipper as ever only days before the wedding.

I was furious with him and gave him a daughterly piece of my mind: "Where have you been Daddy? I have done everything trying to find you, and have been worried sick!" I yelled.

"You know we only have days now before the wedding and because of my fear of what happened to you I still have too much to do to prepare for the ceremony," I began to cry again and Ed hugged me in his arms and whispered a strange thing in my ear.

"Don't worry baby, everything is alright. It is all okay now. No one will ever hurt you again," he said.

I felt better knowing that he had reassured me and decided to move forward. Calls and cards and gifts were coming in now and I was becoming overwhelmed. Nicholas was helping me every day. I had never felt the effects of being spoiled but Nicholas was trying his best to spoil me and promised me everything I ever wanted.

Nicholas and I grew closer every day and our love became stronger as time moved forward. I knew that he was the only one for me and accepted that every other feeling I thought I had for anyone else was a mistake. We spent most of our waking hours together planning for the big day and it was evident that we were in love by the way we treated each other.

With only a few days before the wedding, Nicholas said he had one piece of unfinished business with the Real-estate office to close out. Since I had been let go before Ed became ill, he needed to talk to the manager Billy. He wanted me to go with him although I really didn't want to see them again. When we got to the office I thought I would sit in the vehicle but he asked me to come in. Reluctantly I obeyed.

The women at the front desk began swooning when they saw Nicholas and cringed when they saw me come in behind him and asked, "can we help you?" Nicholas was pleased to answer.

"She's with me," he said firmly.

"Billy will be out shortly," she said.

Billy came out and greeted Nicholas and again ignored me. Nicholas was disturbed with Billy's actions and made his purpose known quickly. He went on to tell Billy that he was removing his land for sale with his real estate company. Billy was shocked and accused me of setting it up because I was terminated.

Nicholas politely told him that I had nothing to do with his decision but he did tell Billy that I had stolen something from him. I was furious and did not know where Nicholas was going with his joke. Billy came unglued and expressed his concern. "What did she steal from you Mr. Francisca, we will press charges against her for you," he yelled. "I knew she was evil!"

"Well, what she stole was my heart and I have already pressed her with charges to be my wife and pay back every piece of my heart she took from me every day," Nicholas said smiling at me. "I am also removing all of my accounts from you as well, as of today. Please send the paperwork for my signature."

Billy was sick! He turned beet red and said well, good day sir!

Nicholas took my hand and we left the parking lot and never looked back. I discussed the thought of looking for another job again but Nicholas had other ideas in mind for me. In the meantime, I would prepare me for the wedding which was only days away.

Everything was going well and everyone for the wedding was there in the little town waiting for the big day. It was one day before the wedding when, I received the information from the historical service agency that Nicholas and I had requested about my family history. I was not sure if I should open it before the wedding and alone so I called Nicholas to come over to be with me. Before he arrived, I said a prayer and realized that whatever was in these papers I would have to accept.

I didn't want anything to spoil my beautiful day with the man I loved.

Ed walked in the room and noticed that I seemed distraught. As any father would do, he stopped to talk with me thinking I was getting wedding jitters.

"What's on your mind, China Doll," he said, sitting beside me on the sofa. He saw the envelope in my hand and read the address on it. He held his head down in disbelief and relief.

"It's the information I requested, dad. I had to know who the rest of my folks are before I get married to the man I love. I don't want to start my life with lies and shadows of who I think I am or who I thought my people were." I said, looking him straight in his eyes. Ed was sad faced and spoke quietly…

"Before you open that, I want to give you something else. I wanted to do this at the restaurant the night you graduated, but it wasn't the right moment. "Now is the right time," he said. He left the room and returned to me on the sofa. He handed me two envelopes. One of them had Grandmother's writing on it. Ed said that Buddy was supposed to give it to me after the funeral but forgot and the other was in a handwriting that I didn't recognize.

I looked at Ed with a puzzled look in my eyes. My heart was racing. I realized that I had three envelopes and each one of them held answers to the myriads of questions I had all my life. I was prepared for this day and wanted to know what was in them. Ed asked me to open Grandmother's letter first. I carefully tore open the top of the envelope. Taking care not to rip it because depending on what it said, I would keep it forever. As I began to read, I was astonished.

Author: Victoria E. Kain

My Dear China,

I don't think I have too much longer, but want you to know the truth about some things. I have always loved you from the time your mama brought you home from the hospital. Your mama was a good woman. She was beautiful and smart and many people envied that. You are smart like her too. The man that owned the company where she worked was the man that violated her that night along with his son. We did not know this at first and neither did your mother. People felt he was a good man, but found out later he was the one.

For a long time this rich man thought he was your daddy and when he got wind of you being born, we believe he wanted to get rid of you both. However, his son was also with him that night your mother was attacked. He was the one that they found in the alley knocked unconscious by the stranger that came in the alley. When the police found him and took him to the hospital, he confessed to the attack and spent a short while in prison.

I was in shock over what I was reading for the first time. It was like that silent moving playing while you see the emotions of the characters but can't hear a sound. I kept reading with eager eyes.

Your mother had gone back to work at the man's factory before his son was released from prison. His father pretended to be kind to your mother and gave her a small promotion to make it look as if he was remorseful for what the town folk thought his son had done on his own.

A few years after returning to work for this man that had attacked your mother, she mysteriously fell ill and died. We later found that she was poisoned and no one talked about it.

They wanted to bring no further issues on the rich man's family. That is when, Ed, the man you know as your dad contacted me from prison and asked me to come and see him. I was hesitant but realized that he couldn't hurt me being in prison so I went.

He was a nice man and we talked quietly at the prison. He told me how the rich man's son had bragged to him about how he and his father had violated your mother and that his father had given him a bonus in his will to take the fall.

Ed also told me that the man who attacked your mother said to him that his father was going to take care of both of you in a negative way, when he got out. He would make sure you could tell no body.

When the rich man's son got out of prison, I started coming to see Ed on a regular basis for more information. He could not trust anyone with what he was telling me for fear I would be hurt and he knew you were with me. I came to the prison and he told me everything. He said that he would help us protect you and he revealed that he was your father.

He had worked at that same factory and told me he had been with your mother before she was attacked and you were his daughter. I reluctantly believed him, but he said he would take care of us and do the right thing and he did. He began sending money each month for you.

Ed asked me to bring you to see him each month so the guards and prisoners would spread the word that he had another daughter. That is when I started taking you to see your dad, but I never insisted that you call him daddy because I still wasn't sure. I knew time would tell.

Author: Victoria E. Kain

He said he had lost one child but would give his life to save you. He then told me who had attacked you that night in your bedroom. It was more information than I could bare.

The hair began to stand up on my arms. I had waited to know who my attacker was for many years. I was exhausted with the nightmares about the incident and would now be able to finally put it away. I continued reading.

After your mother was poisoned Ed knew that the rich man was watching the prisoners and receiving reports on who came to see him. He knew that Ed had gotten close to his son and wanted the wardens to report on Ed's visitors. When they saw that Ed was sending money to you, they leaked the information to the rich man but he still wasn't satisfied. He came to see Ed.

The rich man pretended to be kind and told Ed he would help lighten his sentence so he could get out and be with you and take care of you. Ed knew how ruthless he was and would think nothing about killing him in prison but he played along.

This is when the rich man had his son break into the house and attack you, but you fought him by screaming. I was so glad you did. Now we know who did these horrible things. That is why we had to send you away. I am sorry for slapping your face that day, but I was frustrated about what I knew and scared for you. I wanted you to always stay with me, but I didn't want to lose you like I lost your mother. I am sorry for hitting you. There is more, but Ed will tell you himself when he finds the right time. I love you always my China doll.

Love Grandmother

I dropped the letter in my lap and Ed embraced me. I was in full tears from reading and realized that I finally was putting closure to some of the mystery of what happened to my mother and to me those awful nights in our lives. I did not have any words to say and couldn't think of anything else to feel.

There was a sense of closure to this part of my horrifying past, but I still didn't know who my father was. The skeletons were finally coming clean and I would have no more lies. I had two more envelopes to read which would satisfy my quest and I could move on.

Ed gave me his handkerchief and I dried my eyes. He asked me to wait to read the other letter but I wanted to get it all out in the open while my emotions were fresh. Not another day would go by. I slowly placed Grandmother's letter in the envelope and laid it neatly aside and picked up the next letter. I opened it. Already numb from the first, I continued,

"My dear child." **The letter began. Before I continued, I immediately glanced over at Ed who was now mortified with grief. I continued....**

"Enclosed is a check for $200,000 dollars. This is your graduation present from me. It replaces the money you worked for to pay for most of your education your parents were supposed to give you."

I pulled out the cashier's check, still searching for a name on it but didn't recognize who had given it to me. I continued reading. Still in shock at the amount of the check, I notice that Ed got up to leave the room. "I think you should read this alone, China. Call me if you need me," Ed said, as he walked into the den. I continued to read...

The Blanket of Southern Heat

By now you should have read your Grandmother's letter and are in receipt of mine. I want you to know that anywhere you have been, I was always there. Don't blame the people in your life for the secrets they kept, because they were kept to protect you from yourself and others. We all made sure you had what you needed even if it appeared that you had no one there for you. I was at your graduation from high school in the front row. Enclosed are pictures I took of you and your English teacher and some of your school friends.

I pulled out the photos and searched them like a thief looking for anything I could find. I was amazed that the pictures were taken and how happy I looked. I continued reading...

I was also there when you graduated with your Bachelor's degree. Enclosed are the pictures I took as well. It was a proud moment for me even though I couldn't reveal myself to you at that time, I loved you and walked silently though your life with you. I was even in the restaurant many times where Travis, your Ex-husband, worked and watched you. How I wanted to tell you that he was not the man for you, but I was too late. Lastly, I was there when you graduated with your Master's just weeks ago.

I looked up and searched the envelope for pictures I hoped were there, but there were none. I thought I would put a face to this person, but still could not. Finally I came to the end of the letter.

I am very proud of you China. You are a beautiful loving young woman and I am proud to be part of your life. I loved your mother with all of my heart and hate that she could not witness you accomplishing these things in your life despite the trouble you have endured.

Because the man that harmed your mother finally found out who I was to you, it was necessary to conceal my identity until the coast was clear.

Now it is! I want to get to know you and your new husband and be part of your family. I know about your upcoming wedding and know that your fiancé is the right man for you. I congratulate you both and give you my blessings. Just know that you are all that I have in this world now and I will always love you.

I will reveal myself to you and the final part of this mystery soon.

I will love you always…

All the tears were gone now and I took a deep breath rehashing the information I received. Before I could continue, the doorbell rang and it was Nicholas. He rushed in and hugged me and sat down next to me. He picked up the check and then looked at the letters I had in front of me and asked…

"So, you now know what you needed to know?" "Yes." I responded. "I do."

I gave him the letters I had opened and let him read them. We sat quietly looking at each other and he consoled me. I was glad that I had a strong man who knew where his roots were, since I was just beginning to find mine. The wedding was a day away and although I was ready, I was still conflicted.

I didn't get much sleep that night, but was excited about marrying Nicholas. The wedding day finally came and everything and everybody was in place. Nicholas's family had come from all over and the small chapel was full. I wondered who all of these wonderful people were that had come to see Nicholas marry me.

I knew I would only have a handful of people on my side of the family but that would not spoil my beautiful day. I had the traditional wedding garb with the dress and veil. Everyone was seated and the flowers were neatly arranged.

The ceremony began and everything was beautifully arranged. Some of Nicholas's aunts had helped me with the last minute processes. The Chapel was full of people that I did not recognize at all. As we stood at the entrance waiting for the Chapel door to open, I stood in my beautiful gown with my veil over my face.

Ed held my hand and assured me that I was beautiful and would have a happy life with the man I was marrying today. I smiled a nervous smile, just wedding jitters, I thought and then, the music started and the doors of the Chapel flew open.

The Chapel was beautiful and Ed began to walk me down the aisle towards the platform where Nicholas stood waiting patiently for his bride to be. Every one stood and saluted us, and for once I felt like the China Doll I had been told I was.

We approached the platform and Ed placed me next to Nicholas as he smiled even harder today. He looked extremely handsome in his tuxedo and Nicholas's mother and father sat on the front row along with Ed.

The minister began the ceremony and a flood of thoughts ran through my head. He asked the question…

"Is there anyone here that sees any reason why these two should not be joined together in holy matrimony?" Nicholas turned slightly and looked out in the audience and raised a brow, signaling that no one should respond if they knew what was good for them.

Everyone chuckled and made me feel more at ease.

Then the minister came to the part and asked…

"Who gives this woman to this man?" This is where the father speaks and I was waiting to hear Ed's voice from the front row, but the voice I heard was not recognized.

"I give this woman!" a man said, in a sophisticated authoritative voice as he walked up to me and Nicholas. I was again nervous and could not speak. I quickly searched for Ed's face in the room to confirm what I believed the letter I had read days earlier was being revealed to me.

As my eyes met Ed's, the man, I had known as my father, now nodded a gentle affirmation that this man that had just given me in marriage was my biological father. He had loved, protected, and provided everything I had received monetarily throughout my life.

He was the man at the library in New York that I thought was following me. He was at my graduations and at Grandmother's funeral. I was now weak in the knees and visibly shaken as my father ever so gently lifted my veil to search my face as if he were looking for gold and had found it. He had the true look of a father at his daughter's wedding. He appeared to be remise for words that could describe his feelings at that moment. I could almost hear his heart beating in his chest.

The room was quiet with the altered events taking place, but everyone was poised and waited patiently for my father to finish what he had to say. He expressed to me, "I am your father, Alessio Culpepper.

"This was your mother's married name after we were secretly married." I stood still holding his trembling hands. He continued to speak.

Author: Victoria E. Kain

"I have much to share with you about your brothers and sisters, aunts and uncles who are all here today." Still teary eyed, I slowly looked behind me and as if someone had given the room a cue, the entire room stood up.

All the people there were my relatives from my father's and mother's family. They had been invited to my wedding day with permission from Ed and Nicholas. They felt that this would be the best time for me to begin getting to know my real family. They had kept this last secret from me, out of love.

I couldn't hold back the tears. They came without invitation. All my family guests applauded us as my real father gave me a hug. I looked at Nicholas and he smiled and nodded, indicating his approval. My father Alessio kissed me on the cheek and lowered my veil and placed my hand in Nicholas's and shook it. He took his rightful place on the front row with Ed. The minister completed the ceremony and we became husband and wife that day.

As I walked down the aisle as Mrs. Nicholas Francisca, they cheered when we entered our limo which was taking us back to Nicholas's Grandfather's estate which he had inherited. Nicholas had it remodeled as our new home.

I looked out of the window of the limousine and saw my father Alessio and Ed standing side by side smiling. They both blew me kisses and I returned them with love.

Both men were very distinguished and handsome in appearance. It was easy to see that the family was of Italian descent, looking at all the family standing on the outside of the chapel lawn.

These faces looked like mine and I felt right at home.

I would now have a chance to get to know my new family, and friends as they would join us at the estate for our beautiful reception. I kissed my husband again and again and thanked him for making my day more beautiful than I ever thought it could be!

"I love you Nicholas," I said

"I love you more" he said to me.

We both gazed in each other's eyes, erasing all the hurt I had ever felt in my life. No more skeletons in the closet, I thought as my eyes absorbed the beautiful sight of my family watching the two of us begin our life together.

As the limousine turned onto the country road that would take us to the Vladimir estate, now my new home where I met my true love. I realized it was truly a dream come true and a happy ending. Nicholas did not want to wait to have babies and neither did I. After our first year of marriage, I gave birth to our first baby boy, Nicholas Vladimir Francisca III.

The second year came and went and our little girl was born. We named her after my mother and Grandmother. It was that year that I finally opened the letter from the historical agency about my heritage.

With all the information I had gleaned from the family that my father Alessio had introduced me to, the letter from the historical agency only confirmed everything that had already been told to me by my relatives. I now knew everything I needed to know and loved them all. I finally had the truth.

There were never any more secrets in my life from that time forward and I never looked back on the sorrow I had experienced. The love I had gained was worth every dark step I had taken in life to be brought to this wonderful place of truth and happiness.

Author: Victoria E. Kain

Finally the chain of silence has been broken. My soul can rest knowing that I am loved. I know the truth about my heritage and no longer live in the shadow of someone's dream. No more nightmares and unnatural inhibitions carried in my soul out of innocence and fear of the unknown. I fought to exist, knowing that death was a terrible thing if I had never lived. It is funny how our past can adversely affect our future, but amazing how love can change even the worst things that plague us.

Nicholas and I instilled the love we had for each other in our children. I still miss my mother and Grandmother and made amends with Pearl over the terrible thing she did to me. I forgave her each time I looked into my husband's eyes and clearly understood what true love was and hoped that she would someday find the same.

We finished reading all of the manuscripts together. We traced the work back to his fourth generation Grandmother, the daughter of a plantation owner who married a slave Master. Ultimately, she fell in love with one of their "Slaves." She left her legacy in those words that reached our hearts, the same as my mother, who died much too soon, left her legacy in me to carry life forward.

I have now freed the skeletons in my family's closet never to reclaim them again, only to carry forth a new message of love without prejudice for as long as I live. I am "China Stone." This was my story.

THE END

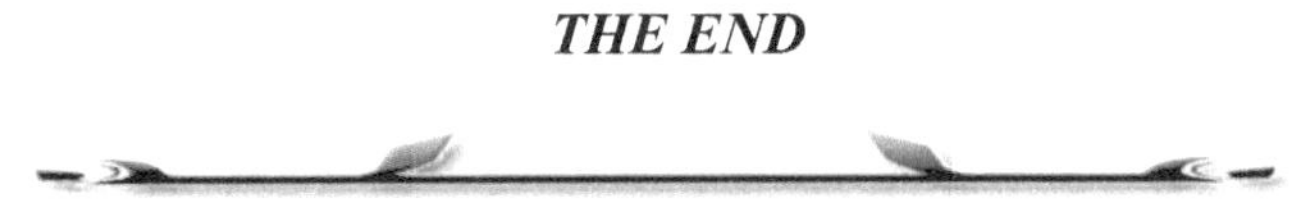

The Blanket of Southern Heat

I would like to give a very special thanks and acknowledgement to

Fycore Publishing
Dr. George R. Monk
Dr. Charles Flowers
Ruthaves Graham
Judy Washington
Beverly Alexander
Carla Tyson
Barbara Jackson
Estell Thomas
Roma Obebe
Jerome Lane
Jamae Jones
Tony Calloway
Kay Horne
Denise Carter
Pat Spard
Eddie Holland
Sarah D. Chavez
… and my Iron Butterfly

I hope the best of life will always meet you in that special place.

Best wishes always,
Victoria E. Kain

Author: Victoria E. Kain